# Dunsvill
## Summer Fun

BY SEBASTIAN ALBERTO DURAN-LOPEZ

DORRANCE
PUBLISHING CO
EST. 1920
PITTSBURGH, PENNSYLVANIA 15238

Dorrance Publishing Co
585 Alpha Drive
Suite 103
Pittsburgh, PA 15238

Visit our website at *www.dorrancebookstore.com*

ISBN: 978-1-6386-7039-1
eISBN: 978-1-6386-7987-5

# Dunsvill
## Summer Fun

# INDEX

# INTRODUCTION

Hello, there. You will read of a present time; many things will happen. These events may be good, bad, horrifying, terrible, disturbing, and so on. And if you think you will not be able to handle what you are about to read, then stop reading NOW! But if you think you may be able to handle what will be lying ahead then, please, join me as we see what happens in this story I'm about to tell.

Ten teenagers get involved with something they never thought they would ever get into. They think it would be fun to go to an abandoned town, DUNS-VILL, and make it a little hang out for the first summer weekend. What they do not know is that they're in for a crazy experience, and this is their tale!

# CHAPTER ONE

# FRIENDLY REUNION

It's a gloomy Thursday afternoon at the high school, and everyone is in class. It's a large school with many classes; some having their own buildings. The school grounds are quiet, even when seniors begin to pour out, filling the outer hallways. The entire graduating class gets out five minutes early for the last week of school. They all head to their lockers clearing them out with joy, knowing that tomorrow is the last day.

One young man is walking by himself; he is a tan, white boy, standing at five feet and ten inches. He's a graduating student with a really fit body, wearing clothes that make people consider him a pretty boy, keeping his hair short with his complexion sharp behind his beautiful, blue eyes and bright, white teeth. As he's walking toward his locker, he signs a couple of yearbooks, writing: "Have a bitching summer and get a LIFE! Will," and draws a winking face at the end. The bell then rings for the lower classmen to exit their classes, and Will rushes to the locker area as students toss their papers in the air. He opens his locker, putting his backpack on a hook that's on the locker door. Staring into his locker, he takes a deep breath. He shuffles through his things and takes out a small photograph, signed by a girl named Rosie with a heart at the end of it. Rosie is a very light skinned, fit Hispanic, with long, straight light brown hair and dark brown eyes. She dresses like a skater with open flannel shirts. She wears fitted caps on backwards and is extremely beautiful.

He smiles at the photo with love-struck eyes, but then someone comes in slamming his hand on the locker next to him, startling Will and taking his smile away.

"Fucking Mark," responded Will, holding the photo to his chest.

Mark is a Filipino who stands one inch shorter than Will. He's good looking and has a skater style wearing skinny jeans, a skate t-shirt and shoes to match. His complexion is light brown and soft, having long dark hair falling to his shoulders.

He laughs, then opens his locker. "Ha-ha, hey, man, what you going to do for the summer?" he asked as he goes through his things.

Will tries to compose himself and replies, "I don't know, probably just kick it with my girl." He opens his backpack, then puts the photo of his girl-friend away in it.

"That's it?" asked Mark.

Will proceeds to clear out his locker. "Yeah, pretty much, since tomorrow is going to be the last day, Rosie and I can do more stuff together," he said, putting his binder and papers in his bag.

"Yeah, but like, what about me, bro?" asked Mark, throwing the stuff that was in his locker on the floor.

Will grabs the last thing in his locker and says, "Nothing for us to do, man; just me and my girl."

"Dude, come on, man, this summer's gonna suck. We have to come up with something to do; like, fuck we…we all been going out and doing shit for the past three years. Plus, you're graduating," said Mark, throwing the rest of his stuff on the floor.

Will closes his locker. "Well, I already told you man, I'm going to kick it with my girl; you find something to do." He then looks at the papers on the floor. "Aren't you going to take your stuff?"

Mark smirks. "We only have one more day of school; I'm not keeping that shit. But really, come on, don't be a little girl; besides, you can't just kick it with her all summer," he said, furiously.

"I can if I want to," said Will, annoyed and begins to walk toward the front gate.

Mark closes his locker and rushes to Will. "Dude, you've been acting this way for over a month now. She can hang out with us, she's my friend, too, you know," he said, calming down and walking beside him.

Will stops and turns to Mark. "Maybe because you tried getting at her at my house!" he said, frustrated with anger.

"Man, I said I was sorry. It was a party, and I was drunk…I didn't know you were with her then," said Mark sadly, trying to ease up to Will.

Will's face turns red, and he grinds his teeth, getting in Mark's face, yelling, "BITCH! WE'VE BEEN TOGETHER FOR FOUR YEARS!"

Some students nearby hear Will and start to close in to see what is going on. Mark slowly backs away and puts his hands up beside his ears. "Just drop it, okay? I was drunk, and I was stupid. I haven't had a drink since. I'm sorry, bro," he said, trying to calm Will.

Will looks up and down at Mark, shakes his head, then says, "Yeah, whatever," rolling his eyes and begins to walk toward the gate again. As he walks away, Mark notices the people staring at him. Not knowing what to do, he waves as he heads to follow Will.

"Hey, that was in the past, alright? And besides, I'm trying to get at someone else," Mark said with a small smile, catching up behind Will.

They arrive at the front gate, and Will finally calms down, then asks, "Oh, yeah, who is he?" joking around placing his bag on the floor.

"It's a girl, and you know her," said Mark with a squint.

Will lets out a sarcastic laugh with a single "HA" and asks, "And who would that be then, huh?" curiously sitting on the side of a flowerbed.

Mark puts a big o' smile on his face. "Christinaaaaaa," he said happily.

Someone walks in on their conversation behind Mark, busting up with laughter. "HAHAHA! Well, good luck, man, you're gonna need it. She wants a real man, not a little pussy, and you, ha-ha, are a pussy," said the voice with laughter.

Mark turns to see who is making fun of him and finds out it's their friend, then quickly tries to come up with something smart to say. "Fuck you, Jose, at least I'm not a 'LITTLE' pussy," he said, shrugging his shoulders going along with the joke.

Jose looks at Mark with disappointment. "Oh, trust me, foo, you're a little pussy," he said giving Mark a stern look, placing his hand on his shoulder. Jose is a rough, good-looking, light-skinned Hispanic who dresses somewhat like a cholo. He is able to pull it off with a fresh buzz cut and goatee to match. He stands at five feet seven inches and is really fit.

Mark smacks Jose's hand away with confidence. "Shut the fuck up, I got this," he replied, smiling.

"HA, YEAH, WHATEVER YOU SAY, MAN! Well, anyways, where the hell is Sebastian? I wanna leave already," Jose said eagerly.

Will, stuck on the screen of his phone, responds, "Chill, alright? We still gotta wait for the girls, and I'm guessing they're getting their things from their lockers really quick." He continues to text.

Jose takes his backpack off and tosses it on the floor. "Ah, are you serious? I wanna leave already," he said, being impatient.

"Well, you gotta wait," said Will with his eyes still glued to his phone.

"But I don't wanna wait; I wanna leave. I'm hungry," said Jose, drooping his body.

Will, already irritated, begins to feel himself becoming more and more annoyed by Jose. "Well, stop complaining, alright? Crying about it isn't going to help. Look, I'm texting the girls right now, so chill," he said, showing Jose his phone so he could shut up.

On the other side of campus, two young girls come rushing out the same room once the bell rings for the lower classmen, throwing their papers in the air as the rest of the students come out after them, doing the same thing.

The two girls hug and run off holding hands as one of them says, "Come on, Lucy! We gotta go get Diana and Rosie." She leads the way.

They're both the same height at five feet five and a half inches, but they look completely different from one another; the one being lead is Lucy, a young Hispanic with long, wavy, dark brown hair, and big, beautiful, brown eyes. She has a tan and the body of a swimmer, dressed fashionably with jeans and a summer shirt. She is gorgeous with a sharp but soft complexion. As she's being dragged through crowds of students, Lucy replies, "Dang, Nallely, slow down."

Nallely is a light brown skinned Filipina, with long, black, straight hair and brown eyes. She dresses like a goth girl and wears black eyeliner. She's really pretty and on the thick side. She slows down a bit when they get to a junior/senior building.

They look around for their friends but can't find them.

"I think they're still in class," said Nallely, walking up to a classroom window, still holding on to her friend's hand. She peeks inside and only sees one of her friends, an older man and the teacher talking together. "Yeah, I see

Diana and…Rosie's dad?" she called out to Lucy, but she is busy on her phone. "Hey, hey I see Rosie's dad," said Nallely, trying to get her attention.

Lucy makes a sad face, then turns toward Nallely. "Huh? Sorry." She puts her phone away. "What happened?" she asked.

"Rosie's dad is talking to Diana and Ms. G.; I don't see Rosie," replied Nallely, looking through the window. Lucy is still in her own world with a pouting smile. Nallely looks at her and notices that she's still not listening. "Hey, what's wrong?" asked Nallely, rubbing Lucy's hand with her thumb.

Lucy quickly looks up at Nallely, snapping out of her thoughts. "What? Oh, nothing; just Sebastian told me he's not coming to eat with us," she answered with a frown of a smile.

"Aw, what? Why not?" asked Nallely.

"Well, he told me already; I just forgot. He's going to help his mom and dad pack for the Land of Diamonds tonight," she said.

"No way! Is he going to?" Nallely asked with excitement.

"No."

"Lame; I would love to go there. Why isn't he going?" she asked with disappointment.

Lucy rolls her eyes, and her smile becomes whole, giving a small chuckle. "He said he doesn't wanna spend his summer without me," she said, as her eyes began to tear up.

Nallely becomes confused and looks at Lucy with a puzzled face. "Okay, so what's wrong? You're acting weird," she asked, letting go of Lucy and putting her hands to her sides.

Lucy closes her eyes to hold back her tears; she shakes her head and takes a deep breath, then says, "I just really need to talk to him." She opens her eyes.

"Oh, my gosh, you're breaking up with him!" responded Nallely with eyes and mouth wide open.

Lucy laughs to herself and says, "No, I'm not breaking up with him, I just—" but then the classroom door swings open.

"Tomorrow, I want you to call me if she does something like this again; this is ridiculous," said Rosie's father to the teacher as he walks out of the classroom. Rosie's father is a tall, Hispanic man, with a rough-looking complexion and a thick mustache; dressed in an old-fashioned style. He turns around and sees Lucy and Nallely. "Have you seen Rosie?" he asked them.

"No, we just got here," replied Lucy.

"You already know she's not allowed to go out right now. If this keeps up, and she's not home, you're not seeing her again," he finished, storming off.

Lucy and Nallely look at each other with bewilderment.

"Wow! That was crazy. You should've come inside and watched the show," said Diana, standing by the doorway, holding the door open.

Diana is a very light brown skinned Hispanic. She has long, light brown hair, dark brown eyes, and wears round eyeglasses that shade in the sun. She dresses like a hipster with a dark brown fedora, standing at five feet four inches. She is beautiful and fit.

The two friends discard what they were talking about and give their attention to Diana. "Heck, no, he's scary. What happened? Why is he even here?" asked Lucy, relieved of the subject change.

Diana lets go of the door and walks up to her friends; they all begin to walk to their lockers as she tells them what happened in class. "Rosie said he was going to come to our class 'cause she didn't go straight home yesterday. So, she snuck out with everyone for the first bell. I thought she was kidding, but nope, he showed up standing outside the window, and when our bell rang, he came right in looking for Rosie."

Nallely quickly turns her head toward Diana. "NO WAY! Where is she now? She's coming with us, right?" she asked.

"Na, she just wants to make it home before her dad, so she doesn't have to deal with him," replied Diana.

Lucy becomes sad and looks down at her feet. "So, my boyfriend and Rosie aren't coming. This was gonna be the first time we all hung out together since the thing at that party; it took a lot to get Will to want to hang out. Now they're not coming," she said.

Nallely gives Lucy a side glare. "Well, what do you expect? They're supposed to be best friends and Mark does that shit. I would have kicked him out the group completely," she said.

"Well, it's not really his fault," said Lucy.

"Yeah, he was drunk," replied Diana with a chuckle. "He was acting stupid before he went after Rosie."

Nallely's eyes widen, and she shakes her head to what she heard. She then looks directly toward Diana, kind of turning her back to Lucy. "So, if a person is drunk, they can do some shady shit? That's what you're saying?" she asked, getting upset.

Lucy goes back to her phone to give her two friends space, seeing Will's text messages.

Diana gets shocked by Nallely's response and looks at her with confusion. "Fuck, no, I'm just saying that he wasn't himself, and he was stupid for getting drunk like that. What are you implying?" she asked.

"Nothing," said Nallely, rolling her eyes and shaking her head.

"Oh, snap, Nallely." Lucy stops walking, and her two friends look back at her. "Mark is trying to get at Christina," she said, clenching her phone with both hands.

Nallely rolls her eyes and turns her head at Diana. "See, it's like he's drunk twenty-four seven. Can't believe you didn't believe me. I had a feeling this was going to happen, he hasn't stopped bugging me about her since Monday," she said, crossing her arms.

"We believed you; I just couldn't believe him for getting at Rosie. For all we know, he really likes Christina," said Diana.

Nallely takes out her phone. "I'll tell her right now." She texts Christina what Mark is trying to do.

Christina replies back with: this guna b fun. ☺

Lucy continues to text in her phone, as well. "Come on, we can get our stuff tomorrow. I told Will we're on our way," she said, as she starts to walk toward the front gate.

They both follow Lucy, and Nallely asks, "Did you tell him Rosie isn't coming?"

"No. He'll just leave, but this might be good anyways. With Rosie gone, it won't be super weird, especially since he's trying to 'get at' Christina," replied Lucy, and then, under her breath, she says to herself, "I hope Will is lying." She sees the guys past the gate. "I'll tell him right now," she said, continuing to walk towards Will.

The three young girls slowly approach the guys, glaring at Mark. Lucy walks up to Will. "Hey, my babe and Rosie are not coming with us," she said, disappointed.

Will's face falls. "What? But she said she was going to come!" he said, with confusion.

"Aren't you texting her right now, dude?" asked Mark, referring to Will being stuck on his phone.

Lucy jumps in to interrupt. "She got her phone taken away for going out to the party with us, remember, and her dad just came to pick her up. There was nothing we could do," she answered, giving Mark a cold glare.

Will gets up, picking up his bag and getting ready to walk home. "Man, if she's not going...I'm-a go home," he said, with sorrow.

Lucy clenches her eyebrows at Will. "Hey, Sebastian's not going, and I'm not going home like a loser. Just come! Besides, you're, like, always with her. Heck, you even joined cheer for her." She spaces out to herself, "Man, if only I could have gotten Sebastian to join the swim team…" she then looks back at Will. "One day without Rosie isn't going to kill you," she continued trying to persuade him to come with them.

Will turns to his friends, looking at them reluctantly.

Lucy looks deep into Will's eyes. "She and I planned this, and you know it! If you don't come, I'm going to tell her how much of a weenie you're being. You know we're like this," she said, making a gesture by crossing two fingers together. "Right, Diana?" she asked turning toward Diana.

She gives Will a half-smile and nods. "Yeah, she'll do it," Diana said, putting her left hand on his right shoulder.

Will takes a deep sigh. "Alright, fine, I'll go," he said, sadly, but then cracks a smile.

Mark looks around and realizes that Christina isn't with them. "Um, hey, Nallely, where's Christina?" he asked curiously.

"Oh, she told me to tell you that you're a bu—" Nallely looks at her phone's messages. "Oh, wait, a 'little' butt-face loser and that she doesn't wanna see your stupid ass face!" she said, with a smile.

Mark pauses for a moment, stunned by Nallely's response. He looks at everyone else, then back at Nallely. "What? She didn't say that?" he asked, confused.

"As far as you know, she'll be here with Jessica in a bit," said Nallely, rolling her eyes.

Jose droops his arms down and asks, "Aw, what? How long is a bit? I'm hungry." He makes a weird face, breaking Mark and Nallely's conversation.

"Not long. Christina just texted me that she's around the corner," answered Diana, typing on her phone.

Jose jumps up and puts on a smile. "Yes, finally! I'm-a go for my van, alright!" he said, happily running off.

Two girls giggling to themselves come passing by the front gate, walking up to the friends. One of the two filled with enthusiasm asks, "Hello, you guys! Are we going or what?" She looks at her three girl-friends, smiling.

Mark walks in her view to make himself seen. "Ah, hey, Christina, we're leaving right now. Jose just went for his van," he said, quickly answering her question.

Christina is a very light brown skinned senior. She has long, shiny brown hair that she has straightened and dark brown eyes. She dresses like a chola, standing at five feet four inches, and is gorgeous, being on the thick side. She snaps a glare at Mark. "Um, did I ask you? NO, I don't think so!" she said meanly, as Mark's expression turns sour. "Ha-ha! Don't get all butt hurt," she ended, giggling.

Mark forces a smile. "I didn't get butt-hurt," he lied.

She looks at him with squinted eyes. "Yeah, sure, you didn't," said Christina, then rolls her eyes, looking at her girl-friends.

Jose then comes driving in his van with his music maxed out. He rolls down his window and begins to yell over his music. "Come on, let's go! Jessica, get my bag!"

"Okay, okay! Come on guys, Jose's buying, ha-ha," she joked holding his bag up.

Jessica is a young, brown skinned Hispanic with long, dyed, straight black hair and brown eyes. She dresses like a chola and wears square eyeglasses. She's very pretty and is five feet five inches and skinny.

They all get into the van, and Mark tries sitting next to Christina, but Lucy had already taken the spot. She looks at him with a smile as he sits next to her.

Jose then starts to drive off to find a place to eat.

# CHAPTER TWO

# DINING OUT

Eight friends had gathered at the front gate of the high school to leave for dinner. Tension is a bit high between everyone from Mark's mistake over a month ago. Lucy is doing what she can to keep the group together, as she deals with things of her own. The eight friends left school and are now riding in Jose's van to find a place to eat. Nallely and Will are sitting at the back of the van with Diana in the middle. Christina and Mark are sitting at the middle of the van with Lucy in the middle. Jessica is sitting in the passenger seat, so she lowers the music.

Jessica turns over toward Lucy. "So, where we going to eat? You haven't told us what you and Rosie decided on," she asked.

Lucy looks slightly embarrassed, giving her a small smile. "She was the one that was going to tell us, but she's not here," she said, with a sad face. "Where do you guys wanna go?" she asked everyone.

"Oh, Big Burgers!" said Mark with excitement.

"Ew, no, that place is nasty," said Nallely, making a disgusted face.

Lucy turns around towards Nallely as if she's about to lecture her. "Hey, that place is good," she said, defending the restaurant.

Nallely does a circle motion with her head as she smirks and says, "Well, Sebastian would agree with me." She then sticks her tongue at her.

Lucy smirks back. "Psh—he doesn't count; he's weird. He doesn't like the awesome chicken nuggets from there, and he doesn't even like candy. Not normal," she said, shaking her head with disappointment.

"Damn, Lucy, you're talking shit about your own boyfriend?" asked Will, smiling and shaking his head.

She then looks at Will. "Yes, MY BOYFRIEND, I can talk smack about him all I want," said Lucy with a smile.

Will continues to shake his head. "Okay, well, what about the Highly Fried Chicken?" he asked, smiling.

"No, Will, no," said Diana, looking at him as if he was stupid.

"Okay, damn," Will responded defensively.

Really eager to eat and not able to come up with a decision, Jose says, "Come on, guys. Alright, we're eating here, then." He drives up to a random diner.

"'Here?' What is here?" asked Lucy.

Jose quickly answers, "Read the sign and find out," being rude as Lucy is trying to look over Christina.

"Man, I'm trying."

Jessica looks at Jose with disapproval. "That wasn't nice; say sorry," she said, softly pushing him.

"Ah, sorry," Jose said apologetically as he parks the van.

"Better say sorry, ha-ha," said Lucy, laughing.

Jose shuts off the engine, "Psh, whatever," he said, smiling.

"So, where are we?" Will asked everyone.

"Like Jose said, read the sign and find out," laughed Diana.

Will opens the van door. "Okay, I will," he said, stepping outside.

They all get out of Jose's van. Diana walks up to Will and asks, "So, where we eating, huh?" She pushes him softly.

"It says Ray's Diner," answered Will, making a stupid smile at her.

"Don't make that face," said Diana with a look of disgust.

"Can if I want to," he replied, sticking his tongue out.

They get in a fifties-style diner with red and white colors; the hostesses are also wearing the same colors that match the era, and there's a bowling alley on the far side with a dance floor. The whole place is lively, packed with people, and old-style high-beat music is playing out a jukebox, filling the area. A hostess, wearing a nametag reading "Wendy" leads the friends to a large rounded booth, placing five menus on the table. "I'll be back with three more," she said, with a smile and walks off.

Mark once again tries to sit next to Christina, but Jessica gets in the booth first following Christina, then Lucy. "Come on, Babe, sit next to me," said Jessica, looking at Jose as she pats the spot next to her with her left hand.

Nallely and Diana sit next to Lucy, and Will takes a seat next to Jose filling up the booth; Mark stands and looks at everyone.

"Well, don't just stay there, dude; get a chair or something," said Will, gesturing toward a different table that isn't occupied.

Mark grabs an empty chair, then sits at the end of their booth. Wendy comes back with the other menus. "Okay, hi, my name is Wendy, I'll be your waitress for the evening. Is there anything you would like to drink?" she asked with a smile, handing out the extra menus.

"We'll all have a Neutral Cola," answered Jose for everyone.

Stunned, Diana quickly says, "Na, I want a Lime and Tingle."

"I'll take a water, please," said Lucy with a sweet smile.

"Yeah, and I'll take a Sizzling Orange," said Mark, changing his order as well.

No one else said anything, so the waitress assumes they want the drink Jose picked for them. "Okay, I'll be back with your drinks," said Wendy, returning a smile, then walks away.

"This guy over here ordering for us," Mark gestured with his hand toward Jose.

Jose clenched his eyebrows. "Shut up, foo. So, what you guys going to have?" he asked.

Christina smirks at him. "Why do you wanna know?" she asked.

"'Cause I just wanna know," he answered.

"Well, you're not going to know," said Christina, smiling.

Jose squints his eyes at her. "We're all going to have the same thing, then," he said, quickly, looking at the menu.

"What the fuck? No, unless you wanna pay for our shit, then, yeah," argued Christina.

"Yeah, what the fuck?" joined in Nallely, backing her up.

While staring at the menu with a stone-cold face, Jose replies, "Jessica said I would," agreeing to pay.

"Wait, what? You're paying?" Will asked, surprised.

"Yeah, we're having the enchiladas; they come with beans and rice," answered Jose, closing the menu.

"That actually sounds good," said Jessica, holding on to her stomach and licking her lips.

Wendy arrives with everyone's drinks. "Alright, here are your drinks. Are you ready to order?" she asked as she serves them.

"Yeah, we're going to have the enchiladas," Jose said, giving her half a smile.

Wendy begins to write in her notebook but then stops. "All of you are going to have the same thing?" she asked, looking at all their faces.

"Yes," Jose quickly answered.

She continues to look at everyone else to make sure no one would change their order. "Okay, your food will be ready shortly," she said, with a smile, walking away once again.

Christina looks at Mark, then at Will, and asks, "So, are we doing anything this summer?" taking a sip of her drink.

"I'm planning on just hanging out with Rosie," replied Will.

Lucy looks at Will with curiosity. "Really? 'Cause when we were planning this, she told me she wants us to go to Southland Beach next month," she said.

"Wow, you wanna go to S.R.F.," Jose said, smiling and shaking his head.

"Heck, yeah," replied Lucy, then looks at Will. "You took her last summer, and the rest of us didn't even go, except for Diana and Nallely."

"Well, yeah; I was the only one down to sneak in, even though I was fifteen, I had to go with Diana, and she didn't want to wait another year."

Lucy smiles back. "Well, we all can go now, and she want us ALL to go, so you best know we are hanging out this summer."

Will clenches his eyebrows and takes a deep sigh. "Why you guys planning stuff behind my back?" he asked.

"Hey! Don't get testy with me," said Lucy with a serious tone, clenching her eyebrows back at him. "We've only talked about it; we've haven't even planned anything yet. You're the one planning to run off with her, and we're just finding this out, just like you are about her just WANTING to go to S.R.F., you butt," she finished, rolling her eyes in anger.

The table gets quiet, and Lucy continues to give Will a cold glare. His face relaxes, taking in a deep breath, then exhales. "I'm sorry. I didn't mean to act like a, like a jerk. I just want to spend time with her alone," he said, looking defeated.

Lucy looks at the table and sees that they are all shocked, pretending to mind their own business. "It's okay, I get it; I want to be alone with my boyfriend, too, but we should all still hang out together. Like we use to," she said, with a sweet tone.

Jose smiles to himself, then says, "I actually got an idea that we can do this weekend...all of us," taking a sip from his drink.

"Yeah? What is it?" Mark asked curiously.

Swallowing his soda, he replies, "Well, I was going to wait later on when we were all together, but I guess I can tell you guys now," Jose said with excitement.

"Okay, just tell us already!" said Nallely and Diana at the same time, eager to know what he has to say.

Jose leans over the table and speaks low enough for his friends to hear. "Okay, I was thinking of some places that would be cool to hang out, and I remember there's some abandoned town in the Unmarked Forest, and I think we should go over and check that motherfucker out! It would be a cool way to get us all together, and if anyone acts up, we'll send them out to another house. We'll be back Monday, what do you say? It will start off our summer," he asked, smiling.

Will shakes his head and smiles to himself. "Mm, looks like you don't have to come up with anything," he said, looking at Mark.

Mark chuckles. "Ha! I guess not. Alright, I'm down to check that place out," he said, with a relieved smile.

Lucy, thinking hard to herself, then looks up with concern. "Wait...you're not talking about um...Dunsvill...are you?" she asked.

Jose gives her an evil smile. "Ha-ha, why, yeah, I am. What, you scared of going or something?" he asked, still smiling; she nods in silence.

Jessica turns toward him and asks, "Why would she be scared?"

"Ha, 'cause..." Jose began but then glances at Lucy with a suspicions smile. "No, you tell her why," he said, letting her answer the question.

Lucy looks at everyone with unsettling eyes, and swallows to clear her throat. "Oh, um, well Ms. G said that everyone was killed in that town by a crazy family; no one knows what really happened there 'cause...no one returns that visits that place. After the town closed, that's when people that went started to go missing," she said, softly.

Nallely jumps with excitement. "Ooh, yeah, I know what town you're talking about now! Yeah, like one hundred years ago, there were some evil possessed family that killed everyone 'cause they were supposedly bored and hungry. First it started with some missing people and then, well, then everyone was killed never to be found except for a brother and sister. Poor kids were scared shitless. Cops from Rickvard were the ones that went over there; they had no evidence or any witnesses but the kids. Weird thing is, is that there's a family called the Duns family, and if you change the V to a K, it spells Dunskill. The only reason why the cops were there was because they got a call from the two kids crying for help; some people say that the kids were part of the Duns family, and that the rest of the family was hiding in the town's old hidden bunker, but like Lucy said, who knows?" she said, feeling smart.

Everyone just stares at Nallely.

"WHAT THE FUCK! THA-THAT'S CRAZY!" Mark projected.

"Shh! Shut up! You're going to get us kicked out," said Diana, kicking Mark from under the table.

"Damn, that's wow…um…wow. I'm not sure if I wanna go," said Jessica, thinking about what she heard.

"See? Now you know why I'm kinda scared to go," said Lucy, showing a sign of fear.

Christina sits quietly and then her eyes slowly get bigger, remembering something. "Oh…my…gosh! And there was some missing workers when they were going to try to take down the town, the whole crew never reported in or something. That's when they sent more people in, but they never came back either, so they just decided to leave it be…Ms. G's class was crazy," she said, with her eyebrows raised, showing her teeth.

"All that shit is fake; you guys swear it's going to happen to us," said Jose, shaking his head.

Jessica clenches her eyebrows and gives him a worried look. "Mm, I don't know," she said, with an uneasy tone.

Jose grabs her hand, looks at Lucy, and says, "Come on, it'll be cool; you've been saying you want us to bond again." He then looks at all his friends. "We can do whatever the hell we want," he said, trying to convince them to go.

"Bond, not die," replied Lucy.

It gets quiet for about a minute, and then Wendy comes by to serve their food. "Okay, enchiladas all around," she said. Everyone reserves their plate. "Okay, enjoy your meal!" said Wendy, walking off to another table.

Jose takes a big bite from his food. "Shit, I'll even cook," he said, with his mouth full.

"Fine, I'll go if Sebastian goes," said Lucy, hoping that he won't agree to go.

"Ha, and I'll go if everyone else goes," said Nallely.

"Alright, then, what about the rest of you guys come on?" asked Jose, hopelessly hoping they'll all go.

Jessica looks down at her food and says, "Let's talk about this later, yeah? I wanna finish eating." She puts a spoon of rice in her mouth.

"Alright, fine," said Jose, eager to know their answers.

The eight of them proceed to eat their food, having a good time rebuilding their friendship.

# CHAPTER THREE

# PREP TIME

The friends have entered a fifties style diner to hang out for dinner. Starting off rocky with Mark and Will arguing back at school, and then Will and Lucy having a dispute at the table. After the tension was broken, Jose mentioned a place he believes would be great to go and rebuild the group's friendship: Dunsvill.

They're all finishing up their food, and Nallely is talking about the time she snuck into the South Rig Festival. "Yeah, it was just like that movie, where that guy helped his friend hop the wall to get into the party," she said, then takes a sip of her drink.

Diana swallows the food in her mouth, then says, "We were making so much noise; I was really surprised we didn't get caught. You should have just went with us Christina, you went last time."

"That was with my ex for my birthday. I just didn't want to go there at the time, but I'm down to go with all you guys," replied Christina.

Lucy finishes the last of her food. "Oh, my gosh, it's going to be a lot of fun; I'm so happy Sebastian waited to go with me," she said, also finishing her water.

"He doesn't like parties or raves that much, so he wouldn't have gone without you either way," said Will, taking his last bite of rice.

Lucy giggles and shakes her head. "Ha, yeah, I know; I told you he's not normal," she said, smiling and thinking about him.

"That's sweet," said Jessica, then softly hits Jose on his arm. "You went without me, you butt, and you told me you were just dropping off Christina and Sam. Ass." She crosses her arms.

"What? I didn't go last year," replied Jose.

"I'm not talking abou-" she pouts, "Ugh, whatever."

As Will finishes his last drink he says, "Hey, let's bowl!" with a big smile.

Diana looks over toward the bowling alley, seeing that it's not so packed as the diner. "Yeah, that sounds fun," she said, agreeing to play.

Will gets up from his seat. "Alright, let's go, then," he said, using Mark as support.

As they all get up from their table to head to the bowling alley, Lucy nudges Will's elbow. "Ha-ha, see, and you didn't wanna come," she said, laughing.

"Yeah, yeah, let's just play," said Will, rolling his eyes with a smile. "We'll do two teams, four versus four."

The friends walk up to the counter to pay for their game; one by one they're getting their bowling gear; as they do, Mark is looking at Christina thinking to himself, *Man, I need to sit next to her...teams of four...I already know Jessica is going to be with Jose, and so will Will...shit Nallely and Diana never split. I have to see if Lucy is down to switch with me...Fuck.*

Christina then goes up to the counter. "I'd just like a ten pound ball, no shoes," she said, to the cashier.

"Ah, you really have to take the shoes," he said.

Jessica becomes puzzled. "Yeah, you do, you're going to slip; it's like the first lesson I taught you," she said, crossing her arms as the cashier nods.

"No, I don't want to wear those nasty things. Plus, I'm already paying for the game. Just take my money," said Christina.

The cashier glares at Christina. "Alright," he grabs a ten pound bowling ball. "Here's your ball," he said, giving it to her, then looks at Jessica. "Do you want shoes?"

"Yes, please, sevens," she replied.

Mark proceeds to get his gear then waits for Lucy to get hers. They all head towards their lane, but Mark taps Lucy's shoulder and pulls her aside to the diner area; walking past a sign reading: "NO BOWLING GEAR BEYOND THIS POINT." Mark and Lucy set there bowling balls down on nearby seats. "Hey, I'm going to be in her team," he said, looking toward Christina as she joins her friends at the bowling lane, then at Lucy.

Lucy raises an eyebrow. "I don't know who she is," she said, acting smart.

"Wow, Christina," said Mark with a dull expression on his face.

She then raises both eyebrows and shakes her head ever so slightly, showing that it's not a good idea. "What about Christina?" she asked.

"I'm going to sit next to her," he answered.

Lucy looks deep into Marks eyes with earnestness. "Um, okay, what are you trying to do, huh?" she asked pushing him softly.

Mark takes a step backward from the push and trips over a chair, falling to the ground. "Wait, what?" he asked from the floor, getting annoyed.

People from nearby tables begin to stare at them. "You heard me. What are you trying to do? Because Will told me you're trying to get at 'Christinaaaaaa.' The heck do you mean by that?" she asked.

Mark begins to get up. "Huh? How did Will tell you?" he asked, ignoring the question.

Lucy walks over to him so he would stay sitting on the ground, looking down at him. "Who do you think he was texting, huh? Now you have us keeping an eye on you. Especially after you tried 'getting at' your best friends girlfriend," she said, putting her hands on her hips.

Mark looks at the tables staring at them, then forces himself up off the ground. "Oh, my…this again? This happened a month ago and I said I was sorry," he said, gesturing at the people to mind their own business.

She crosses her arms and leans back. "WAS? So, you not anymore, and you're just going on to the next of our friends?" she asked, getting heated.

He lets out a sigh and rubs his eyelids with one hand. "I'm still sorry, that was stupid of me, okay? I was drunk, and I haven't had a drink since then," he answered sincerely.

Lucy straightens her posture then tilts her head. "Mm-hmm, okay, then, why are you using Nallely to know more about Christina, huh?" she asked.

Mark becomes more frustrated and begins to pace back and forth. "What? She told you, too? Doesn't anyone keep a secret anymore?" he asked, out loud.

Lucy gets ahold of Marks shoulders, so he'd stop moving. "Not since you messed up with Rosie." She looks behind her to see if anyone is listening, then whispers in his ear, "Did you know you grabbed her boob when you were 'drunk?' You're so lucky I'm the only one who knows about it," giving Mark a serious look.

Mark becomes calm and puts his left hand against his forehead. "What? No way, I don't remember that…why hasn't she told Will?"

She clenches her eyebrows, rolls her eyes, lets Mark go, then says, "I told her not to tell anyone, so we can still keep secrets, alright?"

Mark becomes overwhelmed and takes a seat on the chair he tripped over; he looks up at Lucy and asks, "So, Christina doesn't know; why haven't you told anyone?"

The fact that Christina is still on Mark's mind surprises Lucy. "We've all been friends forever now; I don't think you're a bad guy, just really, really, REALLY stupid and annoying at times…" she sighs, as he stands and looks down at Mark. "Look," she said, taking a seat next to him and continues, "we didn't tell anyone because we don't want the group to break up; once it starts with one of us, it happens to all of us. We planned this dinner, and even though she's not here I don't want you screwing it up. So far, you haven't, let's keep it that way," she finished.

Mark looks at Lucy's eyes and says, "I'm not trying to get at her…" then looks away down at the floor. "I'm trying to get with her," he mumbled softly.

Lucy looks at him in shock. "Wait what? Ha, you're kidding, right?" she asked, but he stays quiet looking at the ground.

Mark becomes embarrassed and covers his face with both his hands, removes them slowly as he takes a soft sigh. "I've liked her since forever," he said, with a hint of sadness.

Lucy squints at him with disbelief. "Really, for that long? Why now?" she asked, crossing her arms.

Still staring at the ground, he replies, "The day I first saw her, I just…I couldn't just…I just didn't, ah; I don't wanna talk about it."

Lucy begins to study Mark as he thinks deeply to himself. A smile begins to grow on her face. "Oh, my gosh, you're serious," she said, then gets up. "This just got better."

Christina then comes from the bowling side and walks up to them. "Hey, you guys coming or what?" she asked.

Lucy smiles at her, picks up her ball and says, "Yeah…Marks on your team," then walks past her.

"Wait, what?" asked Christina, as she stands in place stunned.

Mark walks up alongside Christina. "We'll kick their asses," he said, with a smile.

"Yeah…sure," Christina replied, then walks to their friends. Mark quickly picks up his ball and follows behind her like a lost puppy.

The rest of the friends are seated in their teams, just as Mark thought it would happen. Lucy walks up to them with a big smile on her face, with Christina and Mark right behind her. "Hey! Sorry you guys, Mark was just telling me about how Sebastian really wanted to come here with me," said Lucy, putting her bowling ball on the rack, and as she is about to take a seat next to Will, Jose looks straight at Mark as he comes into view. "Wow, he couldn't text or call you to tell you himself? He's probably pulling a Mark right now ha-ha," he laughed, shaking his head with disapproval.

Lucy stops herself from sitting and begins to tear up. "He's helping his mom!" she yelled at him, then runs off to the restrooms.

Everyone looks at Jose with anger and shock. Jessica stands up and looks down at Jose. "You're a fuckin' jerk!" she said, putting her hands on her hips.

Jose shrugs his shoulders with confusion. "I was just kidding; I know he's helping his mom," he said.

Jessica's eyes become filled with rage. "Fuckin' jerk," she said, once again, then storms off after Lucy, and the rest of the other girls get ready to follow looking at Jose with hatred.

"What? I've said worse," he told them.

The girls then head off to the restrooms to comfort Lucy, and Jose is left alone with Will and Mark who are also staring at him with disbelief. "It's true I have…shit I even said the same thing to Sebastian," he said, trying to defend himself.

"Yeah, but he's a guy, bro," replied Mark.

"Can't believe this but yeah, he's right," said Will, slowly nodding his head.

"Fuck," said Jose, looking down.

Lucy bursts through the restroom door and runs into a stall. She puts the toilet lid down, sits on it and begins to cry softly to herself. Jessica enters and looks around and sees no one by the sinks, she then checks the stalls to see if anyone is in them. Now knowing that they're alone she walks up to the stall Lucy locked herself in. "Hey, girl, want me to come in there with you?" she asked.

The other girls enter the restroom and join Jessica. "We're here for you, Lucy," said Diana.

Lucy siting on the toilet with her feet up on it, and crying in-between her knees, takes a deep sigh then mumbles, "Hold up," wiping her tears.

Her friends wait patiently for her; she comes out with a sad small smile. "Sorry, I know he was kidding. I…we haven't hung out like this in over a month," she said.

"Well, we're all here now; you did a good job," said Nallely, wiping a tear that is falling from Lucy's face.

"Yeah, but Rosie just left and Sebastian couldn't come; ah, if only one of them just came," she said, smiling and rolling her eyes.

Christina smiles at Lucy and crosses her arms. "Bitch, we ain't good enough?" she asked.

Lucy laughs and replies, "Ha, nope," then sticks her tongue at her.

"Wow, ha," chuckled Jessica. "So, you good, then?" she asked, rubbing Lucy's left arm.

"Yeah, I'm fine," said Lucy, then looks at Christina. "There's more important things to talk about, actually," she said, with a smile. "Since we're here."

"Yeah, what's going on? I know you two weren't talking about Sebastian," said Christina, squinting at Lucy, "You were talking about me, huh?" then tilts her head.

Lucy smiles big. "Maybe."

Nallely then becomes heated. "Oh, fuck, what? He's bugging you now! Did he ask you if she has a vibrator?" she asked, crossing her arms.

Christina looks at Nallely with disgust. "What the fuck, Nallely?"

"That's what he asked me, okay? I slapped him, and he said he was 'just being funny,' that sick fuck," replied Nallely, rolling her eyes.

Lucy, also looking at her with disgust, says, "No, that's not what he was asking." She then smiles, shaking her head as she rolls her eyes. "He asked me to let him be on your team for bowling…I think he likes you," she said, looking at Christina.

"No way, you're lying," said Jessica, smiling.

Lucy shakes her head slowly at Jessica then looks back at Christina. "Really, I think he actually might like you, he's been trying to sit next to you all day," she said.

"Aw, and he's not drunk. That's sweet," smiled Diana.

Christina's face goes from disgusted to surprised. "Yeah? Ha, I guess I know who gave me that letter…" she whispered to herself.

"What?" asked Lucy.

"Nothing," she replied. "I find it kind of hard to believe, though; we've known each other for a long time now."

"Well, you are graduating, maybe he sees this as his last chance," says Jessica.

"You really think so?" asked Christina, beginning to blush.

Lucy nods and the rest of the girls begin to smile and get excited except for Nallely. "You got to be kidding me…he tried getting at Rosie!" yelled Nallely as a woman walks into the restroom. She stares at the group of friends and they look back at her. The woman slowly walks backward against the door and walks out.

"He was drunk, and he told me he hasn't had a drink since then. I believe him; he has been hanging out with Sebastian more instead of going to parties," said Lucy, shrugging her shoulders.

"And he's putting up with our shit," added Diana.

Nallely looks at them with disbelief. "Don't tell me you believe this?" she asked, turning toward Christina.

They all look at Christina with suspense; she thinks for a second, then says, "I don't know, this is weird. I did find him cute before but…he comes off as a player at times."

"That's because he is one; watch I bet once he grabs your ass or something and you push him away, he won't care, he'll just be like 'sorry I was drunk' or 'high' and brush it off; like it's no big deal," says Nallely.

"I bet he won't," said Lucy.

Nallely raises her eyebrows. "Really? Okay, twenty bucks he fucks up."

"Twenty if he doesn't," said Lucy, crossing her arms, "and you have to pay for their first date," ending with a smile.

"Shit, then you have to pay her back for her game if he fucks up," said Nallely, smirking at Lucy.

Christina looks at both of them with bewilderment. "What the fuck, you guys? I'm not something for you to bet on."

"What do you have to lose? You just said you think he's cute," said Lucy.

"Yeah, and either way, you have one of us paying for your day," added Nallely.

Diana punches Christina softly on the shoulder. "Yeah, and if he does fuck up, you can kick his ass."

"It's just a game of bowling," added Jessica.

Christina looks at her friends one by one as she thinks to herself, each of them looking straight at her waiting for an answer. "Okay, but this doesn't mean there will be a date after this shit. So, I want some bud if anything," said Christina, smirking at Nallely.

"Ha, deal; I really hope you slap him. It feels good," laughed Nallely.

The friends laugh and Jessica's phone begins to ring; she takes her phone out of her pocket and looks at it. "Hold on," she said, answering the phone. "Yes? What do you want?"

Back at the bowling lane the guys are sitting at their teams' sides, Jose and Will are sitting on the left side and Mark is on the right. Jose is on his phone as Mark and Will watch him in suspense. "Hey, how's she doing?" asked Jose, and through his phone, they hear Jessica raising her voice, "What you said was really fucked up. You need to apologize now, Jose!"

Mark looks at Will. "Damn, they're pissed," he said, and Will raises an eyebrow then nods.

Lucy smirks at Jessica and leans over toward her phone. "It's okay, really. We're on our way right now," she then looks at Christina and says, "Let's go. I think we left him waiting long enough," smiling giving her a wink.

"Shut up," replied Christina.

The girls walk out of the restroom and pass by a rough looking white man, with a thick beard sitting near the back exit and restrooms. He's six foot two around his late thirties; wearing a baseball cap, and clothing that makes him look like a rancher. He watches them approach the rest of their friends, mingling with one another; he continues watching them as they begin to play a game of bowling.

The man starts to observe a group of women in business attire that are at the bar. They're talking and laughing, having a good time with a couple of drinks and tacos. He watches them for a while and proceeds to scan the rest of the bowling alley. He looks at his watch, it's an old style wristwatch with a leather strap, gold casing and roman numerals; it reads five thirty. He stays at his seat drinking water for half an hour watching everyone around him.

Looking over at the friends again; he sees that they have finished their game and are now cheering amongst themselves, still hanging around their bowling lane. He continues to look around for ten more minutes, and then the women at the bar start to say goodbye to each other. Two leave toward the front entrance and one heads straight for the back exit, near the strange man. She passes him and goes out the back door; the woman is a young Hispanic around her early thirties, having beautiful long brown hair. The man follows her.

The back lot is mostly empty with just a couple of vehicles far from each other. Thick trees and a large dumpster are between the cars that are there. The woman heads towards her vehicle by a tree and the man walks up behind her. "Um, excuse me. Can you help me?" he asked with a kind voice.

She turns around to confront the man. "Ah, sure, what's wrong?" asked the woman.

"My car won't seem to start. Can you please give me an upstart, if it's no trouble," said the man patiently.

"Yeah, sure, no problem. Where's your car at?" she asked.

The man points at the car behind the dumpster. "Right over there," he said, shaking his head with a smile. "I been messing with it for a while and took a break. I think if I give it some juice it will start."

The woman opens the door to her car. "Alright, let me just park my car next to yours," she said, getting in. She drives to the car the man pointed at and gets out. "Do you have jumper cables?" she asked.

The man puts on a face of disappointment. "Sadly, no, would you by any chance have one?" he asked.

"Yeah, I do," said the woman going to the trunk of her car. "Luckily my husband puts this stuff in here," she continued as she went through her trunk.

"Thank you; you're a real help," said the man, looking around for other people, and once he saw no one was around, he reaches toward his waist taking a large knife out from its sleeve.

"Oh, no problem, what's your name?" asked the woman, grabbing the jumper cables.

"My name is not important," said the man, knocking out the woman with the handle of his knife. She immediately falls over the inside of her trunk. The man looks around one last time and then ties the woman up with the jumper cables, and puts her body completely in the trunk of her car; putting his knife back in its sleeve. He gets in her car, looks at his watch reading six twenty-eight then fixes his hat.

He dives off with the woman tied up in the trunk.

# CHAPTER FOUR

# THE BIG GAME

The friends have all finished eating and paid for a game of bowling, and Mark then confessed his feelings for Christina to Lucy. After that, Jose caused Lucy to run to the women's restroom to get some space. The rest of the girls went to go comfort her, and all ended up talking about Mark's confession. Once done with their conversation, they headed on back to the guys to play some bowling, as a strange man watches them and the rest of the bowling alley.

The girls walk up to the guys, still seated at their teams' sides. "Hey, boys! Sorry to keep you waiting," said Lucy.

"No, it's okay. I'm sorry for…saying what I said," said Jose with a sad smile.

"It's alright, I forgive you. I'm actually in a betting mood," she said, with a grin.

Will looks at her with suspicion. "What do you have in mind?" he asked.

Lucy takes a seat in between Will and Jose. "Whichever team hits over the most pins, gets to make the other team do a Team Dare, and the dare has to be in here so EVERYONE can see," she said, with a devilish smile.

"Oh, my gosh, yes, I'm down. We're so going to beat you guys," said Diana, grabbing Nallely and Christina by the hand, sitting Christina next to Mark and herself between her girl-friends.

Jessica sits next to Jose and puts on her shoes, as do the other girls except for Christina. Jessica quickly ties her laces. "So, who goes first?" she asked.

"We haven't set the team's names ye—" Mark started to say but is cut off by Lucy, she gets up and walks to the computer and says, "Our team is called Team Lucy!" smiling typing on the keyboard.

"Wow, very original," said Will, getting up and walking toward her. "Here let me do it."

"Too late," she said, entering her teams name. "You guys had all this time to set the teams, ha," she giggles, looking at Will then at Mark. "What's your guys-es name?"

Nallely quickly answers, "The High Ones!" and Diana looks at her smiling as she shakes her head and says, "You would." Nallely begins to laugh. "Oh, come on, I haven't blazed in three days; leave me alone," she said.

Mark nervously rubs his hands together. He takes a glance at Christina, barely opening his mouth about to talk, but he closes it then looks at his hands.

"Okay, done. Jessica you're first!" said Lucy, skipping back to her seat.

"Ha, okay, I got this," laughed Jessica, approaching the front of the lane. She feels the ball in her hands and then begins to feel her right arm swing with it.

Mark thinks to himself for a while then notices that Christina isn't wearing bowling shoes. "Why didn't you get your shoes?" he asked.

She looks at him with squinting eyes. "Are you going to tell me that I'm going to trip and fall on my face 'cause I heard it already," she said.

Mark, stunned by her response, widens his eyes and begins to shift them side to side. "Uh, no I was just wondering…" he said, as he watches Jessica hit a strike.

"Oh, yeah! What's up! You can't touch this!" said Jessica, pumping her chest forward then laughs. "Ha, just kidding." She slowly returns to her seat, giving everyone a sweet smile.

"So, we haven't…" Mark started to say to Christina, but when he turns toward her, he sees her walking away. "Oh, sit your ass down; my turn," she said, walking up to the lane. She picks up her ball, and right when she tosses it; she slips and falls on her face, knocking over one pin.

The cashier begins to laugh and so do all the friends except for Mark and Jessica. Mark immediately gets up and rushes over to Christina. "It's not funny," Jessica said out loud. Mark extends his hand out, offering it to her. She looks at his hand with suspicion and hesitantly gets ahold of it. "Thanks," she said, slowly getting up as Lucy and Nallely look at each other in surprise.

"Are you okay?" he asked with a small smile.

"Yeah, just great," she replied, dusting herself off. She rolls her eyes with regret and looks at Mark. "Could you take my turn, then get me some shoes?"

"Yeah, no problem; need help going back?" he asked.

"No, I got it," she said, walking away then slips and catches herself; after she regains balance, she slowly catwalks back to her seat.

Mark picks up his ball and prepares himself to toss it. "Work that ass Mark," yelled Jose. "You only have one shot so don't miss," said Lucy. He takes a step back then forward lunging the ball down the lane, quickly knocking over eight pins. He turns to his friends and gives them a smile.

"Dang, okay, okay. We're still winning anyways," said Lucy, picking up her ball. "Go fetch her shoes; it's my turn."

Mark heads towards the cashier about to walk past Christina and stops in front of her. "I'll be back with your shoes," he said, giving a wink.

She quickly gives him a cold glare. "And make it quick..." she said, as his face falls, "I'm just kidding," she continues cracking a smile, taking a glance at the floor then back at Mark, "Thanks...size eight's please," finishing slightly blushing. He returns a smile, and she watches him walk away.

Mark blushing approaches the cashier. "Hey, man, can I get eight sized shoes for girls, please? My friend changed her mind and needs them."

The guy looks at him for two long seconds. "Sure, man, that be thirteen dollars," he said, taking out the shoes.

Mark looks at him shocked. "What, why? She already paid bro," he said, a bit frustrated.

"She paid for no shoes, dude. If you want some shoes, you're going to have to pay for them," he replied.

"You can't be serious; come on. I heard you laugh and now you're just being a dick," said Mark, hitting the counter with anger.

"Do you want the shoes or not?"

"Yeah..."

"Thirteen dollars."

Mark looks at him stunned for a while that seemed like forever. He rolls his eyes and takes out his wallet to pay the guy.

"Fifteen."

"What you just said—thirteen."

"Yeah, till I remembered you and your other friend took the balls out of the bowling area; I have to charge you," he replied with a smug face.

"Dick," said Mark, handing him fifteen dollars.

The cashier grabs the money and puts it in his pocket. "Have a nice game," he said, with a smile, placing the shoes on the counter.

Mark looks at him with disbelief, slowly grabbing the shoes then walks off.

He returns back to his friends with Nallely bowling her last turn. He hands Christina the shoes with frustration. "Here you're shoes," he said, taking a seat next to her.

"Ah, thanks," said Christina with a concerned look as she takes the shoes.

Nallely cheers as she knocks over the last standing pins. "Yes!" she said, locking eyes with Diana as they smile at each other, then looks at Jose, "Your turn loser. I know you suck," she continues, walking backwards to her seat, "Sometimes I think that's the only reason Jessica stays with you," finishing with a smile.

Jose approaches the front of the lane. "Shut up! I got this, watch!" he said, as he takes a couple of steps back, then moves quickly forward tossing his ball knocking over three pins. "YEAH!" he yells, celebrating. Everyone laughs at him except Mark who is still stuck on the altercation with the cashier.

"You still suck!" laughs Nallely.

Jessica rushes over to Jose chuckling, she puts both her hands on his cheeks and says, "You're getting better, Babe," giving him a big kiss on the lips. "Now, take out the rest," she said, turning him and spanking his butt.

Jose blushes and prepares himself, taking a deep breath; he tosses the ball and knocks over four pins. He turns toward Jessica with open arms. "My lucky charm," he said, hugging her.

Christina finishes tying her shoes and notices that Mark is still deep in frustration. "You okay, what happened back there?" she asked, putting her hand on his shoulder.

"Huh?" he said, snapping out of his concentration. "Oh, nothing just that guy was a dick; he charged me for the shoes and taking the balls to the dining area, but it's not a big deal really," he finished giving her a small smile.

"What an asshole!" she responded.

"Christina! Your turn, ha I don't want to go yet," said Diana, shoving Christina.

Christina looks at Diana giving her a smile then back at Mark. "Well, thanks again," she said, getting up.

Jessica begins to clap. "Yeah, Christina, you got this! You learned from the best!" she cheered.

"Don't root for the enemy," said Will, smiling.

Christina tosses her ball and hits a strike. "Fuck, yeah, bitch! Watch me get another," she said, smirking at the girls.

"Don't get cocky now just 'cause you haven't gotten any in a while," laughs Diana.

Christina stops herself from celebrating and turns toward Diana. "Bitch, I don't see you getting any," she said, putting her left hand on her hip.

"You don't know my life, foo," smiles Diana.

"Psh, yes, I do," chuckles Christina, shaking her head as she sits back down.

Diana and Nallely take a quick glance at each other and giggle to themselves.

Will gets up and picks up his ball. "Alright, you guys, ready to lose?" he asked, looking at the opposing team.

"We'd have a better score, but the floor fucked me up," replied Christina, laughing then smiles at Mark.

Mark's body begins to shake with nerves and his palms start to sweat. He says, "You did good," giving a weak smile.

"Ha, thanks, I needed that do over," she said, returning a smile. "So, we haven't talked in a while. How's your mom? I miss her."

Mark looks down and frowns. "She's alright," he said, looking back at Christina. "She's working more hours now that she got a different job, so I don't really see her that much."

Christina puts on a sad smile. "Aw, is she still going to work at my old school? It still trips me out that your mom was my second-grade teacher."

Mark smiles. "Yeah, she loves the kids and doesn't want to leave but, she's also working as a part-time waitress overnights and weekends now," he said, then begins to chuckle, "Ha, when my mom and dad picked me up from the movies that day, and you actually yelled out her name. Good times," he ended with a big smile.

Christina rolls her eyes. "Well, yeah! She was my favorite teacher; ha, shit that was so long ago. How is your dad?" she asked, smiling.

It gets silent for a brief moment and Mark takes a short sigh. "He's good, he's been out on a big sales trip for like two months now. I don't know when he'll be back," he replied.

She squints her eyes at Mark and chuckles. "Ha, really? I'm surprised they sent him on a trip for that long. You sure he didn't just go for milk and not come back? 'Cause your dad can't sell a car for shit," she said, beginning to laugh as Mark smiles. "I remember one time your dad's boss came over to your house, complaining about the car he still had in the garage."

"You can't blame him; that car looks like shit," he said, laughing.

Christina laughs with Mark as she proceeds to check him out. "Yeah, we took it out to the river with Jose and Will."

"Yeah…Will blazed me out for the first time as we were setting some shit on fire; we had no idea where you and Jose went," he said, with a half-smile.

"Fuck that was a LONG time ago; but trust, nothing even happen. You can put Jose in the most romantic setting and he'll be thinking about something else. I'm happy Jessica can put up with him," she said, giggling with a smile.

They both stare into each other's eyes as time slows down around them, and as they both were about to say something, Lucy burst with excitement. "YAY! WE WIN, WE WIN WE WIN WE WIN," she cheered, doing a little three-sixty dance.

"Fuck, what happened?" asked Christina, breaking out of their gaze.

"Shit, if you would have been cheering me on and not stuck in la-la land, maybe I would have hit that strike!" Diana replied with excitement.

Christina crosses her arms and tilts her head giving Diana a half smile. "Will just went up though! How's the game over?" she asked, with laughter.

Diana shakes her head and smirks at her. "Mark's eyes were more important, I guess."

"Shut up," Christina said with a chuckle.

Will looks up at Lucy who is staring at Mark with a devilish smile. "Something tells me you already have a dare in mind, and I'm scared to ask what it is," he said, scooting away from her.

Lucy turns towards him with a big grin. "Why, yes, I do, my good friend," she said, then looks at the other team. "Mark has to let the girls dress him up and put makeup on him so he can go dance on the dance floor."

Everyone grows a smile on their faces and slowly look at Mark. "That sounds amazing, I've never seen him dance before," said Christina.

Mark gets up, quickly looks at all his friends and puts his hands up with hesitation. "Oh, no, that's not fair...I thought it was a team dare!"

"What do you mean? It is a team dare, the girls are doing the hard part trying to make you look good; you're just dancing," said Lucy, walking up to Mark and putting her hand on his shoulder.

"I don't know, you guys, he probably can't dance. That's why he never dances at parties," said Nallely with a smug face.

Mark looks down at Nallely. "I didn't go to dance; I went to get fucked up," he said, giving a small smile.

Nallely rolls her eyes with annoyance. "Yeah, we know...You should have been dancing instead. Maybe then you would have been distracted from doing something stupid," she said, with aggravating eyes.

Mark was about to say something, but Jessica quickly butts in. "Just do it Mark," she said, walking up to him. "If you do this, we'll all forgive you and stop bugging you, right Nallely?" she asked, looking at Nallely, finishing with a light smile.

Nallely looks at Jessica with deep thought then gets up and slowly glares at Mark. "Yeah, I'll help fix your face," she said, with an evil smile.

"Ah." Mark begins to back away as Nallely gets closer causing him to bump into Christina. "Just sit your ass down boy," she said, forcing him to sit down.

Christina Diana and Nallely all gather around Mark; Christina goes through her purse grabbing her mirror and makeup, handing them to Nallely. Nallely proceeds to put eyeliner and blush on Mark as Diana plays with his hair.

Jessica grabs an extra bra from her bag. "I had P.E. last period, so it's a little stinky," she said, strapping her bra on Mark. "You're not even in my team," he replied. "Shut up and take it," she said, stuffing the bra with her P.E. clothes. Mark stays seated reluctantly taking the makeover from the girls.

Jose and Will laugh to each other as Jose takes a video with his phone. "This is so going online, right?" asked Will with a compelling smile. "Oh, you know it, bro," replied Jose with a devilish grin.

Christina gets her Bright Red Lipstick putting some on her lips and on Mark's, then writes "LOSER" on his forehead. "Ha, you're our little loser," she said, giving him a big kiss on the cheek leaving a bright red kiss mark.

Diana makes three ponytails on Mark's head; the girls all step back from him and take a glance at their masterpiece. Lucy takes out her phone and starts to take pictures. "Oh, this is awesome," she said, turning around toward Will. "I'm-a send this to Rosie and Babe," she finished with a grin.

Will returns a smile. "Ha, we already sent them a video, I hope her dad watches it," he said, laughing.

Mark stands up from his seat hunching over with an annoyed face then cracks a slight smile. "Okay, let's get this shit over with," he said, fixing the bra.

Jose comes out from behind the girls pointing his phone at Mark. "Well, get to walking bro and shake that ass," he said, pressing the record button.

The bowling alleys dance floor is packed with young adults, dancing to high beat music being played by a young female DJ. It's dimly lit with flashing lights and very little blue fog low to the ground. Mark slowly walks toward the dance floor, as his friends follow behind him laughing and recording him. The people in the area start to watch him, giggling talking amongst themselves. He looks around nervously with his head low; he sees everyone laughing and it begins to fill his mind. As he walks up to the edge of the dance floor, he stops and closes his eyes clearing his thoughts. He cracks a smile bobbing his head, and then does a power slide to the middle of the dance floor.

Over the music everyone can hear the DJ say, "THIS IS DJ FOX ROX, IT LOOKS LIKE WE HAVE A SPECIAL TREAT TODAY! PLEASE MAKE ROOM FOR OUR SURPRISE GUEST," she finished turning up the music.

The people make a circle around Mark and the friends force themselves in the front. Mark pops his chest forward and back repeatedly, and then extends his arms causing them to do a wave motion also moving his torso. The friends are all clapping and jumping to the beat. "Yeah, Mark!" cheered Lucy. "Move that body!" yelled Diana. Mark takes his right foot crossing it over his left, and then turns around dropping his knees on the floor. He places his hands on the ground lifting himself up and begins to spin his body around in circles.

Jose looks at Will with a shocked face still having his phone pointing at Mark. "Damn this foo can dance," he said, as he bobs his head with the music.

Will smiles. "Yeah, it's been a while since we danced," he said, then dances his way towards Mark.

Will and Mark both break dance together swinging and tossing each other around. The rest of the friends join in on the dancing and so do all the people on the dance floor. They have a good time for a while having people cheer Mark on; once finished they leave Ray's Diner laughing and enjoying themselves, not knowing what had just happened out in the back parking lot.

"That was fun," said Jessica, holding on to Jose's arm.

"Yeah, it was," he replied.

The friends get into Jose's van with Mark still dressed funny. Christina sits next to Mark smiling at him and poking at his hair. "You were amazing, now I can watch you dance more," she said, laughing.

"Ha! Yeah, that was the last time you're all going to see me dance," he replied with a big smile.

Christina smirks at him. "We'll see about that," she said, looking away from him.

Jose begins to drive everyone home, and Lucy forces herself to the front in the middle of Jessica and Jose. "You think you can drop me off at Sebastian's? I have to talk to him," asked Lucy.

"Oh, yeah, no problem weirdo," answered Jose, heading for Sebastian's house.

# CHAPTER FIVE

# WE NEED TO TALK

The friends had made a bet over a game of bowling at Ray's Diner. Mark, Christina, Diana, and Nallely, lost having to dress Mark up so he could groove on the dance floor. All the friends ended up dancing with him, as the people cheered them on. Once finished with their fun, they all got in Jose's van to head on home; not knowing that a well-concealed kidnapping took place in the back parking lot.

Jose has dropped off everyone at home except for Lucy and Jessica. He drives up the driveway of Sebastian's house. Lucy opens the slide door to the van. "Thanks," she said, getting out of the van.

"Welcome, don't forget to ask Sebastian about coming with us, okay?" Jose asked, reminding Lucy about Dunsvill.

Lucy stares at Jose as she holds on to the van door. "Mm, okay, I'll try," she said, closing it, not really meaning to try at all since she has other things on her mind. She walks up to the front door quickly knocking as soon as she gets close enough.

Sebastian's mother opens the door. "Hello, I'm guessing you're here for Sebastian," she said, smiling. She's a friendly looking Hispanic lady around her mid-thirties, fit and beautiful. She's wearing jeans with a black summer shirt and sneakers.

Lucy smiles back and gives her a hug. "Hello, yeah, is he home?" she asked politely.

"Yes, he's out in the backyard. Come in," said Sebastian's mother, inviting her inside.

"Thank you," replied Lucy, walking into the house, and heads straight towards the backyard.

Lucy opens the back door seeing Sebastian sitting on a bench, watching something on his phone. Sebastian is a brown skinned Hispanic; five feet and seven inches. He's good looking with a buzz cut, dark brown hair and is nicely fit. Right now, he's wearing comfortable clothing with pajama pants and an old t-shirt.

She closes the door behind her. "Babe?" she called out to Sebastian.

He looks up turning his head towards his girlfriend. "Hey, Babes, you didn't tell me you'll be coming. What you doing here?" he asked, surprised, with a smile.

Lucy walks up to Sebastian. "Psh, I should be asking you that you loner, all out here by yourself, ha," she laughs, "looking like a bum," she said, holding out her hand.

He gets ahold of her hand, stands, and kisses her hello. "Ha, I'm taking a break; my mom has a lot of stuff. So, how was the food? I saw the videos you guys sent me. I can't stop watching them," he said, smiling siting back down.

She sits next to him and says, "It was good, but I wanna talk," looking at him with concern.

Sebastian straightens himself up. "Yeah, about what?" he asked with curiosity.

Lucy clenches her eyebrows looking at the ground as she bites her lower lip. "Um, I um," she said, not knowing if she should tell him what's on her mind. He waits patiently for her to say something; she looks around and then at him as she says, "Ah, um, I ah, ugh, never mind," looking away from him.

He grabs her hand and asks, "What's wrong, Babes?" gently getting ahold of her chin, turning her head so he can look into her eyes.

"Nothing, just forget it," she said, looking at him with half a smile then looks away again.

Sebastian grabs both of her hands and begins to rub them slowly. "Come on, what's wrong?" he asked with a concerned look.

"Nothing," replied Lucy. It's silent, and he patiently looks at her with content. "It's just Jose wants to go to Dunsvill, but I don't wanna go 'cause of what happened there. So, I told him I'll go if you go," she answered, quickly relieved that she came up with something else to say.

Sebastian starts to think to himself, he smiles at Lucy and right when he's about to say something she stands. "NO! Why, why do you wanna go; do you even know what happened there?" she asked, with a worried face.

He laughs. "Babes, I didn't even say anything; how do you know if I was going to say yes?" he asked with a big smile.

Lucy crosses her arms. "'Cause I know you already, Babe, and look you're even smiling," she said, with a serious face.

He gets up from the bench, grabs her by the waist pulling her in close and says, "Well, that happened a long time ago, it's not going to happen again." Lucy stares at him with sincere caution. "Besides, we don't even know if it's true," he continued, but she isn't fazed. "And, hey, it might be fun; you never know."

Lucy continues to stare him down as he lightly looks into her eyes. She sighs, then says, "Fine, but if I die, I'm going to haunt you forever, okay?" giving a small smile.

"Ha, don't worry, I'll protect you," he said, giving her a kiss on the lips.

Sebastian leads them to sit back on the bench and Lucy's phone begins to ring. She looks at it rolling her eyes and says, "Oh, gosh, it's my dad," then looks at her boyfriend.

"What are you going to tell him?" he wondered.

Lucy thinks to herself as she looks at her phone. "Well…I can ask to see if I can sleep over here for the night," she said, smiling at Sebastian.

He becomes shocked by her response that he almost falls off the bench. "Ha! Okay, ask him," he said, fixing himself, "Oh, and put him on speaker yeah? I wanna hear this," he finished with a big grin.

"Ha, okay, shh," she said, answering the phone and puts it on speaker:

**Lucy:** "Hello?"
**Dad:** "Where are you it's getting late?"
**Lucy:** "Oh, um, I'm at Rosie's house."
**Dad:** "Why? You should be home."
**Lucy:** "After we finished eating, she asked me to help her with something, and we're not done, I was about to call you if I can spend the night, so can I, Daddy…please?"

**Dad:** "Mm, just because it's almost the summer, you think you can start sleeping over your little friend's house? Next time call me to let me know where you are alight, have fun, I love you."

**Lucy:** "Okay, thank you, Daddy, love you; bye!"

**Dad:** "Bye." (call ends)

Lucy puts her phone away, then gives Sebastian a kiss on the cheek.

"Ha, wow, Babe, really?" he asked, shaking his head smiling.

"Ha, what?" she asked, giving him a hug. "You know my parents hate you. If I told him I was here, he would have come to pick me up," she said, giving him a big kiss on the lips.

Sebastian's mother walks in on them and says, "Sebastian, we're just about ready to leave for the airport. Could you please put my last bag in the car."

"Oh, shit, yeah, I'll be right there," said Sebastian, wiping his lips.

"Hey, watch that mouth. When is your dad picking you up Mija?" she asked Lucy with a warming smile.

"He's going to pick me up at eight," Lucy lied, smiling back.

"Mm, okay," she said, then looks at her son. "Well, your dad and I are almost ready, so do it right now please, Chaparrito."

"Okay, Mommy," he replied as his mother leaves to finish getting ready.

Sebastian and Lucy look at each other and Lucy says something first. "Hey, it looks like we're getting the house to ourselves, huh, Babe?" giving a little wink.

"Ha, yeah Babes, looks like we are," said Sebastian with a big smile.

They are seated holding hands looking deep into each other's eyes. She gives him multiple quick kisses on the lips, continuing to do so as he proceeds to stand up; holding his hand with her left, and with her right hand gently "forcing" him down by the side of his neck, so he'll kiss her.

"I have to go," he whispered over her lips then kisses them.

She gives him a slightly big kiss. "No, don't. She can take her own bag," she whispered over his lips, giving a sweet smile then kisses him again.

"Oh, wow," he said, rolling his eyes with a smile.

"I'm just kidding," she said, giving him one last kiss. "Go," she finished, still holding his hand smiling at him.

Sebastian walks away and Lucy holds on to his hand up to the fingertips; she watches him walk through the door and her smile slowly disappears. She looks at the ground and then closes her eyes about to cry. "Babes, you want something to drink?" he asked, popping out from behind the doorway, scaring and stopping her from crying.

"Ah, ha yeah," she replied, chuckling then gets up. "Water, please," finishing with a smile and fluttering her eyes to take back the coming tears. Once she composes herself, she follows him inside.

They're both in the kitchen as Sebastian grabs a cup for Lucy's water. *He loves me, I know he does…I have to tell him. He…he won't hate me, he won't.* She begins to torment herself in her thoughts.

"Here you go, Babes," said Sebastian, handing Lucy the cup.

"Thanks," she replied with a weak smile.

"Okay, I'll be right back," he said, giving her a kiss on the cheek, then rushes off to finally get his mother's bag.

Lucy stands in the kitchen alone holding the cup with both hands, looking down at the water. She raises her head and slowly walks toward the living room; once there, Sebastian's mother hurries in.

"Do you see my…" she was saying, though as soon as she glances at Lucy, she notices her distress. "What's wrong, sweetie?" she asked, walking up to her slowly.

"Nothing, I'm okay," answered Lucy with the same weak smile she gave her boyfriend.

Sebastian's mother looks at her with suspicion. "Are you sure? You look distracted," she said, putting her hand on her shoulder and sitting her down on the couch.

"Yeah, yeah, I'm fine really," Lucy replied, looking straight into her eyes.

Sebastian's mother squints at her and begins to study her body language; she raises an eyebrow, then says, "Is everything okay at home?"

Lucy looks at her with shock. "Uh, yeah, why do you ask?"

"Well, I know your dad isn't going to come and pick you up," she answered with a smile. "Sebastian told me about what happened at your house a while ago," she said, crossing her arms.

Lucy's jaw drops, and embarrassment begins to fill her eyes. "He…he told you?"

"Of course, he did. He's my son and I expect him to…" she said, then takes a short sigh, "Look, I can't control you guys, you're going to do what you want. I just want you two to be responsible," she begins to chuckle, "and to tell you the truth, I trust you more than I trust Sebastian," she finished with a smile.

Sebastian's father then walks in from the hallway holding his wife's purse. "You ready?" he asked. He's also of a Hispanic descent, is fit and has a clean-cut hair style; he's handsome around his early forties and is wearing jeans with a button up blue collared shirt.

Sebastian's mother stands up and so does Lucy. "Yes," she replied fixing herself then turns to Lucy. "Just don't do anything stupid when we're gone, okay?" she told her giving a wink.

Lucy responds smiling with embarrassment, and they all walk out the front door. Sebastian is by the car, trunk open, trying to fit all the baggage in it.

"Mijo what are you doing? You're supposed to put my bags in not take them out," she said, smiling shaking her head.

"What? You have a lot of stuff; I have to make it fit," said Sebastian, struggling to put a large luggage in the trunk.

Sebastian's mother laughs to herself. "Honey, please help him," she said to her husband.

He goes to help as his wife stands with Lucy. "I got it," he told his son.

Sebastian heads over towards Lucy and his mother. "Thank you anyways, Mijo," said his mother, giving him a kiss on the forehead. "I wish you two were coming with us," she finished with a smile.

Sebastian's dad closes the trunk to the car. "Okay, ready!" he said, then gets into the driver's seat.

"That was fast," Sebastian's mother said, surprised. "Well, I guess we'll be leaving now. De amo me Chaparrito. Take care of each other." She gives Sebastian a kiss goodbye on the cheek, then gets into the car. "Bye!" said his mother and father as they drive off.

Sebastian and Lucy both wave goodbye as they disappear into the street. They walk into the house. "So, we have the whole place to ourselves what do you—" He was beginning to say but Lucy silently gets ahold of his hand from behind. "Babe…" she said, interrupting him.

They stand in the living room and he turns toward her smiling. "Yeah," he said, putting his hands around her waist.

Lucy softly pushes him away. "You told your mom about my brother catching us?" she asked with a worried look.

"Yeah…" he hesitantly replied, and she stares at him in shock. "What? I had to tell her. Your mom kept calling me, telling me she knew where I live," he said, frantically moving his eyes.

"AND YOU BELIEVED HER!" yelled Lucy, slightly hitting him on the chest.

Sebastian takes a step back. "Well, yeah…what do you expect? To think your mom's a liar?" he asked, putting his hands up.

Lucy squints her eyes at him. "This isn't a joke Sebastian…" she said, giving him a serious face.

"And I'm not joking, Babe; your mom really freaks me out. I never really met your parents till after I went over to say sorry," he replied as she gives him a stern look. "My own mom scares the crap outa me, I know not to fuck with moms," he finished, returning the same stare.

"Ah," she grunts and takes a seat on the couch. She hunches over and covers her face with both her hands.

Sebastian frowns with confusion and takes a seat next to her. "Was I not supposed to tell her?" he asked, slowly fiddling with his thumbs. "Like she was going to find out anyways."

"I don't know, but you should have told me you told her Sebastian…" she said, tossing her hands down to her side and looks at him. "Like she's known for over a year and you haven't told me," her eyes quickly widen, and she punches him in the chest. "Did you tell her about Flag Mountain? Oh, my gosh, Sebastian, if you told her I…ugh!" she said, continuing to hit him gently.

Sebastian gets ahold of her hands. "Babe, I don't tell her things she doesn't need to know, and it's not like I give her details, Babe; come on now," he said, proceeding to give her a hug, but she slightly pushes him away then turns her back to him. "What's wrong? My mom loves you. Why would I tell her if she was going to start hating you?"

Lucy quickly looks toward him. "But you didn't tell me Sebastian…" she said, getting up crossing her arms and turning her back to him again; she puts her head down then whispers, "you didn't tell me." *I haven't told him*, she thought to herself. "Look, Sebastian, I—" she proceeded to say as she rubs her eyelids.

"Could you please stop saying my name like that?" he said, interrupting her. "It makes me feel like I'm in trouble…Am, I in trouble?" he asked with hesitation.

Lucy sighs. "No Se…bee, you're not in trouble," she snickered.

Sebastian begins to frown as he slowly looks at the ground. "I'm," then raises his head looking at his girlfriend, "I'm sorry I told my mom without telling you," he said, with sad eyes and a weak smile; he sighs as he stands, "You're right; I should have told you. From now on, anything that involves us, I'll tell you everything," he finished, strengthening his smile.

"You promise?" she asked sincerely, walking closer to him.

"Yes, I promise," he answered, hugging her.

Lucy presses her head on his chest closing her eyes, and Sebastian rests his head on hers then starts to say, "I got some cookies and cream ic—"

But she pushes him on the couch and says, "I'll go get the ice cream and you find something to watch." Then runs off to the kitchen.

Sebastian chuckles; grabbing the remote.

Lucy rubs her tummy as she opens the freezer. "We're going to enjoy this," she whispers as she takes out the cookies n cream ice cream. She grabs a bowl and the scooper, then proceeds to slowly put two scoops of ice cream in it; she stares at the bowl as she places the scooper down, beginning to think over and over, *I need to tell him.* She closes her eyes and takes a deep sigh then smiles. *I'll tell him later,* only taking one spoon with her.

Sebastian flips through the channels, and Lucy walks into the living room holding the bowl of ice cream. She rushes over sitting next to him grabbing the spoon from the bowl.

"Where's mine?" he asked.

"Right here," she answered, feeding him some ice cream.

The both of them cuddle and watch a movie together sharing a delicious treat. Time passes and they are in the middle of their film.

Television:

A man and woman are in a master bedroom on top of a king-sized bed, under a single cover with their heads out. They are having sex and the woman has her legs over the man looking down at him. "Are you sure no one's home?" asked the man. "And why are we always under the blanket?"

"Because I like blankets," said the woman as she puts her index finger over his lips. "Now shut up before my brothers hear you."

Lucy hits Sebastian on the shoulder. "Did you pick this movie on purpose, you butt!" she asked, giving him a stern look.

"Ha, no, this is a new movie. I've never seen it," said Sebastian, laughing.

"I still can't believe you told your mom we got caught having sex," she giggled, rolling her eyes.

Sebastian sits up. "Shit, if you would have remembered to lock the door, then your bother wouldn't have walked in on us," he said, tilting his head smiling.

"Don't cuss at me boy," she said, with a smirk and crosses her arms. "If you would have been listening, you would have heard him coming!"

"So, you heard him coming?" he asked, squinting his eyes.

Lucy blushes. "No, I was too busy enjoying myself," she said, raising an eyebrow smirking at him.

"What? And I can't enjoy myself?" he asked.

"Nope, not allowed," she said, starting to crawl on top of him.

Sebastian slowly rests his back on the seat cushions. "Wh…what are you doing?" he stuttered, checking her out as he moved his eyes in all directions.

"What does it look like?"

"But the movie…"

"Shut up and do your job," she said, kissing him and biting his lip.

They both close their eyes as they kiss, letting things go from there.

# CHAPTER SIX

# UNDER SOME STARS

Jose and Jessica dropped off everyone at home after dinner except for Lucy, who needed to go speak with her boyfriend, so they took her to his house. Lucy found out he didn't tell her something and with her being overwhelmed, she now doesn't know how to tell him what he needs to know. She's now sleeping over there making the best out of the night.

Jose took Jessica to a nearby park. The park is thirty-two acers large with five entrances, having a black brick wall embedded with black bar fencing. The brick wall arches over the main gate, and on the top is a sign that reads "Riverbank Park." A rolled up banner is on top of it ready to cover the sign. The entire area is filled with dark green trees grassy planes and hills, having a large river flow through it over two-thousand five-hundred feet wide. Near the front entrance is an outdoor stage decorated with college banners. Three tall hills are surrounding the stage, each having a picnic area decorated with small white lights, and the tables with bright red and gold covers. Jessica and Jose are now on one of the hills by the stage, happily lying on the grass; Jose is on his phone with one hand, as Jessica holds the other looking up at the few stars that are in the sky. "Aren't the stars beautiful?" she asked, smiling at them.

"Ah, yeah, I guess, you know we can do this every night when we're at Dunsvill," said Jose, glancing at Jessica.

She looks at him. "Yeah, but I like the park," she said, giving him a sweet smile.

"Well, I bet the stars are a lot brighter over there," he said, smiling back at her.

"Well, I think they're bright enough right here," said Jessica, gazing at the stars.

"There's only like three stars up there," he smirks at her.

Jessica looks at him in shock. "There's ten, you ass. If you would just stop being on your phone," she said, rolling her eyes.

"I'm trying to look up some pictures of Dunsvill, and if I can find out where exactly it is," he said, scrolling through his phone.

Jessica elevates herself. "You don't even know where this place is and you want us to go there?" she asked, tilting her head and squinting her eyes at him.

Jose looks back at her with excitement. "Mrs. G said that it's somewhere in the forbidden side of the Unmarked Forest, but I'm just double checking," he said, moving his eyebrows up and down.

She stares at him with disbelief. "Are you fuckin' serious? There is no way we're going there," she said, clenching her eyebrows.

He chuckles. "Ha, don't be scared; I bet we'll find it in no time—"

"You want us to drive over eight hours to a place that might not even be there?" she asked, interrupting him and continues, "What if we don't find it, huh? What if we get lost? What the fuck are we going to do about gas? I'm sure there's no gas station there," she finished crossing her arms.

"Actually, there is one in the forest, for the park rangers that are there. See, it's not that bad," he replied showing her his cell phone with a smug face.

She takes a deep sigh closing her eyes, slightly shaking her head. "Just stop. I don't wanna hear it anymore." She then smiles and leans in toward Jose. "Let's just enjoy right here right now, okay?" she asked, going in for a kiss.

He rejects the kiss and quickly says, "Come on, just come with us. It'll be fun."

Jessica looks down at Jose with anger. "Is that all you can fuckin' talk about? Is that stupid ass town!" she asked, with great annoyance, ripping some grass from the ground and throwing it at him.

Jose flinches. "Well, I just wanna know if you'd come," he said, not getting the message.

Jessica, with her mouth open and eyebrows clenched says, "You know what? Fine. I'll go if it will make you shut up about it already! That's all you've been talking about since we got here."

Jose puts up his phone between them with excitement, meaning to text his friends. "Okay, awesome, now I just need to find out if the others will go," he said, happily as he makes a group message.

"Oh, my fuckin' goodness, man, I'm leaving!" Jessica said furiously. She gets up, retrieving her things then storms off.

Jose looks up at her as she walks away. "What? Wait, where you going?" he asked, confused.

As she continues to walk, she yells, "Home!" without turning back.

Jose sits up on the grass. "But why?" he asked.

She stops, then turns toward him. "'Cause all you fucking talk about is that stupid ass town!" Jessica answered back with her arms crossed.

"Okay, I'm sorry, I won't talk about it anymore; come back yeah?" he asked, as he taps on the grass, trying to get at her good side.

Jessica throws her arms down in a fit and stomps her left foot with anger. "What the fuck? No! I'm mad at you, I'm going home," she said madly, beginning to walk down the hill.

"Come on, you're not going to walk home by yourself; it's like 10:00 P.M.; come back," said Jose, trying to get her to lay down with him.

"It's 9:45! And I can, and I will, so bye," said Jessica, trudging while frustrated and trying to calm herself down at the same time.

"Well..." Jose begins to get up off the ground, then says, "let me at least give you a ride, you're going to get in trouble," dusting himself off.

Jessica suddenly stops and crosses her arms. "Fine," she said, rolling her eyes with an angry tone.

They get into Jose's van and drive off. Jessica is looking out the window with her arms crossed. It's silent for five minutes and as they come to a red light, Jose turns to Jessica. "You still mad at me?" he asked.

Jessica just rolls her eyes and says, "Yes! Just don't talk to me; you're going to end up talking about that fucking town again, just take me home."

The ride continues and she is still looking out the window with her arms crossed. He looks at her and sees that she won't even look at him. Time passes and it's still silent in the van, even outside in the dark streets.

"Hey, I'm sorry, I just—"

Jessica interrupts him by saying, "Okay, stop; I'm not mad at you, just don't talk about the town to me right now," finally looking at him.

Jose makes a sad smile and asks, "Alright, so do you wanna talk to me now or…?"

"No just, just take me home," she answered, looking back out the window.

"But I thought you said you weren't mad?" asked Jose, wanting to talk to her.

Jessica rests her head on the headrest and closes her eyes. "I'm not mad; I just wanna go home, I'm tired," she said.

"Alright," Jose said with a sad face.

They arrive at Jessica's house and she quickly unbuckles her seatbelt, getting her things ready. Jose drives up the driveway and says, "Okay, we're here," parking his vehicle.

Jessica opens the van door. "Thank you, bye," she said, getting out closing the door, and starts walking toward her front door.

Jose's eyes widen, and he takes in a deep breath, he turns off the engine then gets out of his van. He rushes around his vehicle and calls out to Jessica, "Wait!" He runs over to her, hugs her, and gives her a big kiss on the lips.

"Mm, see now that's what I wanted to do instead of talking. Kiss me again," she said, grabbing his shirt and starts making out with him.

They stop and Jose walks her up to her house door. "I'm sorry I just want—"

Jessica puts her left index finger over his lips. "Shh, I know. It's okay; we'll talk about your stupid little town tomorrow, okay?" she said, with a sweet smile.

"Okay," said Jose, returning a smile.

They give each other one more goodbye kiss, and Jose leaves after Jessica goes inside her house.

# CHAPTER SEVEN

# CHARMING

When the friends had finished their dinner and betting on a game of bowling, Jose dropped everybody off at their locations. After Will was left at home, he entered his house and stopped in front of a portrait of a military man. He lit the candles surrounding the photo then saluted it giving a small smile. He proceeded to go to his room and got an extra change of clothes to take a shower. Once finished freshening up, he checked in on his mother to find her asleep in bed. He put on his shoes and grabbed his phone, sending his mother a text message letting her know he will be out late. Before leaving he gave one last salute saying, "I'll be home soon, Sir." He blew out the candles then closed the door behind him.

Will is walking in the night through his neighborhood, dressed nice and clean, focusing straight ahead of him. He arrives at a two-story blue brick house. He slowly creeps up the side of the large living room window, and peeks through the curtains seeing Rosie's father. He's sitting on a lazy boy comfy chair made of leather, watching an action movie off a big flat screen television. Will backs away from the window, and then heads toward the left side of the house, next to a wooden rectangle trellis. He picks up small rocks from the ground, looks up at a second story window and begins to throw them at it.

The girl from Will's photo signed Rosie, opens the window as a rock flies straight between her eyes. "Aw, fuck," she said, quietly rubbing her forehead with a smile, then whispers out loud, "Ha, what you doing here, you creep? That hurt," she chuckles, leaning out playfully glaring at Will.

"Shit, sorry, you okay?" he asked, biting his knuckles.

Rosie rolls her eyes. "Yeah," she looks behind her. "Hold on, okay?" she asked, turning back to Will. She walks up to her bedroom door, as action sounds come from her hallway, and locks it. She is still able to hear the movie from downstairs as she returns to her window, she whispers out, "Alright, come on."

Will climbs the trellis and enters her room. He walks up to her embracing her. "Hey, Babe, I missed you," he said, kissing her lips.

She smiles and closes her eyes as she receives the kiss. "I missed you, too," she replied, slowly opening her eyes. "What are you doing here? It's late."

He holds her by the waist and looks into her eyes saying, "I just had to see you. I was really hoping you would come with us."

"Yeah, me, too, Babe; my dad came to the school before the bell rang. He told me he would, so I left before he came; ha, sorry, I didn't tell you," she said, hugging him then leads him to sit on her bed. "Did you have fun?" she asked.

"Ha, yeah," he chuckled. "Mark earned his spot back in the group. Wanna see what he did?" he asked, smiling and grabbing his phone from his pocket.

They look at the videos the friends recorded at Ray's Diner. "Oh, my gosh, this is gold. It already has over ten thousand views. He's so lucky it's the end of the school year," said Rosie, scrolling through the comments.

"I think he'll like the attention; just wait till tomorrow," he said.

Rosie smirks at him. "So, you guys good now? Are we all good?" she asked, slightly pushing him.

Will rolls his eyes. "I guess, I don't know. He was all over you," he replied with a frown. "What if he grabbed you or something?"

Rosie's eyes widen then quickly go back to normal smiling. "For the last time, Babe, he's your best friend. You guys practically known each other since birth, he's like your little brother."

Will then becomes heated and raises his voice a bit. "Well, brothers don't do that shit!" he said, clenching his eyebrows.

"Shh, okay, okay," she said, rubbing his back calming him down. "You know, you, Nallely, and Christina are the only ones that have a problem with Mark. He's already said sorry like thousand times."

"Why did you forgive him?" he asked, looking at her with a weak smile.

"'Cause I know he means a lot to you, Babe," she answered, smiling back gently and rubbing his cheek. "Plus, he was really fucked up; I've never seen him so far gone before," she said with worried eyes.

Will looks down and thinks to himself.

"Why did you dance with him if you're so pissed?" she asked, crossing her arms.

He smiles. "I forgot I was mad at him I guess; in the moment it just brought up old times," he said, looking at her with sad eyes.

"You two should talk, Babe, cry on each other's shoulder or something," she said, giving him a wink.

They both chuckle as Will's cell phone vibrates in Rosie's hand; she looks at it and unlocks the phone's screen then raises an eyebrow.

"What is it?" he asked.

Rosie looks at Will raising the other eyebrow. "When were you going to tell me about Dunsvill?"

"Ah, I was gonna tell you right now," he said, with a grin.

She shakes her head smiling. "You're such a bad liar," she said, pinching his cheek as he smacks her hand away; she looks back at the phone. "Jose said Jessica is going, so if we don't go we're all punk ass losers."

"Wow, really? I'm surprised he convinced her," he said.

"Yeah, me, too; I remember when she didn't want to go in that hunted house at Flag Mountain; I had to wait with her 'cause she didn't trust the people in costumes ha," giggled Rosie.

They both laugh and the movie from downstairs suddenly stops. "Oh, shit, my dad is coming!" Rosie whispered, pushing Will off her bed.

"What? How do you know?" he asked as she continues to push him toward her window.

"I just do! I'll meet you on the roof; now, go!" she said, shoving him out of her window.

"Rosie! What are you doing in there!" shouted her father, wiggling the door's handle. "Why is this door locked? Open it now!" he said, banging on the door.

Rosie gives Will a stern look as she says, "Give me a second! I'm putting on my pj's!"

Her father continues banging on the door. "You already have your pajamas on! Open this door now!"

"I wanna wear different ones, damn…" she called out.

As Will climbs up to the roof, Rosie quickly changes her pajamas. "You have till the count of five! ONE, TWO!" her father proceeded to count down.

Rosie struggles to put her legs through her pajama pants, as she squeezes her head and arms pass her shirt. "I'm coming I'm coming gosh!" she yelled, tumbling to her door.

"THREE, FOUR, FI-!" he said, stopping at five because Rosie opens the door quickly.

"What? What happened?" she asked, shrugging her shoulders with an oblivious look.

Her father forces his way into her room. "Why was your door locked? What were you doing, huh?" he asked, inspecting the area.

Rosie crosses her arms. "I already told you, I was changing," she said, following her father. She sees her boyfriend's phone on the floor near the window. "I'm cold; are you cold?" she asked as she walked up to the window and kicks the phone under her dresser.

"Why was the window open in the first place if you're cold?" he gives her a stern look continuing to interrogate her, "and who were you talking to, huh? I heard voices."

"Huh?" she turns to her father with shocked eyes. "Oh, that was me, I was talking to myself," she replied with a weak smile.

"Don't lie to me," he said, walking up to the window. "Who was in here? I heard a boy." He opens the window and looks out in his front yard.

"What? No, no one was in here, Daddy. It was me."

Her father gives her a stern glare. "Mm, go to bed it's getting late, and I don't want to hear any noise, or you're not allowed to go to S.R.F.," he said, walking out her room slamming the door.

Rosie rushes over locking her door, and then grabs her boyfriend's cell phone from under the dresser. She climbs out her window and heads up toward the roof, hanging herself off the edge of the house with her arms, looking at Will with a sweet smile. "Before we go to Dunsvill, let's go on a little field trip tomorrow."

"Wait, you wanna go?" asked Will.

She lifts her body, and does a front walkover gently landing on the rooftop as she says, "Well, I'm no punk ass loser," then quietly walks over toward her boyfriend. "And who knows? It might be romantic," she said, sitting next to him giving a wink.

"What if we don't even find it?" he smirks at her. "No one has been there in years, and you can't find the address anywhere because of its history," he said, smiling as he tilts and shakes his head.

"Well, then, make sure to bring your big tent 'cause I guess we're camping," she answered, smiling small. "Perfect bonding time," she said, now closing her eyes placing her hands under her chin.

He chuckles. "Ha, wow, that's what Jose said."

She opens her eyes and punches him softly. "See! Jose knows what's up; but I wanna go to the beach first. We can go at lunch since we're having that boring ass Last Day Party. I'll text everybody right now and tell Jose to get his van ready," she said, typing in Will's cell phone.

"Alright, you gonna want to go in the water, huh?" he asked.

Rosie quickly turns her head toward Will. "Duh, why do you think I wanna go there; my dad won't let me use the pool," she said, with an annoyed tone rolling her eyes. "So, we going to the beach just in case there's no lake at the town," she continues with a smug face, that suddenly turns into shock when hearing a faint sound of a window sliding open. "Fuck!" she jumps to her feet looking at the edge of the roof. "Babe, run…" she finished with a whisper.

Will, still sitting down, asks, "What, what happened—?" glancing at the area she is staring at.

The top of her father's head begins to rise slowly; Rosie gets in front of Will so she will be blocking him from her father's view. "Go before my dad sees you!" she loudly whispered, helping him stand.

"Rosie what in the world are you doing up here? Who's there with you?" he yelled, lifting his upper body, giving his daughter a cold glare as she turns to look at him.

She quickly starts pushing her boyfriend screaming, "RUN! GO!" leading him to the backyard.

"Where am I going to go?" Will whispered, panicking trying to find a way down.

Rosie looks at her dad one last time and sees he has one foot on the roof. "Just jump in the pool!" she said, forcing him to stand above her pool.

Her father stops himself from getting up completely. "DON'T YOU DARE!" he yelled, preparing to go back inside; and once he sees his daughter's companion take a running start, he quickly gets into the house.

Will leaps off into the pool causing a cannonball and begins to swim to the swimming pool ladder. As soon as he gets out of the pool, Rosie's father comes bursting out the back door while she watches from the roof. She looks at both her father and boyfriend, then realizes she still has Will's cell phone. She clenches it with her hands. "Run, my little princess!" she yelled out, embracing the phone against her chest, watching him jump the fence to the neighbor's house.

"Get your ass back inside, Rosie! NOW!" yelled her father with anger then looks over the fence Will jumped over. "AND THAT BETTER NOT BE YOU, WILL!"

# CHAPTER EIGHT

# HI MY NAME IS

The friends have all rested up from their long day; having a delicious dinner at Ray's Diner, betting on a game of bowling that likely saved their friendship. Couples, spending time together and sharing their thoughts to each other. Now it's a new day and plans for the beach are already made.

Christina and Jessica are walking toward the locker area at the high school, talking to each other while a random student follows them. He's a dark-skinned Filipino sophomore, standing fairly tall. He has a big round head and wears faded t-shirts and jeans.

"He rejected your kiss?" asked Christina in shock.

"Yeah! I had to say I would go to that stupid town so he would shut up, but that didn't even work," said Jessica with a stern look.

Christina shakes her head, smiling, and says, "Like I said, the boy be clueless. I don't know how you can deal with it."

Jessica rolls her eyes. "He can surprise me sometimes, and he can be sweet when he puts his mind to it," she said, with a tiny smile. "Once he actually stood out my window with a radio playing our song, it was cute; my baby brother threw a water balloon at him."

"What no way! When did this happen?" asked Christina, surprised.

Jessica begins to grin big. "A long time ago, ha, I told him I wouldn't tell anyone, but fuck that, it's too funny. My dad even got mad at him for waking him up," she said, laughing.

The girls arrive at Christina's locker and they both look inside it, including the random student who they haven't noticed behind them. "So, you're really going to Dunsvill?" she asked, going through crumbled paper balls.

"Yeah, I guess. I don't think it's a good idea but, Rosie and Will are going so there's no doubt Lucy will go if Sebastian hasn't already convinced her. I don't want to be left behind," replied Jessica.

Christina finds the balled up piece of paper she was looking for; she takes a knee putting it in her purse and begins to ruffle through her things. "Oh, talking about Rosie; are you ready for the beach—?" she was asking turning to Jessica as she takes out a plastic bag of marijuana, but she then notices the random guy watching them. "Oh, shit fuck, the fuck," she quickly puts the bag away. "Who the fuck are you?" she asked, startled.

"Hi, my name's James," he answered, sticking his hand out toward the girls.

They raise an eyebrow and stare at his hand then his face at the same time. "The fuck you want?" asked Christina with disgust.

"I hear you're going to Dunsvill," answered James, smiling.

Christina glares deeply into his eyes with concern. "How the fuck did you hear that?" she asked, continuing to interrogate.

"Yeah, were you following us?" joined Jessica, clenching her eyebrows.

"Fuckin' creep," added Christina, closing the locker and picks up her purse.

The girls are about to walk away but James steps in front of them, blocking their path. "Can I come with you guys?"

Christina glances at Jessica in shock. "Fuck, no, you can't come, the fuck?" she said, looking at him up and down. "What kind of fuckin' question is that?" she asked, trying to get by him.

"You really like that word, huh?" he asked, not letting her pass with a grin.

"Fuck, yeah, now fuck off!" projected Christina.

They both push their way past James, and he follows behind. "Aw, come on! Don't be like that," he said, trying to keep up with them.

The girls begin to walk faster. "Boy, I said fuck off! How much more of a bitch do I have to be for you to leave us the fuck alone?" asked Christina, rolling her eyes.

James follows their pace and looks at Jessica giving her a small smile. "I bet you want me to go, huh?"

"What? Ew, no! Why you say that?" she asked, avoiding eye contact.

"Well, you're having problems with your man, right? Maybe I can make the trip more interesting?" he asked, giving her a wink.

Jessica becomes nervous and Christina stops to get in James' face. "Okay, what the fuck is your problem, huh? Does 'no' not mean no anymore?" she asked with anger.

"Hey, I'm only playing," he gives out a chuckle. "I just really want to go," he said, putting his hands together. "Please! I'll do anything," he pleaded.

Christina becomes curious and asks, "Why do you wanna go so bad, huh? Do you even know what happened there?"

James' eyes brighten up. "YES! That's why I want go!" his grin begins to grow. "A real live ghost town, with a crazy back story! We would be the first to actually go there in over a hundred years, we'll make history!" he said, with an open smile.

"Well, yeah, we are going," said Christina, pointing at Jessica and herself. "Not you," she finished, walking away once again.

"Aw come on, please! I said I'll do anything," he continues to plead with puppy dog eyes walking alongside her.

"How about you go die, once you're dead you can come, okay," she answered with a condescending smile.

James' faces falls, and he stops walking with the girls. "That's not nice!" he yelled out to them as they leave.

"I DON'T GIVE A FUCK!" Christina yelled back.

The girls continue to walk down the school's hallways and Jessica begins to laugh. "Damn Christina," she said, with a smile.

"Ha, what? He was being a total fuck. I had to say something to get him to leave," she replied, laughing.

The morning class bell rings as Jessica says, "I hope we don't see him again," and they start to walk to their classroom. "What did you get from you locker anyways?" she asked.

"Oh, nothing, just a letter from a secret admirer," she answered.

"What about Mark?"

Christina opens the door to their class. "What about him?" she asked, with a chuckle.

Jessica smiles shaking her head as they both walk into their class.

# CHAPTER NINE

# SPAM CALLER

Several classes end, and the Last Day Party begins for all the students in the school. The friends head to their favorite spot on the stage in the large quad. Rosie and Will come in holding hands, talking about how she's going to go on the trip; since she's grounded. Nallely is walking with Diana arm in arm. Jose and Mark come in while talking to other students about Marks dance, as Jessica and Christina are a good distance behind talking about them. Sebastian, who's now dressed like a skater with skinny black jeans and flannel shirt with sleeves rolled up, comes in with Lucy with his left arm around her shoulders.

"So, when we going to the beach, you guys?" asked Sebastian, smiling with excitement.

Jose leaves Mark with the students, turning to Sebastian and the others. "Once they start the music, we'll go," he answered as Jessica and Christina come standing by his side. "Hello there beautiful," he said, with a smile kissing his girlfriend on the lips.

"Ha, hi," blushed Jessica.

Rosie jumps in place. "You guys brought my surfboard right, Babe?" she asked, rubbing Will's cheek.

"Yeah, it's on his van," he answered with a smile, pointing at Jose.

"Yes, thank you! We're going to my favorite spot," she said, hugging Will, then looks at her friends. "The water is perfect at this time!"

Mark says goodbye to his new friends. "Man, I fucking love this day!"

he said happily. "Everyone's been showing me some love because of yester-day."

"And it's only gonna get better, thanks to Nallely," said Christina, secretly showing her friends the bag of marijuana, and Nallely winks at her with a smile.

Diana's eyes widen. "Oh, shit, I almost forgot!" she said turning towards Nallely. "Hey, come with me yeah?" she asked, grabbing her hand.

Diana and Nallely rush over to the Auto Shop hand in hand. Once there Diana sets her backpack down and begins to look through her now old workstation.

"What are you looking for?" asked Nallely.

Diana ruffles in the back of her desk saying, "My pipe, I know I left it here."

Nallely walks up to Diana's backpack and asks, "Isn't it in your bag?" going through it.

"No, you can check, but I know it's here somewhere," she replied, pulling out a metal sheet from the desk.

As Nallely is looking in Diana's things, she sees that her cell phone is vi-brating receiving a call. Once she picks it up the call ends, and she notices that there are twenty-seven missed calls from someone named Adriana.

Diana comes out from under the workstation. "Found it!" she said, happily showing it to Nallely, but she's still fixated on the phone.

"Why is Adriana calling you?" Nallely asked, looking at her with concern-ing eyes.

Diana stands. "What? I didn't even know she was calling, I been with you the whole day," she said, walking up to her and reaches for her phone.

Nallely moves it away from her. "She called you like thirty times," she said, squinting her eyebrows.

Diana looks at her in shock. "Why she calling me if we had class," she said, trying to grab her cell phone. "She was in class, right?" she asked, getting ahold of the phone.

"I don't know you tell me," she said, crossing her arms. "Call her and find out what she wants and put it on speaker."

"Okay, dang. You don't have to be worried," said Diana, calling Adri-ana back.

As soon as it starts to ring Adriana answers the phone, crying and talking frantically:

**Adriana:** "Diana! Oh, my gosh, please tell me you guys saw my mom at the stupid diner. Tell me you guys talked to her and she told you where she was going."

**Diana:** "What? Slow down, what are you talking about?"

**Adriana:** (sniffle) "My mom! I know you guys went to Ray's Diner, I saw the video you guys did there, and she was even walking past one of them. Please, tell me you know something."

**Diana:** "Oh, no, I'm sorry we didn't know she was there, where are you?"

**Adriana:** "I'm at home waiting for my dad; he's at the police station right now, but he said he wants me and my brothers to go with him and look for my mom. She didn't come back home at all last night." (cries quietly)

**Diana:** (looks at Nallely in shock) "I don't know what to say."

**Adriana:** "You don't have to say anything, I was just hopin you talked with her or something…" (sniffles) "I gotta go bye."

**Diana:** "Bye." (call ends)

Nallely and Diana look at each other with disbelief. "Still think I don't have to worry," said Nallely, raising her eyebrows. "Is her mom really in one of our videos?" she asked with worried eyes.

"I don't know let's see," said Diana, looking up the videos Jose and Lucy recorded yesterday.

It didn't take long for them to find the video Adriana's mother is in. She was walking in the background when the girls were giving Mark a makeover. Diana and Nallely glance at each other with wonder.

"What do you think happened to her?" asked Nallely.

Diana puts her things away in her backpack then puts it on. "I don't know, but I hope she's okay," she said, grabbing Nallely's hand and gives her a sweet smile; music begins to play throughout the school. "Come on, they'll be at the van waiting for us."

They both walkout of the Auto Shop, heading towards the student parking lot.

# CHAPTER TEN

# RED AND BLUE

The school is having a big Last Day Party for all the students, and the friends are all getting ready to leave school grounds to go to the beach. Diana and Nallely went off to retrieve something and got a depressing phone call. Moments later when music began to play in the school; the friends went to the students' parking lot to wait in Jose's van except for Will, Rosie, Diana and Nallely. Jose is sitting in the driver's seat with Jessica in the passenger's, Christina is in the back with Mark next to her in the middle seat, while Lucy and Sebastian are in the trunk of the van, looking over Mark and Christina's seats.

Jose is tapping his fingers impatiently on the steering wheel, as Jessica is talking to him while the others talk to one another.

Jessica rolls her eyes. "He just kept following us, and he even said he can make the trip more interesting for me," she said, looking at Jose with unimpressed eyes, and notices that he's not paying attention. "Hey! Are you listening?" she asked, pushing him slightly.

"Where's Rosie and the others? She the one who wants to go," asked Jose, turning over and looking at his friends in the back.

"Guess not…" whispered Jessica, crossing her arms.

"They're coming," answered Lucy.

"Ugh text them and tell them to hurry their slow asses up!" he said, throwing himself back on his seat eager to leave.

"Ah, fine," said Lucy, rolling her eyes as she pulls out her cell phone to text Rosie:

> **Lucy:** Hey, Jose told me to tell u guys to hurry.
> **Rosie:** Well, u can tell the punk ass bitch to wait…we're almost there.
> **Lucy:** lol ok

Lucy puts her phone away and says, "They said they're coming."

"Alright, well, I'll give them one minute," said Jose, starting his van.

"Ha, wow, you suck, man," said Mark, laughing.

The rest of the friends then come rushing over getting into the van. Christina moves toward the middle seat of the vehicle, leaving Mark behind. "You guys take the back since your favorite people are there," she tells Rosie and Will with a smile.

"Rosie! Yes, come back here!" said Lucy with excitement patting the headrest of the seat. "I can't believe your dad didn't catch you with Will's phone. You're like a ninja!"

As Diana is taking her seat, she says, "Wow, Sebastian, you always wanna go back there, don't get too crazy you two ha!" she giggles.

Once everyone gets settled in the van; Jose drives off to Rosie's secret spot on the beach. They're halfway there until….

Jose lowers down the music with a quick flick. "Fuck! It's the cops. Hey, Sebastian, Lucy get down!" he said, pissed off as the siren wails and lights flash behind him.

Rosie quickly turns to Christina. "Shit, the weed! Hide it, Christina!" she said, panicking. Christina grabs the bag of weed and raps it in a blanket that was under the seat. "Okay, okay!" she said, putting the weed under the seat just as Jose pulls over and the siren stops.

An old white male officer with a gray beard wearing sunglasses; walks up to the driver's side window.

"Um, is there something wrong officer?" asked Jose nervously.

The officer slowly takes off his sunglasses and looks at everyone in the van with curious eyes. "Yeah, you were speeding; may I see your license and registration please?" asked the officer politely, putting his glasses in his shirt pocket.

Jose reaches over toward the glove compartment, getting his license and registration. "Ah, yeah, here," he said, handing the officer what he asked for.

The officer examines the papers and without looking at Jose he asks, "Shouldn't you kids be in school?"

Jose quickly answers, "It's the last day of school sir," with a smile.

He then looks up at Jose. "Then why aren't you guys in school for the last day?" asked the officer with his eyebrows clenched, looking at everyone else in the van.

The friends stay quiet as the officer continues to stare them down. "Where you guys headed, hmm?" asked the officer with his eyebrows still clenched, getting a little closer to Jose.

"The beach, sir," answered Jose, looking away from the officer then back at him.

"So, you're ditching the last day of school to go to the beach, huh?...Ha, ha, okay, go; just don't let any other cop pull you over, because they might not be as okay with this as I am. Have a nice day," said the officer with a smile.

"Ah, thank you, sir," said Jose with a relieved sigh.

The officer walks back to his car, but then he sees Sebastian and Lucy in the back. "Um, excuse me, who's back there?" asked the officer, going back to the driver's window.

Jose quickly answers. "No one, sir."

The officer slowly approaches Jose. "Oh, please, don't lie to me; I hate it when people lie, especially if I just let you go. NOW, who's back there?" he asked again.

"My friend Sebastian and his girlfriend, we—" Jose started to say, but Lucy interrupts him and says, "Hey, what I'm not your friend?"

"Oh, my, please...shut up," said Jose, putting his hand on his forehead, and sliding it to the back of his neck then looks at the officer.

The officer takes out a notebook. "That isn't safe to have two people back there, I was going to let it slide, too, but you just had to lie to me. I'm going to have to give you a ticket," he said, about to write up a ticket.

Jose puts his hands together and begins to beg. "No, please! I'm sorry sir; please my dad would kill me! Please, don't; please give me no ticket, please."

The officer gives him an uneasy glare. "Hmm? I guess I can forget you lied to me, give me hundred pushups and I won't write you up, okay?" he asked, working up a deal.

"Alright, I can do that!" said Jose getting out of his van.

All the friends stay in the van as they watch Jose do pushups out the right side windows, some looking over each other's shoulders.

"Come on, Babe! Work them mussels!" yelled Jessica.

All his friends continued to root him on as he reached closer and closer to one hundred. "Yeah, come on! Ninety-one, ninety-two, ninety-three, ninety-four!" cheered the friends. "One hundred!" they yelled with excitement, including the officer.

"Ah, yeah! Done! Phew!" said Jose happily and pumped up from his small workout.

The officer puts his notebook away. "Ha, yeah, you're done, now get outta here, before I change my damn mind," he said, with laughter heading to his car.

Jose gets in his van and starts to drive off to the beach.

"Damn the cop was chill," said Nallely.

"Ha, yeah, he was cool," laughed Rosie.

"Cops are all the same to me, bitches," said Will with a serious face.

Rosie punches Will's shoulder. "Calm your ass down, Babe, just because they caught you with weed...and stealing," she said, making fun of him.

"What? No way!" said Christina in shock.

Rosie pinches his cheek and says, "Yeah, he's not the good boy you think he is," then embracing his arm.

Will rubs his cheek. "Ah, thanks a lot Rosie, I didn't want them to know!" he said, madly.

Rosie quickly lets go of him, crossing her arms and does a circle motion with her head. "Mm, so, I'm Rosie to you, now, okay I see," she said, with a mad face.

Will's face goes pale. "Wait, no, I'm sorry, Babe," he apologizes.

"Mm, yeah, okay," she said, looking away from him.

"Ah!" grunted Will, putting his head down.

She hugs him. "Ha, you're so cute when you're mad, Babe; it's okay," she giggled, giving Will a big kiss on the cheek.

"Well, let's all be happy the cop let us go and he didn't find the weed," said Jessica with a smile.

Christina's eyes widen, and she begins to laugh. "Ha, oh, yeah, I forgot about the weed," she said, grabbing the weed from the blanket under her seat.

"How can you forget about the weed, Babe, ha," said Mark with laughter.

It gets really quiet in the van, and Christina just looks back at Mark with a serious face for calling her Babe. "What? Oh, shit, sorry, Christina…" said Mark feeling stupid.

"Mm, yeah, okay," said Christina, slightly blushing.

It gets quiet for about three long minutes. Lucy sits up so she can see everyone. "Well, this is um awkward, ha-ha, so we almost there?" she asked, with a smile.

"Yeah, we…" Jose began to say but stops himself when he sees Lucy in the rearview mirror, "get down I want no ticket; Christina there's a blanket under your seat, give it to her please," he said, with an irritated voice.

"But we're almost there why should—" Lucy started saying, but Sebastian interrupts her. "Babes just get the blanket," he said, with a wink. "Oh, okay, Love," Lucy said grabbing the blanket.

"Ha, wow, really, you guys? Even if you're under the blanket we can still hear you," said Rosie, laughing.

"Ha, as long as you can't see, it's all good," said Lucy under the blanket with Sebastian. "It smells like weed," she giggles.

"Well, do that shit later; we're here!" said Rosie with excitement.

# CHAPTER ELEVEN

# BEACH DAY

The friends have left school early, and on the way to the beach they were pulled over by a police officer for speeding. Jose almost got away with no problems, until he lied about people being in the trunk of his van. He ended up having to make a deal to avoid getting a ticket. Now they have arrived at their destination, parking on the side of an old abandoned sandy road by the beach.

A warm shore breeze rolls in as the friends all get out of Jose's van. They walk to a gate with a sign reading: "NO TRESPASSING!"

"Wow, do you and Jose have some kind of problem with being in places you shouldn't be?" asked Jessica, laughing and shaking her head.

"What can I say, I love the thrill of doing something wrong," replied Rosie with a big grin.

Crossing through the soft coarse sand; the friends make their way to a secluded area, leaving the surfboard on the van. They find a spot with lots of boulders and rocks to sit down at, Christina then takes out her bag of weed while searching her pockets. "Fuck!" she said, frantically patting herself down.

Jessica gets a little startled. "What?" she quickly asked.

"I fucking forgot my damn fucking piece!" answered Christina, rolling her eyes in anger.

"Ha, it's a good thing I brought mine," said Diana, taking out her glass pipe and hands it to Christina.

Christina's eyes brighten up while grabbing the pipe. "Yes! Thank you!" she said, happily with a smile.

They all have been smoking for a while except for Lucy; she sits by herself on a rock away from the weed smoke.

"Hey, (cough, cough), Lucy, (cough), want some of this shit?" asked Mark, struggling to speak.

"No, thanks," she answered with a smile.

Sebastian then looks at her with curiosity. "Why not, Babes? You didn't smoke last time we hung out; don't you smoke anymore? And what you doing over there for?" he asked, grabbing the pipe then begins to take a hit.

"I do, but I don't want any right now, and I don't want any smoke in my face either," Lucy answered, still smiling, picking up a nearby stick.

Sebastian holds his breath for a few seconds, then says, "Ah, but it's been like almost two months," blowing out smoke as he passes the pipe to Will.

Lucy looks down at the sand. "I know but, I don't know I just don't want any," she replied, picking at the sand with the stick.

"You want me to go over there?" asked Sebastian, proceeding to stand.

She gives him a wink and says, "No, finish smoking, it's okay. I'm not going anywhere."

Sebastian gets comfortable again and they all smoke a couple of more bowls. "(cough) Alright…this is some good shit," said Will with a rough throat.

Nallely with her eyes half-closed, asks, "Yeah, it is, ha what did I give you again?" stoned out of her mind.

Christina retrieves the pipe from Will. "Imaginative," she answered with a big stoner smile, then takes a long puff.

"Hey, come on, let me take a hit!" said Diana wanting to smoke some more. She grabs her pipe and begins to smoke out of it, managing to puff out two smoke rings to impress her friends.

Jose begins to laugh to himself. "Nice. Ah, I'm hungry now," he said, while holding his stomach.

"Psh, me, too! It's the weed ha, fuck Christina your eyes are red as fuck!" said Mark with an open mouth smile.

Christina looks at him unimpressed. "Ha, 'cause I'm high stupid ass!" she said, laughing it up.

"Ha, funny! Damn Diana stop hogging the shit!" said Jessica grabbing the pipe from Diana.

Diana then quickly grabs on to Jose's shoulder. "Ha-ha…(cough)…sorry… (cough) gosh damn! Hey, Jose, hee, hee, I'm going, I'm going! Yup! I'm going, too, you…you? What? Huh? Wait what the fuck? Okay, um? Oh, yeah, I'm going with you to the um yeah, ha, ha, ha, too the what-ever place ha, ha!" said Diana cracking up.

Everyone stares at Diana and laughs together. "You mean Dunsvill sweetie," laughed Nallely. "I guess I'll be going, too."

Rosie jumps to her feet. "We all gotta go now, unless you wanna be called a little bitch," she said, staring down at Mark.

Christina puts her hand on his shoulder. "Na he's going, he's gonna be my escort," she said, with a smile.

Mark looks back and forth at Rosie and Christina. "I am? I mean, yeah, I am!" he said, finishing with a smile, "No little pussy here!" then glances at Jose.

"Ha, okay? Fuckin' weirdos; alright, so we're all fucking going, yeah!" said Jose with excitement.

Rosie begins to force herself to tear up. "(sniffle) It's so beautiful seeing the gang get along," she said, giving Mark and Christina a big hug.

Mark shakes his head in bewilderment. "You just called me a bitch," he said, patting her back.

"Beautiful," replied Rosie, smiling and still hugging them with her eyes closed.

"Ha, you guys are way too high, I can hear you all the way from here," laughed Lucy from afar.

Nallely points straight at her. "Hey, hey, hey, there is NO SUCH THING as being too high," she said, smiling.

"Ha, yeah, you got that right. Come on, you should have some," said Rosie, waving her hand to Lucy for her to come. She notices the signs that Lucy wants to come over but there's something holding her back. "Ha, ha, no thank you," said Lucy, smiling shaking her head. She squints her eyes at Lucy. "Whatever; you're missing out," Rosie said, taking another hit as she wonders what's going on with her.

"Ha, well, I'm done, no more for me, I'm-a go with my babes," said Sebastian, getting up and walks toward Lucy.

Lucy gets up rushing over to Sebastian grabbing his hand. "You're done, Babe? Let's go for a swim, yeah?" she asked, smiling as she leads him to the water.

"Alright, Babes." Sebastian kissing his girlfriend's hand as she drags him.

Rosie jumps with joy. "We should all go!" she said, forcing Will off his rock.

"Ha, yeah, we should! Come on, let's go!" said Nallely with laughter, grabbing on to Diana's hand.

They all get up and head over to the water, but Christina then turns toward Mark. "Hey, Mark and I are going to go for a walk alright!" she said, smiling.

Mark looks at her with shock and confusion. "We are? I mean, yeah, we are. We'll meet up with you guys later!" he said, happily looking at Christina.

"Okay, let's go!" said Christina smiling, grabbing Mark's hand and starts to walk off with him.

# CHAPTER TWELVE

# HANDS OFF

Some of the friends smoked marijuana to start off their day at the beach. While enjoying time together, they had all agreed to go on the trip to Dunsvill for the beginning of the summer. Once finished, they go for a swim in the water except for Mark and Christina.

Christina and Mark are walking alongside the beach shore as they hold hands. Mark is extremely nervous and slightly confused that she asked to walk with him, let alone holding his hand.

Christina looks at Mark and sees that he's practically sweating. "So, ha-ha, what's up?" she asked, trying to break the awkward silence.

"Nothing really, just walking with you," he said, with a smile.

She giggles, then says, "Sounds lame," pushing him.

Mark's smile becomes nervous. "Ha, ha, not really," he said, then takes a big gulp. "So, what made you wanna walk with me?" he asked, trying to continue the conversation.

Christina begins to laugh. "The weed! Ha, if I wasn't high I wouldn't be here with YOU," she said, letting go of his hand then holds on to her sides.

Mark's smile then falls. "Oh…I see, ha-ha," he said, stopping in his tracks and looking down at the sand.

Christina stops in front of Mark and gazes deep into his eyes. "Mm…you know what else," putting both hands around his waist, "I wanna do besides walking?" she giggled, bringing him closer to her.

Mark, hypnotized by Christina's beautiful eyes, says, "No, what else?" grabbing her butt.

She immediately pushes him away from her and gives him a stern look. "WOW! I was going to say make a sandcastle!" she said, holding on to her butt cheeks.

Mark's face becomes pale, and he begins to stutter. "Oh, um…I'm…I'm sorry…I didn't um…I'm sorry…" he said, feeling really stupid.

"Was it the 'weed' this time, huh?" she asked, clenching her eyebrows then crossing her arms.

He becomes shocked. "What? No! I'm so sorry. Shit, I fucked up, I'm fuck," he said, covering his face. "Shit, I'm sorry," he finished, giving her a weak smile then begins to walk away.

Christina's eyes widen in surprise, and rushes over to him grabbing his hands saying, "Hey, it's okay; come here," putting them around her waist smiling at him.

Mark's heart begins to race. "Yeah?" he asked, not knowing what she wants.

She pulls him in closer so that her chest and his stomach are touching, standing on her tip toes to get her lips near his ear and whispers, "Kiss me," then quickly moves back raising a finger at him. "But don't grab my ass!" she said, giving him another stern look.

"Is that the weed talking or—" Mark was saying but is interrupted.

"Just fucking kiss me, already!" said Christina smiling, as she shakes her head.

Mark, once again trapped in her gaze, moves in to kiss her but then…. "AH!" a loud scream comes from the area Jose parked his van.

Christina quickly puts her hand on Mark's face causing him to kiss her palm instead. "What was that?" she asked, scared out of her mind.

Mark grabs her hand away from his face and begins to take her back to their friends. "I don't know, let's check it out," he said, with a worried tone.

They head towards where they were smoking and before arriving, they see Diana wet only in her underwear running toward them. "SHIT, YOU GUYS GOTTA COME!" she yelled.

Christina quickly pushes Mark aside. "What's going on?" she asked, approaching Diana.

Diana grabs on to both of Christina's shoulders and continues to yell, "Some guy…just came…and grabbed Rosie!" frantically between breaths.

Mark walks forward next to the girls. "What the fuck!" he said, in shock.

Diana then turns to him with wide open eyes. "Yeah…and Will! Oh, my… go help him!" she said, pushing him.

Mark takes a couple of steps, looking for Will. "Alright, where is he?" he asked with a serious expression.

Diana then begins to run up the hill of rocks. "Over here, come on!" she said, leading them to the location they parked at.

Mark and Christina follow behind her to see if Will and Rosie need any help. When they arrive, they see all their friends are in their underwear, dripping wet blocking the view of the commotion. Sebastian and Jose are chanting, "KICK HIS ASS!" as Lucy Nallely and Jessica are comforting Rosie, while Nallely yells with the guys.

Diana and Christina rush toward Rosie.

"Are you okay?" asked Christina, embracing her.

"Yeah, yeah, I'm fine," she replied, pushing her away. "It's Will. I don't want him to get fuckin' hurt, that dumbass…Will, just let it go!" she yelled out to him.

Will is confronting a strange man standing just a bit taller than him, near Jose's van.

The man looks like a hairy rough white trucker, with ripped blue jeans, dragging along the sandy concrete, bare foot, and a gray tank undershirt stuck to his sweaty body. His teeth are so rotten some are missing, as he clenches the remainder together giving out an ugly grin. "Hey, man, I'm sorry, alright? I didn't know she was with you," he said.

"So? You still shouldn't be grabbing her!" Will yelled and Rosie comes running to his side grabbing on to his arm. "Babe, I said let it go!" she said, pulling on him.

The man looks at Rosie. "You should listen to your slut," he said, giving her a wink.

Will points straight at him screaming with anger, "YOU STUPID MOTHERFUCKER!" yanking on his arm so Rosie can let go. "You're dead!"

"Kick his ass already!" yelled Sebastian, punching the air.

"Fuck that bitch up, Will!" yelled Nallely with Sebastian.

Rosie turns to them with an irritated look. "You guys aren't helping!" she said with vexation, but they all continued to riot.

The stranger puts his hands up and takes a few steps back. "Hey, man, I'm just playing, I'm-a just be going now," he said, slightly turning away, then quickly takes out a six-inch knife and looks Will straight in the eyes. "Come on, bitch!" he roared, swinging his knife left and right.

The friends, in shock, all take steps away from the crazy stranger. "Put that shit down, fucker; grow some fucking balls!" yelled Will with fiery rage.

Rosie starts to pull on Will even harder. "Come on, Babe, no, just leave it alone! You don't know what he can do," she said, trying to get him to walk away.

The stranger points his knife at Rosie. "No, bitch! You stay out of this. It's me and this fag, and once I'm done with his ass, HA, HA, HA, YOU'RE NEXT!" he laughed with a creepy smile.

He licks his knife and runs straight towards Will to try and stab him. Will pushes Rosie towards their friends, causing her to fall to the ground. He dodges the knife and kicks the stranger in the ankle; the stranger trips on to the sand and the knife nicks him in the left arm.

The man try's getting up but before he can, Will kicks him in the face then gets his knife. Will grabs the man by the hair. "What now, you peace of shit?" he asked, putting the knife next to the man's neck.

"Babe, no!" said Rosie, rushing to Will to stop him.

"Ha, ha, ha, come on! Kill me, you don't have the balls, boy!" said the stranger, smiling with laughter.

Rosie then pulls Will off the man and puts one hand on his face, saying, "Babe, no, it's not like you," and with the other hand grabs the knife away from him.

The man quickly gets up and rushes Will. Will pushes Rosie out of the way once again, then gives him a straight right jab between his eyes. The man becomes dazed for about a second and then tries to kick Will, but Will gets a hold of his foot twisting it; the man falls flat on his face. He gets up and they stare at each other.

"Yeah! Beat the shit outta him!" yelled Christina.

"Babe, be careful," Rosie said to herself in fear.

The man gets a hand full of sand and throws it at Will's face. Will quickly rubs the sand out of his eyes, and sees the man running straight toward him.

"WATCH OUT!" yelled Rosie, covering her eyes.

Will throws a left hook at the stranger's face following with a right-handed uppercut. The stranger quickly shakes it off and throws two punches of his own. Will blocks both of the stranger's punches by swiping them to the side, then punches him in the stomach and does a spin kick to the man's face. The stranger was in the sand once again.

Will grabs the man's shirt and gets his fist ready to punch him in the face, and the man puts his hands up covering his eyes. "Alright! Fuck...you win," he said, with anger spitting out blood on to the sand.

"Then stay down, fucker," said Will, roughly letting go of the man's shirt, then stands up.

Everyone rushes over to Will, praising him. Rosie jumps into his arms. "Oh, my gosh, Babe! Are you okay? I didn't know you can fight like that!" she said, with excitement.

"Ha, well, now you do," said Will, hugging Rosie and smiling.

"Yeah, I do," she said returning a smile then kisses him on the lips.

The friends all focus on Will and forget about the stranger except for Jose. "Fuck, yeah, man! You kicked his ass, ha," he laughed, looking at the man on the floor as he stares back deep into Jose's eyes. Jose becomes uneasy, turning his attention back to his friends.

"Hey, he can protect us when we go to Dunsvill tomorrow, ha," said Lucy, laughing.

Sebastian turns to Lucy and grabs her by the waist. "What? I can protect you, Babe," he said, smiling.

She looks up at him with an eyebrow raised. "Psh, yeah, sure you can, Babe," she said, with a sweet smile.

"Wow, whatever, Babes," said Sebastian, shaking his head while rolling his eyes and smiling.

"I'm just kidding, Babe, of course you can," said Lucy, putting both hands on Sebastian's face, forcing him to kiss her on the lips.

"Hey, um, where the fuck did the guy go?" asked Mark, looking around for the man.

They all scan the area, trying to see if the man is still nearby.

"Ah, who gives a fuck? That foo got his ass beat by Will!" said Sebastian, still excited about the fight.

"Yeah, forget him, we should be heading out, school about to end, and I don't plan on getting in trouble before tomorrow," said Jose, unlocking his van.

"Yeah, he's right, I need to pack anyways. Come on," said Christina, grabbing Mark's hand as they head toward their things.

Mark looks back at his friends in shock while being pulled away, and they all say to each other, "It's the weed," nod and follow them.

The friends all get dressed and Rosie puts the knife away in her bag. They all head back to the van and take their seats.

They drive for a while and are now in their city, with Rosie still praising her boyfriend. "Damn, Babe, I still can't believe you can fight like that," she said, hugging him.

"Yeah! You kicked ass," said Nallely happily.

Will begins to smile. "Ha, I was just looking after my queen," he said.

"And you did a good job with that man! Shit, you didn't need any help," said Mark, laughing.

"Yeah, he didn't, and we were all ready to jump in and beat his ass," said Sebastian, nodding.

"Yeah, we were! I was all pumped up and shit," said Jose, honking his horn, and they all begin to cheer.

"Oh! I even told Mark to go help you out, see I got you," said Diana with a big smile.

"I just heard a loud ass scream when I was with Christina, and then Diana told me to go help you out, she was like, 'Oh, strong and powerful Mark, go help Will he can't fight for shit,' and I was about to help you but then I saw you had it," Mark said, smirking.

Christina quickly pushes Mark's head. "Shut the fuck up, psh, this guy. But, yeah, Rosie you scream fucking loud! How did he even grab you?" she asked, looking at Rosie with her eyes wide open.

"Ha, I was scared, okay? Gosh, I just went back to get my surfboard, and that guy just came out from behind a rock and grabbed me. I thought I was going to DIE! But now I know I got a kick ass fighter of a boyfriend," said Rosie, kissing Will on the cheek.

His face begins to turn red. "Oh, my, you guys," he puts his hands up next to his shoulders, "as much as I like you guys talking about how awesome I am, I'm going to have to ask you to stop," he said, clapping his hands together. "Ha, what am I saying? Keep talking about me, I'm liking this," he continued, enjoying the praise.

"Well, what you did was awesome! Like that guy had a knife," said Lucy with enthusiasm.

"Okay, okay, really no more about my babe, but yeah, Babe, you were awesome, I feel safe with you now," said Rosie, smiling and resting her head on Will.

"What you didn't before?" asked Will, looking at Rosie.

"Well, ah, no not really, I thought you were weak and lame. Still think you are, so I kept the knife," said Rosie, smiling at Will as she holds on to his arm.

Will rolls his eyes and says, "Wow, okay, Babe."

"I'm just kidding, Babe, it's a souvenir," said Rosie, smiling placing her head on his chest.

"Well, okay, Sebastian get the fuck off, I'm dropping you off first 'cause I don't want shit going on in the back," said Jose, stopping the van in front of Sebastian's house.

"Aw, what? But we weren't doing anything," said Sebastian with disappointment.

"Psh, still doesn't mean you guys won't do anything, now get out," he said, pointing at his house in a demanding tone.

"Shit, fine," responded Sebastian, rolling his eyes. "Bye, Babes, I'll text you," he said, opening the trunk door to the van, then gives Lucy a kiss.

"Okay, Babe, bye…" she said, with a frown then grabs his shirt, "wait… just one last kiss," kissing him goodbye with a sad look.

Once Sebastian closes the van door Jose drives off.

"You're messed up, now I'm all alone," said Lucy, throwing a ball of paper at Jose.

"Well, I don't wanna hear 'aah ugh, harder!' In the back," said Jose, slightly smiling.

"Oh, shut up! We weren't even doing anything you butthole," said Lucy, pouting and crossing her arms.

"Yeah, 'cause we got to the beach just in time," said Rosie, quickly adding to the conversation.

"Ah, whatever we weren't even going to do anything," said Lucy, rolling her eyes.

"Ha, well, you didn't make it sound like you weren't going to do anything," said Nallely, giggling.

"We were messing around! Duh…" she replied, rolling her eyes again.

"Ha! Okay, then, when we go to Dunsvill tomorrow, you two aren't going to do anything?" asked Jose.

"No, just make out and stuff," answered Lucy.

"Ha! Okay, let's bet on that! And we're here Diana, off," Jose said, quickly stopping the van.

"Aw, this was getting all good," said Diana, giving Nallely a silent goodbye by squeezing her hand as she's getting off.

"Okay? Well, come on, bet on it five bucks?" asked Jose, driving off.

"Fine, you butt!" said Lucy agreeing with the bet.

"Okay, but you guys can't do anything, not even 'make out and stuff,'" he said, smiling.

"Ah, fine!" pouted Lucy in shock.

"Ha, wow, you guys. Babe, drop me off next. I live close to Diana," said Jessica, wanting to go home.

"I'll go with you, Jess, if that's cool? I wanna walk home," said Nallely with a weak smile.

Jessica looks at Nallely with surprise. "Why walk when you have a driver?" she asked.

"I don't know, I just feel like it," replied Nallely.

"Okay," she said, with a bit of suspicion. She turns to Jose. "Please?"

"Alright," said Jose, heading to Jessica's house.

Jose then drops the rest of his friend off, and then goes home himself.

# CHAPTER THIRTEEN

# DRESS UP

It's 10:00 P.M. in the town of Dunsvill; the man from the diner is waiting out in front of a big, white, two-story house. The house is on a small hill with a white picket fence. At the front, there are three steps going up to the porch; there's a table and chairs on the left side, and a white wooden rocking chair that the man is sitting on the right. A car approaches the house parking in front of it; the man from the beach gets out of the vehicle, and as he opens the gate the other walks down the three steps to meet him halfway; he notices his black eye.

"Hello, brother," said the black-eyed man.

"Hello...you didn't bring anything?" said the man from the diner with a puzzled face.

"I got...I got in a bit of trouble, Victor," said the man, looking away from him.

"I can see that. What happened to your face?" asked Victor, inspecting his brother's bruised face.

His brother slaps his hand away and says, "I got into a fight," looking at him with hate in his eyes.

Victor looks at him stone cold, and with an unpleasant tone, he says, "Yeah... and it looks like you got your ass handed to you. Where did you go, Devin?"

Devin quickly answers, "The beach," looking at his brother's eyes with anger. He tries to walk past him; but Victor immediately gets in his way.

"Ah…and why would you go to a public area like that?" he asked, shaking his head slowly.

"I didn't. I went to the part that's not open to the public, usually they have stupid teenagers there…and there was a couple. I ended up trying to take some guys girlfriend named Will, and well…ah," said Devin with the most hated look, as he relives the fight.

"Where's your knife?" asked Victor with a serious tone.

"They have it…" he responded, rolling his eyes.

Victor glares at his brother with an unreadable yet unhappy look. "Mm, maybe I should tell mother the truth; that you're not capable for this. I am done covering for you. I keep on giving you chances to prove to me that you are able to do this, but I end up cleaning after you every time you fuck up." He breaks his unreadable face by clenching his eyebrows and raising one of them. "What are we going to do, huh?" he asked putting his pointer finger to his brother's chest. "I was counting on you to do this. The woman ended up not being suitable and you know that. We did not eat yesterday, and I guess we have to eat what we got in the garden today," he gestures to the house behind him, "and there's not much. What are we going to do for tomorrow, hmm? I am not sending you out for hunts anymore," he said, letting out a deep sigh.

Devin rolls his eyes. "What about our sisters? They're out right now," he said, slightly tilting his head.

"It's Sophia's first time out; she's not bringing them back fresh, and you know this," he replied.

"I can fix this," Devin insisted quickly.

"And how exactly will you do that?" asked Victor with a serene tone.

"It seems that the teens from the beach know of our little town, and they plan on coming over tomorrow for some summer fun; there are about ten of them. We can be set for a good while," said Devin with a calm tone, placing both hands on Victor's shoulders smiling at him.

Victor's eyes widen. "Ten…yes, we would; okay, set some traps in the woods, I'll let our parents know…go!" he said, pointing toward the woods.

Devin nods and walks away.

Victor walks inside of the house; he sees his mother and father sitting down, working on Adriana's mother that is tied to a coffee table in the living room. It's a large living room with dark wooden floors and a hand carved spiral staircase, leading to a balcony on the second floor; the walls have white paint with red top trimming going around the room, and a candle chandelier hanging from the middle of the wooden ceiling. His mother is sitting on a wooden four seat black cushioned couch, and his father on an old fashion black cushioned recliner. There are bookshelves filling the room and the balcony; there's a doorway to the right leading to the kitchen and a glass door behind the staircase for the backyard.

Adriana's mother is awake and cannot move a muscle, only her terrified eyes are able to move across the room. There is an IV attached to the back of her neck, with a needle going down her spine. Her arms, broken backwards by the elbows; and ankles are tied to the legs of the short coffee table. She's barefoot with her finger and toenails ripped clean off. Blood freshly runs down her nail beds, falling on to a white tarp. She is wearing a clean white dress and has a red rose pinned to her chignon style hair.

The mother is an elderly white woman with long brown/gray hair, five feet three inches and fit for her age. Her skin has some slight wrinkles, though at the same time appears ageless and her eyes are bright light blue. She is wearing a long black dress with red flowers on it. She is humming a song as she is sowing Adriana's mother's mouth shut, who is also forcibly humming the same song in fear.

The father is an elderly white man with balding white/gray hair, five feet eight inches, and is slightly less fit then his wife looking sickly. His skin is wrinkly, and his eyes look lazy and tired. He has a clean-cut beard and is wearing a black suit with a white tie.

Victor's father pierces Adriana's mother's left eye lid with a needle about to sow it shut, but stops when his son begins to speak…leaving the needle in her eye lid, with the tip resting on her eyeball as she looks across the room rapidly.

"Mother…Father, Devin did not bring any bounty, but…" said Victor, closing the door behind him.

His mother and Adriana's mother stop humming. "I didn't say stop, sweetheart. You keep playing me some music; you know the song by now, right?" she asked, softly stroking her left check, and then she continues to hum while tears of blood run down her face; "There you go," she said, looking at her son with a light smirk.

Victor walks up to the coffee table. "Instead, he got ahold of some valuable information," he said, looking back and forth at his parents.

"And what would this information be my son?" asked the old woman, placing down her needle and giving her full attention to him.

"After Devin got a beating, he found out that we will be having guests sometime tomorrow. Of course, I do not know if his information is authentic, but if it comes to be true…we should be prepared," said Victor, taking a seat on the couch next to his mother.

"And what do you suggest we do?" she asked, tapping her fingers together.

"Welcome them…We make them comfortable, so they settle in and become part of the town. Then we consume them," said Victor with no emotion whatsoever.

"H-h-h…how…how many?" asked his father, wiping off the bloody tears going down their victim's face.

"Ten, Devin is setting some traps as we speak," he replied.

His mother's smile starts to grow. "Good…good!" she laughed as she gets up from her seat. "Help me prepare in the kitchen," she said waving toward Victor and walks to the kitchen.

# CHAPTER FOURTEEN

# CELEBRATE

Jose dropped everyone at home from their trip to the beach, after they had an encounter with Devin of Dunsvill. Will had to save his girlfriend Rosie, who almost got kidnaped by him.

Christina is now in her bedroom listening to loud music. Her clock reads 10:30 P.M., and she has just gotten out of the shower. She's wearing a short purple bathrobe dancing around, waving her wet wavy curly hair around as she's finishing packing up her stuff; but her father then walks in and lowers her radio.

"Hey, Daddy," said Christina, zipping up her suitcase smiling at her father.

He's a big, muscular man in his forties and dresses like a cholo. He is a light brown Hispanic with a buzz cut and goatee. "'Hey', what are you doing?" he asked, examining her suitcase as he closes the door behind him.

His daughter smiles zipping up her last suitcase. "Ah, I'm leaving tomorrow for the weekend," she replied.

He crosses his arms, then says, "Wow, where you think you're going? I didn't say you can go anywhere, you have rehearsals on Monday," giving her an angry look.

Christina rushes to her father's side, grabbing ahold of his arm. "Oh, sorry! My friends want me to go on a road trip with them to start the summer, and they're leaving tomorrow. I really want to go with them since I might not see them again; please is it okay if I go, Daddy?" she asked, apologizing with big puppy dog eyes while squeezing his arm.

"Mhm, for the whole weekend? I don't know," he said, raising an eyebrow in deep thought.

As she's holding on to him she bounces in place and pleads, "Come on, Daddy! It's just for the weekend; I'll be back Monday for rehearsals! You'll be home with Mom alone…you can take her out and stuff," she said, putting ideas into his head.

"Mm," hummed her father, squinting his eyes at her.

"Please, Daddy, I really wanna go," she continued, looking up at him once again with big puppy dog eyes.

He stares at her for five seconds, then rolls his eyes giving her a stern look. "Okay, you can go," he agreed, giving her a smirk, "but if you're not back by Monday morning, there's no way your mom and I are going to let you go to S.R.F."

"Yay! Thanks, Daddy!" said Christina with excitement giving him a hug and kiss on the cheek.

"Have fun and go to bed already; it's getting late," he said, giving her a hug and kiss in return.

"It's Friday, Daddy, and I'm going out on a date with someone," she said, giving a weak smile.

Her father looks at her in shock. "Why am I finding these things out last minute?" he asked, crossing his arms.

She shrugs her shoulders. "I found out last minute, too; things just pop up," she said, pouting her lips.

"Mm, and who you going out with?" he asked, unfazed.

"Mark," she answered with a sweat smile.

"HA! Really?" he laughed.

"Yes, don't laugh. He's cute, and I've known him for a long time now so why not try it? I already told mom about it, she said it was fine," she said, with a smug look.

Her father smirks at her. "Okay, go," he said, then mumbles, "If he even comes," walking out the doorway, shaking his head smiling at her as he closes her door.

Christina rolls her eyes, locking her bedroom door; she moves her suitcases aside then throws herself on her bed. She grabs her phone beginning to text Mark.

Before Christina finished packing her bag for the trip; Mark was in his living room watching television; he lives alone with his mother in an old run-down house. It's a small house containing a tiny kitchen with a bar separating the living room, one bathroom and only one bedroom; Mark sleeps in the living room.

It's 10:20 P.M., and Marks mother walks through the front door with an arm full of groceries. She's a really short skinny Filipina around her early thirties with a very light tan; she is beautiful, has long black hair wrapped up in a bun, and is wearing a blue and white diner's waitress outfit with skater shoes. "Hey, sweetie, could you please get the other bag and meet me in the kitchen," she said, stumbling across the living room.

"Okay," he said, getting up from his couch bed. He heads outside and grabs the last bag of groceries, then goes back inside setting the bag on the bar, and sits at the living room side facing the kitchen.

His mother rolls her eyes and giggles. "I said the kitchen, not your room. Come on and help me put the stuff away, I want to talk with you," she said, with a warming smile.

He goes around the bar into their tiny kitchen and begins to put the groceries away. His mother scoots over toward him. "So," a smile begins to grow on her face, "guess what?" then quickly looks at her son. "I finally got some time off this summer! I even got this weekend off so you and I can go to Up-Rock City, to see the High Kings concert and also go to the lake," she said, as she grabs two cans of food and starts to dance in place. "There's a pier there with a Ferris Wheel and other cool little things to do," she puts down the cans and gets ahold of her sons face gently rubbing his cheeks. "I know I been really busy, and I haven't been able to do anything with you since your dad left," she continued, opening a cupboard, "but that's going to change thanks to my diploma!" she finished, taking out a bottle of wine.

Mark continues to put the groceries away with a shocked expression saying nothing back. His mother bumps him with her butt. "Well, come on! Grab the glasses we're going to party!" she said, with a big smile.

"Ha…but I'm not twenty-one yet," he chuckled.

She pushes his head softly. "Oh, shut up and get the glasses. I'm a nurse now, so I got you," she said with a smile.

Mark grabs two wine glasses from one of the cupboards quietly, while his mother is putting the last of the groceries away. She then takes the wine bottle proceeding to pop the cork. He places the glasses down on the bar counter and takes a seat, looking at his feet. She begins pouring the wine into the glasses still smiling and dancing in place. "So, we leave tomorrow afternoon, we should get there by around 6:00 P.M., so we can eat before the concert at nine," passing him a glass of wine. "There's this fancy restaurant I really want to go to. I already made reservations for us. We have to be there by seven," she said, holding out her glass, so they'll clank them together, but Mark continues to stare at his feet as he holds his wine. "What's wrong?" she asked, placing her hand on his shoulder.

He turns to his mother. "Oh, nothing, Mom. I just don't drink," he said, with a weak smile.

She gives him a smirk. "Boy! You would be coming home at 2:00 A.M. after parties with your friends, and you can't have a glass of wine with your dear old ma to celebrate her success?" she asked, giggling continuing to hold out her glass.

Mark hesitantly taps his glass against hers. "Na ma, I'm happy for you," he said, putting his wine down.

"Then come on let's party!" she said, chugging her wine. "I'll go pack you should do the same!" she finished, pouring herself another glass and rushes to her room.

He takes in a deep sigh as he stares at his glass of wine. His phone makes a quick ring; and as he looks at it, he freezes in place once seeing the caller identification.

Christina: HEY LOSER!!!!!!! lol wat u up to?

Mark stares at his phone as his heart beats through his chest. He begins to think to himself. *Ah, she's…she's texting me? Shit, ah, what do I say, ah, oh, man.* His phone makes another quick ring.

Christina: hello? U there!?!?!?!

Mark continues to stay paralyzed, then his phone begins to ring from an incoming call. His eyes begin to widen. *She's calling me…*he thought to himself hovering his thumb over the answer button and as he's about to press it the call ends. "Fuck!" he yelled out then covers his mouth.

"You okay, sweetie?" called out his mother.

He rolls his eyes and smacks himself on the forehead with disappointment. "Yeah, ma…I'm fine, just hit myself," he answered back.

"Well, be more careful!" she called out once more. "Don't need you hurting yourself before we even get there!"

Mark puts his head down, makes a grunting noise and then his cell phone starts to ring again; he quickly answers without hesitation this time. "Hello!" he said, putting the phone against his ear.

Christina is holding the cell phone with her shoulder while painting her toenails; she smirks and slightly shakes her head. "Ha, hey, why didn't you pick up the first time, huh? You're not drinking, are you?" she asked, giggling.

Mark glances at his wine. "Ah, no, I was talking to my mom, ha. Ah, what are you doing?" he asked with a nervous smile and he hears, "Just painting my nails while I dry. I'm so wet," almost dropping his cell phone. He gets a full grip on his phone and with a shocked expression slowly asks, "Wha— what was that?"

Christina lifts her foot near her mouth and begins to blow on her painted toenails. "I just got out…the shower…" she puts her foot down and starts painting on her other toenails, "And I was thinking about you when I was in there."

Mark's jaw drops, and his eyes begin to shift. "You were?" he asked, then giving out a weak smile.

Christina giggles. "Yeah, we never finished our walk since Rosie almost DIED, and I was thinking maybe we could go to Royal Plaza and finish what we started," she said, and she hears him say, "Really?" She rolls her eyes, then says, "Yes, really; I wanna hang out a little more before we go to Dunsvill."

Mark, without thinking, asks, "Why?" then smacks his forehead closing his eyes with regret. He takes in a deep sigh as he hears, "'Cause I want to see if it's worth keeping you as my escort. Ha," his eyes widen; "Have you asked if you can go yet? My dad said yes," coming out of his phone. "Oh, no; not yet. I'm just waiting for the right moment. But even if she said no, I would just sneak out," he laughs nervously. "There's no way I'm missing out on this trip."

Christina finishes painting her last nail. "Wow, look at you, all bad. That means you can pick me up in an hour," she said, slowly getting up from her bed. As she walks toward her closest, she hears, "But I don't even have a car," then giggles while going through her clothes. "Just take your mom's since you're so bad; or the one that's never left the garage," she said, taking out three different types of shirts, then places them on her bed. "Oh, wait, your dad took it on his sales trip, huh?" she asked shaking her head as she walks back to her closest. "Well, then, yeah, your mom's," she said.

Mark is now standing with suspense as he hears, "See you in an hour," and the call ends. He begins to smile grabbing the glass of wine and does a little controlled dance in a circle; once he was turned behind him about to take a sip, he sees his mother looking at him curiously.

"What was that?" she asked, titling her head a little.

He looks at her in shock and puts his cell phone away in his pocket. "Oh, just Christina," he said, giving her a weak smile putting the glass on the countertop.

"Oh, and what did she say? What's this trip you guys were talking about?" she asked, crossing her arms.

He takes a deep gulp and says, "Um, well…my friends and I are going on a road trip this weekend since some of us are graduating." His mother's face begins to fall. "I was going to tell you when you got home but…" her eyes start to water, "You were all happy… 'cause you…grad…uated. Then you told me all these plans you made. I didn't know what to say," he said, trying to avoid eye contact.

She takes a quick breath, closing her eyes then opens them saying, "I don't know, how about you rather go with your friends than your own mom."

"Ah, Ma, don't say that. See, this is why I didn't know what to say. I knew you'll say something like that," he said, looking at her completely.

His mother puts her hand up and looks away from him. "You know what; just go…you're planning on going anyways without my permission, so go. I'm already use to your father leaving me, I'm sure I'll be fine with a weekend to myself," she said, turning around to walk off.

Mark rushes over to keep her in the kitchen. "Mom, what about the reservations for dinner?" he asked with sad eyes.

"They give wine there, and you're not twenty-one," she said, then looks at his wine on the counter. "Besides, I'm sure I can find someone who wants to go with me," she continues as she picks up the glass. "Excuse me, please," she finished, chugging the glass of wine, then puts it down on the counter.

Her son steps aside and once she passes by him tears start to fall down her face. "Wash that glass," she whimpered, heading toward her room.

Mark stays where he's at till he hears his mother's bedroom door slam shut. He walks up to her door and once he knocks on it loud music begins to play. He then goes to his room with his head held low. Grabbing a towel to take a shower, he smiles knowing that he now has a big date.

# CHAPTER FIFTEEN

# FIRST DATE

**PART ONE**

Christina got permission to go on the trip, and then she called Mark to see if he was able to finish the walk they were having at the beach. At that time Mark's mother was talking to him about a trip of their own. He let his mother enjoy her moment as he spoke with Christina about the walk and going to Dunsvill; that's when his mother found out their trip wasn't going to happen. Mark is now waiting outside Christina's house in the car his father was trying to sell.

Mark sits in the car dressed nice like a pretty boy, with his door open thinking to himself, *Ah, man, this is happening. This is really happening.* His cell phone vibrates and he looks at it.

Christina: Where u at foo! Better not make me wait. ☺

He holds his phone tightly as he looks at her front door; he then takes a step outside, slowly walking up the brick pathway to her house. He approaches the door and as he's about to knock, it swings right open with Christina's father on the other side.

He clenches his eyebrows looking down at Mark. "Oh, my…so it's true?" he asked, letting out a chuckle. "When Christina told me you were coming, I couldn't believe it. Psh, I bet my wife you wouldn't even get out your car to come get her," he continued as he placed his hand on Mark's back leading him inside.

"Ha, what do you mean?" asked Mark with a nervous laugh.

"Oh, come on, now; I saw you out there sweating. Never saw someone walk so slow to pick up their date. You make it seem like it's your first," he said, smiling at him as he gestures so he'd take a seat in the living room.

Christina's mother then comes out from the kitchen into the living room. She's a dark-skinned black woman who's as short as Christina and has shiny brown long curly hair; she is gorgeous, skinny, and also dresses like a chola. "Oh, leave him alone, honey, so what if it's his first date," she said, taking a seat on the couch with her husband putting her hand on his lap. "How you doing, Mark? I haven't heard anything from you for over a month now. I would ask Christina, but she would always get so angry. So sorry if we are a little surprised you two are going out," she said, looking at Mark with a sweet smile.

"Ah, oh, I just messed up really bad, but I'm making up for it," he replied, smiling weak, nervously looking back and forth at both her parents.

"How's your mom and dad?" asked her father, putting his arm around his wife.

Christina then comes rushing out the hallway with nice straight hair, wearing dark black skinny jeans, a red and black flannel with a tucked in black tight shirt and new white shoes saying, "Hey, Daddy, leave him alone," walking into the living room. "Come on, Mark," she said, putting her hand on his shoulder. "Let's go."

As Mark and Christina walk out of the house, they hear, "Have fun, you two!" said her mother standing on the porch holding her husband by the waist. Mark opens the passenger door for Christina, and she takes a seat inside. "And you're taking her in that thing?" called out her father, and his wife hits him on the chest. "Oh, stop it, Daddy," Christina yelled out, giggling. "Let's go," she said, smiling sweetly at Mark.

Mark enters his car, while her father yells out, "You better treat her right!" then closes his door nervously turning on the car, slowly puts on his seatbelt.

They're both sitting in the car as Mark has both hands on the steering wheel, looking ahead having himself a little panic attack. Christina smiles at him, then asks, "Hey, you okay there?" rubbing his shoulder.

"Is he still watching us?" he asked.

Christina turns and sees her father with her mother standing on the top step of their porch. He does a gesture with his hand pointing at both his eyes then points at them. "Ha, yeah, don't worry about him, let's go," she said, patting him on the back.

It's a quiet night as they drive through the neighborhoods. The sky is clear and the moon lights their way to Royal Plaza. Mark looks straight ahead having trouble to focus on the road, and not at Christina's breasts squeezing out of her tight shirt.

"So, your dad didn't take this piece of junk with him, huh?" she asked, giving him a smirk.

He thinks for a while leaving it quiet for three seconds, then says, "Ah, he gave it to me before he left."

"I thought you said you didn't have a car?" she asked, crossing her arms.

Mark takes a glance at her chest. "Well, this is my first time driving it; I forgot it was mine till you told me to drive it," he replied, giving a hesitant smile.

She squints her eyes and says, "Mhm, okay, if you say so."

They drive out of the neighborhood and on to the main road. They pass billboards that Mark notices; one having a couple embracing each other, walking through a plaza with flashy signs showing different stores and the caption: "ROYAL PLAZA: TREAT HER LIKE ROYALTY AND BE THE **REAL MAN** SHE DESERVES!" and another with a man caressing the woman's cheek as they kiss each other, and her reaching into his back pocket taking out a condom having the caption reading: "TAKE CONTROL AND DOMINATE THE NIGHT!" Mark takes a big gulp then takes another glance at her cleavage.

Christina then looks down at her shirt, lifting it to completely cover her breasts, then turns to look at the back seat. "Damn, I remember some crazy times back there," she said, with a smile.

He forgets all about the sexual messages from the billboards and clenches his eyebrows in confusion. "What do you mean?" he asked, slightly shaking his head.

Christina sits back and smirks at him. "Jose would take me back here and...well, we pretty much fucked," she said, letting out a soft giggle.

"What? I thought you said nothing happened at the lake!" he stated quickly, looking back and forth at her and the street.

"Who said this happened at the lake, ha?" she asked, starting to laugh and he looks at her in shock and disgust. "Oh, come on, who do you think he takes back there now when we use to come over?"

"AH, WHAT! No fuckin' way," he said, becoming even more disgusted.

"Yeah, you might wanna talk to him about it now that it's your car," she said, with a sweet smile.

Mark becomes speechless as he tries to focus on the road, and Christina proceeds to stretch and yawn; she sticks her chest out slowly and her shirt begins to go back down. "Ah, don't be mad; it was a long time ago," she said, reaching out and rubbing his shoulder; Mark's eyes go off the road and immediately gaze at her cleavage. He slowly starts to drive on to the opposite side of the road, that his left tire begins to ride over the road studs. "Hey! Watch where you're going, foo!" she said startled, turning his head so he'd look in front of him.

He quickly goes back on his side of the road and with widened eyes says, "Shit, sorry."

"What are you looking at, huh?" she asked, giving him an angry look.

"Ah, nothing," he said, looking straight ahead.

She squints her eyes at him and says, "Well, you better keep your eyes on the road and not at 'nothing'," then crosses her arms. "I'm not planning on dying in a car crash," she said, smirking.

Mark looks at her and notices that she isn't wearing her seatbelt, as he takes a brief glance at her breasts again, then says, "Well, maybe you should buckle up, so you won't fly out the window," looking at her with a smile.

She turns his head again to face the road. "Don't tell me what to do, foo, I do what I want!" she said, doing a circle motion with her head.

"Watch it happen to you one day," he said, slightly turning his head at Christina then back at the road.

She gently hits him on the shoulder. "Don't say that! That's like one of my deepest fears," she said, giving him a stern look.

"Then put your seatbelt on!" he said, laughing. "There's no airbags, remember."

She squints her eyes at him while she slowly puts on her seatbelt; she then looks at the airbag label and rolls her eyes. "Shit, I hid my bud in here," she said, reaching for the glove compartment opening it, and takes out some old papers placing them down at her feet. "My CD should still be here," she continues, biting her lower lip letting out soft groaning sounds. She struggles to take out the top part of the compartment, to get into the dashboard, using both her hands to see if her item is still there; causing her chest to be compressed, so that her breasts spill out her shirt some more.

Mark's eyes dart back and forth at Christina and the road, while she searches the inside of the dashboard where the airbag used to be.

She grins and her eyes widen once she gets ahold of her old CD. "Yeah! Here it is!" she said with excitement, taking it out and begins waving it in front of his face.

"Hey, ha, I'm driving!" he giggled, trying to look over her CD.

She smirks. "Oh? Okay, now you wanna look at where you're going," she said, shaking her head, "I saw you looking at my boobs," putting her hands to her sides.

Mark begins to blush. "Huh?" he asked, quickly shifting his eyes. "Well, they're all out," he answered, smiling weakly. "What am I supposed to do?" he asked, shrugging his shoulders looking forward.

She pushes him slightly. "You're supposed to be mature about it, duh. But I guess you can't handle," she said, buttoning up the top button of her flannel.

"Aw, what? No, don't cover them, I can handle!" he said, with a shocked face.

"Mm, why do you wanna see my boobs so bad?" she asked, crossing her arms.

He begins to sweat, then replies, "I don't!" she raises an eyebrow. "I do." Her mouth drops. "I mean I do, but not right now," he said, nervously.

She clenches her eyebrows. "So, then, you wouldn't mind me buttoning my shirt," she said, smiling, continuing to button up the rest of her shirt.

"NO!" he yelled out, then covers his mouth. "I mean, I just want you to be comfortable," he finished with a nervous smile.

Christina jerks her head back in shock then rolls her eyes. "Well, I'm comfortable with my shirt buttoned up! Thank you very much," she answered, returning a sweet smile. "Or is this all you want from me?" she asked, looking at him up and down while grabbing her breast, and lifting her hair with her other hand then gives him a wink, blowing out a quick kiss.

Mark freezes like a deer in headlights, he briefly looks toward the road and sees another billboard; there is a beautiful woman in a black bikini holding a wine bottle between her chest, and with the caption: "IT'S TAUNT IS HOT, IT'S ALL YOU'LL WANT," he then see's the Royal Plaza's welcome sign. "Oh, won't you look at that, we're here!" he said, giving out a small sigh of relief.

"Alright, nice save," she said, smiling and shaking her head. "Now just park so we can finish our walk."

They park and Mark gets out of his car rushing over toward Christina's door. He opens it, offering his hand; she smiles getting ahold of it, and they walk off into the heart of the plaza. Royal Plaza is large with a big red carpet covering the entire walkway; it has a clear glass roof with small lights imitating sparkling stars filling the ceiling, making it seem like the night sky is shining. There are many different shops and restaurants, all with big bright flashing signs packed with a lot of people. Tables, chairs, benches also fill the red carpet with customers enjoying their time. Palm trees and stone statues of Heroic Nudity are placed throughout the carpet, and a giant artistic water fountain at the heart of the plaza.

They walk along the red carpet hand in hand, laughing and talking about the past. Even though it's extremely crowded, the both of them are in their own world avoiding anyone who comes near them; it's as if there's a spotlight following everywhere they go. They look up at the star lights in the ceiling, and the lights begin doing a wave affect by having some turn brighter. The two smile at each other as they watch the lights do many tricks. Once they arrive at the water fountain live jazz music begins to play, and Christina leads Mark toward the other side of the fountain. There's a band performing with two saxophone players on the rimming of the water fountain, a drummer at the bottom with a string bass player, and a singer/trumpet player interacting with a full crowd that is formed around the band.

Christina makes her way to the front holding Mark's hand, and the spotlight continues to shine on them. When they reach the singer, he sees the great excitement in her eyes, he plays a quick solo then places his trumpet down grabbing ahold of her hand. He begins doing some easy swing steps and Christina follows with no problem. They then start to swing dance as if they practiced together before. Mark watches with a beaming smile, his eyes glued to her as she soars through the air; all he sees is her.

She spins on over to Mark grabbing both his hands. "Let's dance!" she said, pulling on him.

He resists, giving her a smirk and replies, "Nope, nope, I told you the diner was the first and last time."

"Wow, you butt, I see how it is, I'll just keep dancing with him," she said, slightly pushing him.

Mark grabs the hand she pushed him with. "Well, it would be a pleasure to watch an angel fly," he said, then kissing her hand. "I miss watching you dance."

She squints her eyes and pulls her hand away. "That was so cheesy," she said, walking backwards toward the singer. "I'll get you to dance with me dork."

Christina dances for a bit longer as the crowd cheers her and the band on. Mark continues to watch, imagining that she is dancing with him, having fireworks going off in the background. The song finishes and she takes a bow then rushes over to Mark hugging him.

While Christina embraces him, she looks up into his eyes and says, "I'm hungry, let's go eat at that sushi restaurant we always go to!" then drags Mark behind her.

They walk up to a large restaurant with a big red door; Mark opens it gesturing to Christina to go inside. She walks by him giving him a wink getting ahold of his hand. The place is lively, having many waiters and chefs serving tables. It has some gray stone walls and other parts painted red, also having pillars in the color red. The tables are made of black marble and the floor is made of shiny bright red wood. There are at least two chefs at each table cooking the food, and waiters serving drinks and bringing in the raw food. A hostess greets them and leads them to a rounded table with other people eating, and three chefs in the middle severing them; one chef tosses a shrimp up into the air and lands it perfect in the glass drink he's holding, and then hands it to the costumer. The host leaves and a waiter comes by giving them a glass of water, and they order their sushi and drinks. The chefs all help each other cook everyone's meal, doing tricks with fire and their knives. The waiter delivers the fresh ingredients handing it over to the chefs. One of them proceed to slice up the fish while the other tosses the noodles round. The one working on the noodles sprinkles some special spices causing it to quickly light up in flames; he hands them over to Christina and she takes some chop sticks feeding it to Mark.

"I love this place, it's so bomb," said Christina, putting a couple of noodles in her mouth and closes her eyes chewing slowly.

The chefs all do a couple more fancy tricks and give them their last meal; they then begin working on the desert, making a hot fudge volcano cake. Mark and Christina eat their sushi enjoying the different flavors, and Christina talks about James. While she explains how James wanted to go to Dunsvill, Mark stays hypnotized by her beauty. Christina then begins making some jokes about how things may be on their trip.

"If the place really is haunted, you're going to be the first one to die," she said, giggling.

Mark breaks out of his gaze on her. "What? What makes you say that?" he asked.

Christina gets ahold of his cheek and Mark looks at her in shock. "'Cause you're easily distracted," she answered, caressing his face.

He immediately begins to blush and his whole body starts to shutter. "I… I…" he said, but an eruption of hot fudge comes out the volcano cake, grabbing their attention.

One chef stabs the middle of the cake causing the fudge to come out of its side; he cuts two slices and gives it to them. They eat their cake enjoying each other's company; Christina looks at Mark and smiles at him. She takes a piece of her cake offering it to him; he smiles back at her taking a piece from his offering some back. They cross their arms together eating the delicious hot fudge volcano cake. Once finished with their food, Mark goes ahead and pays for the meal.

Christina rubs his back. "Don't worry, Nallely's gonna pay you back," she said, giving him a wink.

"Really? Cool!" he replied with enthusiasm.

They get out of the restaurant hand in hand continuing their late night walk. Christina rushes over to a statue of a medieval shirtless strong man, and Mark takes some pictures then heads toward a statue of a medieval naked woman, with leaves covering the private parts. He poses with the statue and Christina joins him taking pictures together. As Mark gets ready to take one more picture, Christina sees the Royal Arcade and jumps with excitement.

She pushes his cell phone aside. "We gotta go to the arcade!" she said, tugging on his shirt.

He glances at the store. "Ha, wow, I haven't been there since middle school," he replied, putting his phone away.

She begins walking backwards toward the shop, saying, "Yeah, that's 'cause you and Will got those lame ass Diamond Consoles. Unlike your lame asses,

I haven't stopped going there," she gestures for him to follow with her head, "Come on! Let's go play some games, so I can kick your ass!" she finished, running off to the entrance.

As they approach the arcade, Mark notices a large crown on top with neon letters spelling Royal Arcade. "That's new," he said, looking toward his left to look at Christina, but she wasn't there. He looks around and sees her running inside as rumbling, and shouting sounds come out from the arcade. "Hey!" he yelled out, chasing her. Once he opens the front door, he immediately hears high beat notes, lasers, explosions, and many others different sounds. He enters seeing four different gaming posters hanging near the entrance: a Racer, a Shooter, a Fighter, and a Speed Runner. The place is large with lots of flashing colored lights; it's crowded with young adults and teenagers all chanting, "Coup d'état, Coup d'état!"

Mark looks around trying to find Christina. He wanders mindlessly searching for her as people run past him with excitement. A group surrounds an arcade game catching his attention. Pushing his way through he sees Christina playing a two-dimensional racing game. She bobs back and forth and side to side, hunched over the controls while the crowd cheers her on. Mark gets close behind her and as she finishes the game, she shouts, "Fuck yeah!" Everybody celebrates.

Mark grins clearing his throat. "Hey, there, cutie," he said, tapping on her shoulder.

She turns around raising an eyebrow. He looks at her in shock noticing that it's not Christina; she's Hispanic with a tan and soft complexion wearing the same attire as her. She looks at him from head to toe then gives him a sweet smile.

"Oh, sorry I thought you were someone else," he finished, returning a smile.

"Oh? And who did you think I was?" she asked, fluttering her eyes, slowly getting closer to him.

The crowd begins to chatter with one another as they watch them communicate.

Mark becomes nervous and his eyes start to shift around. "Ah, my date," he replied, proceeding to check her out. Now that he can see her completely, her body is slim having large breasts and thick hips.

She puts her right hand upon his cheek. "Is that some kind of pick-up line, or did you truly lose your date?" she continued to ask questions stroking his face.

"Oh, snap!" yelled someone within the crowd.

His jaw drops remaining speechless, he tries to back away, but the girl grabs his hand with hers. "Ah," he struggles to speak.

Her fingers slide down to his chin and down to his chest. "Are you going to answer me?" she asks.

He freezes in place.

"What's going on!" yelled out a familiar voice. "Get out of my way!"

The crowd immediately clears a path and Christina comes rushing out, as they mumble, "Race Queen."

Mark quickly backs away from the girl and puts his hands up; Christina gives him a stern look and walks between them. "Mark! Where the fuck were you? I turn around for one second and you're gone!" she said, pushing him softly.

The girl backs up a little to watch them.

"Ah, you ran off and left me!" he replied defensively.

She crosses her arms. "I expected you to keep up! I wanted to show you something!" she said, grabbing both his arms, and then turns toward the random girl clenching her eyebrows. "You..." she hissed.

She smirks and gives her a small bow. "Hello, Race Queen," she said, looking into her eyes. "Got you," she continued stepping aside, showing the monitor of the game she was playing.

On the screen is a list of the top ten players, all the spots are marked with "RACQ" except for first place marked as "GOTU."

"I know who you are!" she said, stepping closer to her. "Mary Sue..." she grunts and begins to look at her attire. "So, first you steal my style, then you take my people, and now you're trying to feel my man!" she said, getting in her face.

"OH, SHIT!" someone yelled out. "You tell her!" yelled another.

The girl smirks while she rolls her eyes. "Just like these titles you left him alone for the taking," said Mary, walking past her and stands next to Mark. "Don't worry, I won't leave you alone like she did," looking deep into his eyes as she intertwines her fingers with his, then glares at Christina.

Mark becomes stiff looking at Christina with complete disbelief spreading his fingers apart. She gets ahold of his arm and yanks him towards her side. "Taking my kingdom ain't that easy bitch!" she said, walking back up to Mary. "You have to race me, and your brothers can't help you."

"Oh, trust me, I know the rules," said Mary, crossing her arms. "I beat your time in all the racers, now we fight on stage."

"You're on. I hope you have your second," replied Christina, wrapping her arm around Mark's.

She grins. "Yeah, I do, and I can't wait till you see who it is," she said, then walks off into the crowd.

Some of the people follow Mary and in unison yell out, "Coup d'état!" then begin chanting, "Stage Battel! Stage Battel!" while some stay with Christina waiting for her to say something.

Someone quickly comes holding a stool, setting it down in front of Christina; she stands on it and addresses the crowd. "My subjects of Royal! The fuckin' Sue Family continues to threaten our arcade! Preaching their damn lies about using the royal funds for us all; these bitches will end the Monthly Feast and replace it with their Family Weekend! Their reign in Southland Beach proves it! They never follow the quarter rule and kick gamers off their games, just because they own the stage. Now they think they can take the homeland!" she projected, raising her hands wide open.

Mark gazes up at her in awe as the room slowly turns dark leaving a single light on her.

"They've held three of the Seats of the Four Royals since the stage was built, constantly after the Throne of Royals, MY THRONE! And when they threaten my throne, they threaten my people! But I am not afraid and will not run; they came to the wrong arcade," she finished, standing tall while the crowd cheers; she steps down, and the people depart chanting, "STAGE BATTLE!" and she turns toward Mark with a sweet smile.

He looks at her with confusion and asks, "What's going on?"

Christina's smile turns into a smirk, she rolls her eyes saying, "Right, you're an outsider. Things have changed since you guys stopped coming here."

"Yeah, I can see that but I didn't think you were this into games," he replied with a chuckle.

"Jose kept bringing me here even though you guys stopped coming, and I just fell in love with the place. I continued to come after we broke up," she replied with joy.

Mark raises an eyebrow. "Jose hasn't told any of us about this place; why don't we know about this if I see some people from school here?" he asked, crossing his arms.

"We don't talk about this place outside, no one wants to get fucked up for playing Kings and Queens, and luckily for me Jose stopped coming here before it got a makeover; plus, I don't want you guys coming here trying to take what's mine," she said, smiling big, and then her face becomes serious getting really close to him. "If you tell any of them about my little 'nerd out' here, you'll have to answer to me, the Queen," she said, pushing him slightly with her pointer finger.

He looks at her smiling wide. "Oh, of course, as you command my Queen!" he said, giving a small bow.

Christina stands tall. "That's right, you…" she was saying but catches a glimpse of someone familiar. "What the fuck…James! What the fuck are you doing here?" she asked, walking up to James enraged.

He stays in place with a neutral grin. "Hello, your highness, it's good to see you again," he said, with a nod.

"Don't act like you belong here! Why the fuck are you following me?" she asked, getting aggravated.

His grin becomes bigger. "Aw don't be like that; I'm Mary's second for the Stage Battle, I've been training with her for over a year, and I gotta say… I think she might just beat you," he said, with a smug face.

Her eyes widen and one begins to twitch. "You dare doubt my abilities, boy!"

James takes a deep sigh. "Look, before she started coming here, she had me spy on you, to see when you come and when you're not here; and when you're not sitting on your throne, she's here getting the peoples favor. Saying that she's nothing like her brothers; that she'll give out free tokens to everyone in the Kingdom, on the first Saturday of the month while still hosting the Monthly Feast." He crosses his arms. "Many of your subjects will aid her once she gets the Reinforcements Coin. She's prepared, but I'm willing to sabotage her game if you let me go with you guys to Dunsville," he said, as his eyes lighten up.

Mark and Christina look at each other with bewilderment. "Is he serious right now?" he asked.

"Yeah, he's the one that was staking me at school," she replied, then looks at James. "At least now I know why; listen you fuckin' creep," she said, getting closer to him, "You're not coming with us, okay? And I definitely don't need your help. Now please stop asking to come and leave me the fuck alone!" she yelled, pushing him slightly.

At that very moment, a blackout happens throughout the whole plaza. Everyone in the arcade moans and groans with disappointment. The stores backup generator turns on some red lights and intercoms, repeating a message in a deep voice, "Attention People of Royal, darkness has fallen upon us, thus we must close the gates; we apologies for the inconvenience. Please gather your goods and head toward the front exit in a calm manner; thank you. Attention People of Royal..."

Christina rolls her eyes. "Just great, I didn't even get to play one game," giving James a death glare then grabs Mark's hand. "Come on, let's go."

They head for the front doors.


## FIRST DATE

## PART TWO

**M**oments before the sun sets, with the skies painted red; two ladies are driving into the city. The driver has a freckled face and light brown hair slightly ruffled. She is a pretty woman five feet, five inches in her late twenties, fit with bright white slightly crooked teeth; wearing a flannel shirt and overalls. The other is laying out in the passenger seat, taking a nap with her eyes open; she's slightly shorter and in her early twenties. She has long dark brown hair with a soft complexion, beautiful with big bright brown eyes, wearing a blue jean collar shirt that has the sleeves rolled up to her elbows, and a long dark blue skirt.

"Hey, Sofia, wake up! We're here!" said the freckled woman, shaking Sofia slightly. "Sista, wake up!"

"Ahh what, are we there yet?" she asked, grunting looking out the window as she rubs her eyes. She sees many different stores and restaurants with a bright red glow illuminating from the building's edges. "It's beautiful..." she said, with a smile. "So, where we going, Lesley? The park, the movies, oh! The mall! I've always wanted to go to one!" she finished with excitement.

Lesley begins scanning the street signs. "Ooh, I know exactly where we can go! Victor took me to this plaza, and it's amazing at nighttime," she said, then sees a Royal Plaza billboard, "There! That's where we're going," pointing at the sign. "The place is amazing; alive with many different people," she continues as she grabs her hand, "I really think you're going to love it."

Sofia quickly reads the billboard squeezing her sister's hand. "Oh! We have to wear dresses! Please! I've never wore one before...Mother only lets the guest use the ones we have," she said, giving her puppy eyes.

Lesley gives a small smile and places her hand on her cheek. "For you, anything; and lucky for us, dresses are in season," she said, as her smile grows.

The sun is now set, and the sisters arrive at Riverbank Park; passing by the main gate they see vehicles fill the entire parking lot, with some college graduates hanging about dressed in fancy clothing.

Sofia looks at Lesley with confusion. "What are we doing here? I thought we were going to the plaza!" she said, crossing her arms with disappointment.

Lesley parks the car and turns off the engine, she then places her hand upon her sister's left cheek. "Don't worry, we're still going. This is where we're getting our dresses. It'll be fun, trust me," she said, giving her a peck on the lips, "Come on, let's go," she finished with a sweet smile.

Sofia smiles and rolls her eyes as she watches Lesley exit the vehicle, she then gets out herself closing the door behind her. "So, what are we going to do?" she asked, opening the trunk to the car, taking out a handbag; but Lesley's cell phone begins to ring.

She looks at the caller identification clenching her eyebrows, then answers. "Yes? Really? Okay, Sofia and I are going to stay and have a little fun...What? No, we wouldn't do that. We're just going shopping...Okay, bye," she said, talking into the phone then hangs it up. "That was Ma; we don't have to take anyone back home. We have the whole night to ourselves," she said, giving her sister a demonic smile.

They reach the main entrance of the park walking through the crowd of college graduates, barriers are set around the river that "prevent" anyone from getting near. A couple of young adults are skipping rocks along the water; two tanned skinned women, and two handsome men are having a time talking with one another. "This is fun and all, but aren't we kind of old for this?" asked one with a red high-low dress and light blue jean jacket, as she chucks a stone into the river.

"Yeah; where are the drinks you promised?" asked the other women in a white empire waist dress. She takes a seat on the grass where a large black blanket is set for them. "Or are you guys going to be playing with rocks all night, and not with us?" she asked, giving the man with a dark blue structured suit a wink, as she arches her back.

The two young men look at each other in shock. "We got the drinks; they're in the ice box on the pier," answered the other man in a black fitted suit. "Come on, dude, let's go," he said, skipping one last rock.

The two young men rush off toward the pier, leaving the two women on their own.

The woman in the red dress lies down next to her friend. "Boys," she grunts taking a deep breath and closes her eyes.

The lady in white looks up at the sky. "Tell me about it; I can't wait for the fireworks to start," she said, as a damp cloth wraps around her face.

"I can't wait for those drinks!" said the other women opening her eyes right as a cloth goes over her face.

They both struggle for a couple of seconds, as Lesley and Sofia look deep into their eyes. The ladies go unconscious, and the sisters smile at one another. "I love this dress and this jacket," said Sofia, taking the jean jacket off the woman.

"I can't wait to show you the plaza," said Lesley, slowly taking off the woman's white dress. "Mhm, she's really pretty," she whispers to herself as she slides her fingertips down her breast. "You brought the rope, yes?" she asked, turning toward Sofia.

"Yeah, it's in my bag," she answered, taking out a long rope.

"Good. Leave the dresses and help me tie them to the trashcan," said Lesley, dragging the women to the metal outdoor trashcan near the river.

Sofia lays the other women next to her friend. "What are we going to do with them?" she asked, handing over the rope to Lesley.

Lesley begins to tie both their ankles together. "Here, tie this to the trashcan," she said, giving her the other end of the rope. "We're going to turn them into mermaids."

Fireworks of all different colors fill the night sky. The two sisters gaze up holding each other's hand, intertwining their fingers. "I never seen anything like it, it's beautiful..." said Sofia giving a small, sweet smile as she watches the colorful explosions.

"Not as beautiful as you," said Lesley, tugging her sister's arm to get her attention.

They look into their eyes as they see the lights illuminate upon each other's faces, kissing one another.

As they hold each other in their arms Lesley smiles, then says, "Help me with this," giving her one more kiss then grabs ahold of the trashcan.

The sisters tip the can over and roll it into the river. The trashcan quickly floats down pulling the two women with it. They stand hand in hand as they watch the women getting pulled into the water. "I wonder if they'll wake up in the water," said Sofia, leaning her head on her sister's shoulder. Once the women were completely under water, they open their eyes in shock and fear wailing their arms trying to swim. "Yay!" she said, clapping with excitement.

All these women can see for their final moments, are the two sisters smiling over them and the colorful fireworks. They begin gasping for air causing water to fill their lungs, continuing to fall into darkness.

"Wow, it's so deep. I can't see them. Can you see them?" asked Sofia, squeezing her sister's hand with a smile.

Lesley stares in the water, scanning the area with her eyes not seeing any sight of the women anymore. She looks at their reflection as fireworks light up the sky around. "No; they're gone; let's go get those dresses," she answered, slightly blushing.

They walk back to the blanket to find the two young men looking confused and holding a couple of bottles of vodka. "Where they go?" asked the man in the black suit picking up the jean jacket.

Sofia and Lesley walk on to the blanket. "They ran off in their underwear, they told us to tell you to find them. They might already be naked," replied Lesley, picking up the dresses, and hands over the red one to Sofia.

The young man's mouth drops. "Dude I told you they were freaks! Comes on!" he said, rushing off dropping the jacket behind him. The other man follows his friend as he hugs the bottles.

Lesley picks up the jacket. "Boys," she said, rolling her eyes.

The car's clock reads 12:27 A.M., and the sisters arrive at Royal Plaza wearing the dresses of their victims; Sofia is wearing the red high-low dress and light blue jean jacket, and Lesley the white empire waist dress; both with big smiles on their faces. Lesley parks the car and they head straight into the plaza. Sofia's face brightens as she sees the lights and different stores.

"This is amazing! Thank you, sis!" Sofia cheered, jumping into her arms; she closes her eyes giving her a big kiss on the lips. They rub their bodies together as saliva spills out from their mouths.

People nearby give quick uncomfortable faces to one another and stare as they make out. The sisters then open their eyes looking back at the crowd, while continuing to share tongue. The people notice it wasn't going to end so they slowly walk away from them, trying to go on with their night.

Sofia becomes unhappy and begins to pout at Lesley. "Did you see how they looked at us...I just got here, and they already ruined everything!" she said, clenching her eyebrows.

"It's okay. I have an idea," she replied, kissing her on her forehead.

Through an alley between stores is a door marked with an electrical sign. Inside is a power room generating electricity for the entire plaza. Lesley leads Sofia by the hand to the end of the room; where there's a large on and off switch.

"No one will bother us here," said Lesley, flipping the switch, turning off the power throughout the plaza.

Orgasmic sounds echo inside the power room in complete darkness. "Ugh! Thank you!" moaned Sofia.

Moments not to long after the blackout, a maintenance man is walking through the alley. "Damn kids. I told them we need to replace that lock," he mumbled to himself. As soon as he opens the power stations door, he hears the sexual moans and groans quickly shutting the door.

He stands in shock with his back against the door, looking up and down the alley. He turns around and puts his ear against the door, listening to what's happening; with wide eyes he opens it slowly peeking his head inside. The echo begins to fill the alley way once again, so the maintenance man rushes in closing the door behind him. He takes out his flashlight and starts searching the room, getting closer and closer to the noise. He reaches the switch, not having seen the sisters, turning on the power for the plaza stopping the echo. Cheering can be heard from the outside and the man stands stills listening to his surroundings. Not hearing anything he turns to leave but immediately sees the two sisters, unclothed holding hands smiling at him.

Sofia looks at Lesley as she bites her lower lip. "Look what we have here.

You didn't tell me you invited someone," she said, then gets closer to the maintenance man.

"Mm, well, I thought you might be hungry," replied Lesley.

He drops his flashlight and puts his hands up. "Um…y-you're not aaloud…ugh um," he stuttered as Sofia puts her hand on his chest, pushing him against the wall.

"Shh, don't talk. I don't want you to talk," Sofia said, sliding her hand down to his belt. She kneels not breaking eye contact with the man.

He breathes in deeply looking at Lesley; she walks up to him as Sofia proceeds to take off his pants and pleasure him. Lesley grabs his hair and begins to kiss him. He lets loose going along with the two sisters.

"Ugh, yes," whispered the man.

All of a sudden, his face becomes horrified, mouth wide open with disbelief.

Lesley chuckles. "What's wrong?" she asked, taking a step back away from him.

He looks down and sees Sofia with a full mouth as she stands; then looks at his lower half and notices that his penis is missing, dripping blood. He looks straight at Sofia in confusion; and she takes a big gulp swallowing what was in her mouth. "I told you, no talking," she said, with a demonic smile.

His body begins to shake, and lips start to quiver. The realization of the outcome slowly sinks in, as the adrenaline gradually fades away.

Lesley walks up close to his ear and whispers, "We're gonna eat you up," then licks the inside of his ear.

"AAAAAAHHHHHHHHHH!"

# CHAPTER SIXTEEN

# INTERRUPTED

Mark and Christina have spent their night in Royal Plaza eating, taking pictures, listening to music, and then ended up at the arcade. A blackout caused by Lesley and Sofia hit the entire plaza and forced everyone outside.

The plaza is filled with upset people, complaining about the power. Mark and Christina squeeze themselves through the crowd. "Come on, this happens sometimes. They say it's because of all the power this place uses," she said, leading Mark by his fingers.

"Where are we going?" he asked while apologizing to the people they shove out the way.

Christina doesn't answer turning a corner; a gas lamppost is placed in the middle of a small circle garden. There's a few couples hanging about in the dark, kissing and cuddling with one another. They stop under the light and she looks at him with a sweet smile. "You got lucky," she said, intertwining her fingers with his.

Mark flinches. "What do you mean?" he asked.

"I was hoping we could play Race Con," she answered.

"The game we use to play? They still have it?" he asked.

She blushes and reaches into her pocket taking out a piece of paper. "Yeah, I got your letter," she said, handing him the paper, "and I wanted to finally kick your ass, since you got me into it. But that stupid hoe ruined everything."

Mark's eyes widen as he looks at the wrinkled folded up paper. He opens it slowly taking quick glances at Christina.

The paper reads:

Every time I see you, I get nervous and can't get myself to show you who I am. From the very first day I saw you in the Arcade my heart fell, and I found it extremely difficult to even speak. At the time you had someone which made things harder for me…not to mention my stupidity. Now you're graduating and this may be the last chance I get to tell you how I feel. Hopefully, I can do that before it's too late.

Secret Admirer

He looks at her in shock. "Ah, you have a secret admirer, huh?" he asked with a weak smile.

She rolls her eyes. "It's you, dork," she chuckles, giving him a push. "Not gonna lie, I found it weird till Lucy told me everything."

"WHAT? She told you…she wasn't supposed to…" he said, rubbing his eyebrows.

"You're lucky she did; she pretty much saved your ass," she said, pulling him closer. "I know you have trouble telling me how. So, why don't you show me?"

Mark takes a deep gulp and goes in for a kiss. The power of the plaza suddenly turns on and cheering fills the area. Mark and Christina look around in surprise, and Christina then sees Nallely and Diana smoking out of a glass pipe; Diana takes a large inhale out from the pipe and holds in the smoke. "Look, it's Diana an—" she was saying, but Diana then blows a straight stream of smoke into Nallely's mouth, and Christina's jaw drops.

Mark looks at her with a puzzled expression. "What happened?" he asked, turning around and sees Nallely and Diana kissing as smoke rises from their faces. He, too, becomes speechless as they watch their two friends making out.

Christina punches Mark's arm. "What are you looking at?" she asked, startling him.

"You told me to look!" he replied, rubbing his arm.

She tilts her head and places her hands on her waist. "NOT STARE!" she said, with frustration.

Nallely and Diana slowly separate their lips from each other, gracefully opening their eyes with big smiles. Nallely hears a faint ruckus; she turns her head and notices Mark and Christina arguing. "Oh, shit…" she whispered, covering her face.

Diana takes a look. "Hey, it's Christina and…shit. They saw us didn't they," she said, turning away, closing her eyes, and taking a deep breath.

"Yeah…yeah, yeah, yeah, yeah, yeah…mm," said Nallely, massaging her temples.

Diana sighs. "Well, let's go say hi," she said, grabbing her hand standing up.

"Are you crazy?" she asked.

"Crazy for you," she replied with a weak smile; she then becomes serious. "We both knew this was going to happen," she said, tugging on her hand.

Christina rolls her eyes and glances at her friends. "Shut up! Here they come," she said, hitting Mark. "HEY! What are you guys doing here?" she asked, with a big smile.

Diana and Nallely walk up to them as Nallely quickly lets go of Diana's hand, rubbing her hands together.

Nallely forces a smile. "Oh, nothing we were just smoking," she said, constantly looking down and back at Christina.

"And kissing," added Mark, raising an eyebrow and Christina hits him on the chest. "Ow, stop hitting me!" he complained, rubbing his sternum.

Christina gives him a sharp look. "Then stop being an idiot!"

Diana rolls her eyes. "It's okay, really," she said, with a smile.

"No! No, it's not okay!" shouted Nallely with frustration. "This is exactly why I didn't want anyone to know. Now Mark is going to fuckin' tell the guys, and they're gonna be all weird about it," she said, sitting on the edge of a flowerbed, then covers her face with her hands. Diana sits next to her and puts her arm around her. "I just don't wanna deal with bullshit," she mumbled though her fingers.

Diana and Christina both give Mark a death stare. He takes a deep breath and sits on the other side of Nallely. "Hey, I'm sorry. I was just joking and, this wasn't the time," he said, with a sigh.

Nallely takes a deep breath. "I just don't want to deal with jokes right now," she said, giving him a weak smile.

"It's going to happen. Shit, you guys make fun of me all the time," he said, smiling shaking his head.

Nallely giggles. "Ha, yeah…I'm just not ready," she said, looking at Christina and Mark, then grabs on to Diana's hand.

Diana looks at Mark with worry and says, "Please don't tell anyone."

He clenches his eyebrows, relaxes his face, then says, "Why not? They're not going to say anything bad," Christina kicks him. "Ow, okay, I won't," he said, rubbing his shin.

Nallely takes one last deep breath. "Can we change the subject? How was your date? Am I gonna be broke?" she asked, forcing a smile at Christina.

Christina begins to blush. "What no, the nights not over yet. He still needs to take me home," she said.

Diana and Nallely look at each other in surprise. "You have a car?" they asked him at the same time.

Christina smirks. "His dad gave him THE car," she said.

Nallely's jaw drops. "No, way! The one you and Jose would always—" she was saying.

"Okay, yes, that car," Mark said interrupting her with eyebrows clenched.

Diana laughs getting up from her seat. "Does this mean you can give us a ride home?" she asked, helping Nallely up.

He sighs. "Yeah, I guess, I just need to take Christina home first, your dad freaks me out," he replied, looking at Christina.

"Ha, he won't kill you, trust," she said, grabbing his hand, "but we should get going, we leave in like five hours," she finished looking at her phone.

The four friends are in Mark's car listening to Christina's CD. They all sing and have their own little party as they arrive at her house. Mark parks and lowers the volume to the music. He stares at her front door with anxiety; Christina places her hand on his and begins to rub it. "You gonna walk me to my door?" she asked, smiling at him.

Mark stays quiet and Nallely goes between the two front seats. "Don't be scared, you loser. Go finish your date," she said, nudging him.

He takes a deep breath and gives them a weak smile opening his door, without a word he steps out of the car walking toward the passenger side.

Christina smiles rolling her eyes. "He's so nervous," she said, looking at her friends.

Diana begins to blush. "This is so cute," she said, as Mark opens the passenger's door, "Aw," and then he reaches out his hand to Christina, "AA-AWWWW!" she finished and grabs ahold of Nallely's hand.

Christina flutters her eyes as a shy smile starts to grow. She takes his hand, and he helps her out closing the door behind her.

Mark and Christina slowly walk to her front door hand in hand, as Nallely and Diana giggle watching them through the car window. Mark feels his body tingle, to the point that he starts to breathe in deeply and slowly. As they get close to her house he opens and closes his mouth, having trouble speaking.

Christina examines him, noticing his struggle. "I had fun tonight," she said, as they stop in front of her door. "Thanks for taking me out," she finished, slightly lifting his forearm with her fingers, sliding down to his hand holding on to it. Her head is slightly down while still making eye contact.

Mark's face turns red, and he grabs her other hand; he slowly leans in to kiss her with his eyes closed. Christina smiles and rolls her eyes, then closes them leaning in for the kiss. Their lips are about to touch and suddenly the door swings open as the porch light turns on. Christina's father glares at Mark with murderess intent. "What the hell! You guys actually had a good time? And you're ending it with a kiss!" he said, pulling Christina into the house, "Get inside!" he continued, getting between them. "What did you do when you weren't here, huh?" he asked, getting closer to him.

Mark freezes in place, too terrified to move. "I…uh…we, I…didn't mean to…uh…I'm," he stuttered.

"Leave him alone, Daddy, nothing happened," said Christina, tugging on her father's biceps.

He looks at his daughter. "He's not going on the trip, is he?" he asked.

"Huh? No," she quickly answered with wide eyes.

Her father squints his eyes at her, then walks away.

She places her hand on the door gazing at Mark. "I'll see you later," she said, with a smile closing the door.

Mark still doesn't move from his spot, staring at the door in fear. He begins to think of the things her father can do to him, and then a voice calls out from behind him.

"Ha! You loser! You failed, now take us home! We still need to pack!" yelled out Nallely.

Mark snaps out of his torment, turns around and sees Nallely sticking her body out the window. He walks back to his car in disappointment; he opens the door taking a seat inside.

Diana leans in close to Mark. "Hey, there, buddy, you doing alright?" she asked, rubbing his shoulder.

"Yeah," he replies looking down at his lap.

"That's good, that's good. You think you can take us to my house now?" she asked, patting his shoulder.

He nods placing his hands on the steering wheel, driving off.

# CHAPTER SEVENTEEN

# PACKING

After the friends had their fun at the beach, Mark and Christina went out for a late night date. They ended up meeting with their friends Nallely and Diana, who were having a date of their own in secret. Mark then took everyone home so they can get ready for their trip.

It's now the next day around 8:00 A.M. and the friends are finally out of school; Jose is in his van heading over to Sebastian's house. He parks and begins to honk continuously. Sebastian comes out carrying three suitcases to the van. "Hey, man! Help me with this shit!" he yelled.

Jose gets out of his vehicle rushing over to Sebastian. "What's all this? You packed for your girlfriend or something?" he asked, confused.

"I have an idea for tomorrow; we're having a party. Don't tell the girls, okay?" he replied, lifting a suitcase on top of the van.

Jose helps him tie everything down. "Wow, mister romantic over here. This why you wanted me to get drinks?" he asked, tying the stuff down.

"Fuck, yeah!" he said, with excitement. "I'm-a go in the back kay, go get Lucy," he said, walking to the back of the van, opening the trunk. He looks around and begins to search; he leans over to the left of the van looking at Jose. "Where's the blanket?" he asked with a smile.

"Wow, really, it's back there just keep looking; it's probably under the cooler," he answered, smiling shaking his head, then enters his van.

"Nice, alright, let's go!" said Sebastian hopping in the back as he moves things around.

Jose drives off to pick up Lucy and he begins to laugh. "Ha-ha, dude, you know I made a bet with your girl, right?" he asked, with a big grin.

Sebastian gets up placing his arms on the back car seats. "No? What's the bet?" he asked.

"Eh, she didn't tell you, well, we made a five buck bet that you guys are not going to do anything in the back, no make out or full on dick in va-jj sex," he said, looking back and forth from Sebastian to the road.

"What? Nah, she didn't tell me, psh, I might as well give you the five bucks now for her ha-ha," he replied, rolling his eyes.

"Ha-ha, wow, foo, you're stupid," said Jose, shaking his head.

"I'm-a ask her about this shit," he said, laying back down.

They arrive at her house and see that she's sitting on the sidewalk, waiting for them with a backpack and small suitcase. Jose parks his van next to her so the trunk is facing her.

Sebastian opens the trunk to the van. "Hey, Babes, come back here," he said, showing her the blanket.

Lucy gets up. "Wow, Babe," she said, smiling at him. "What's with all the bags? You told us not to bring so much," she said, projecting her voice so Jose could hear her.

"Ask Sebastian, he's the one with the surprise," replied Jose.

Lucy quickly turns toward Sebastian. "Surprise? What surprise?" she asked, putting her bags next to the cooler, then gets in the back of the van.

"Wow, thanks, bro," he replied, closing the trunk; he looks at Lucy smiling. "Don't worry about it, you'll see if we find the town," he replied, holding her hand.

"If we find the town? Come on, tell me," she said, tugging on his hand, giving him puppy eyes.

He tilts his head slightly. "No, 'cause you kept something from me," he said.

Her eyes widen, clenching her arms together. "W-what did I keep from you?" she asked with hesitation.

He smiles. "Jose told me about the bet you guys made."

Jose leans back turning his head a bit towards them. "Yeah, you better have the five bucks on you!" he said, with a smirk.

Lucy lets out a breath of relief. "You better have mine!" She then lies down, pulling Sebastian with her and hugs him tight giving a quick peck on the cheek. "What are you gonna do about it?" she asked with a smirk.

He smiles. "Break up with you if you do it again."

Her face goes pale and softly pushes him away. "Wow, really?" she asked with sad eyes beginning to water.

He reaches out to her and try's to grab her hand. "No, I'm just kidding." She rejects his hand, then says, "Sure you are…"

"I am!" he replied with a chuckle. "Come here, you know I love you."

She reluctantly gives him a smile. "You don't even like hanging out with me; you'd rather smoke."

He looks at her in shock. "What? I always hang out with you. Even when we first got together, I hardly saw our friends," he said, raising an eyebrow.

Jose slightly turns his head toward them while still looking at the road. "Yeah! You took him from us for like two months, we thought he was dead," he said, with a chuckle.

"We were on our honeymoon, bro!" replied Sebastian, intertwining his fingers with hers. "I love you," he said, kissing her hand.

Lucy's cheeks turn rosy red with a small smile on her face, remaining silent, looking deep into his eyes.

"NO FUCKING, YOU TWO!" yelled Jose, breaking her line of sight.

"We're not! Chill!" she snapped back.

They arrive at the park parking lot, and see their friends arguing with James. Jose parks his van next to them and Will opens the trunk, as they hear Christina yelling in the background, "YOU'RE NOT COMING YOU FUCKEN CREEP!"

"FINE!" yelled James, then leaves.

The friends then focus their attention on themselves. Sebastian sits on the rear bumper of the van. "What was that about?" he asked.

"Just some stupid kid that wants to come with us," answered Christina, annoyed.

Lucy comes from behind Sebastian and wraps her arms around him. "How does he know we're going somewhere?" she asked.

"He was listening to us talking at school," answered Jessica with wide eyes, shaking her head.

"Wow, what a creeper," said Lucy with a horrified face.

Christina walks over to the side of the van and opens the slide door. "Tell me about it! That foo wouldn't shut the fuck up, he's really annoying," she said, plopping down on to her seat inside the van.

Jose gets out of his van with a rope in his hand. "Alright, well, come on; help me tie all this shit on top of Sebastian's shit," he said, giving one end of the rope to Mark.

Mark looks at the suitcases with bewilderment. "What's all this?" he asked, looking back at Jose, and then starts to put the other's stuff on top of the van.

"Why are you guys asking me? It's his surprise," he answered, pointing at Sebastian.

Everyone quickly stares at Sebastian. "Wow, again, thanks," he said, rolling his eyes at Jose. "You guys will find out if we find the town."

They all clench their eyebrows looking at each other.

"If we find the town?" asked Nallely and Diana at the same time.

Lucy takes a quick glance at Sebastian. "That's what I said!" she said, giving her friends wide eyes.

Sebastian smiles. "And I'll tell them what I told you…" he said, giving her a kiss on the cheek, "Yes, if we find it."

Mark and Jose put their friend's things on top of Jose's van and placed the rest in the trunk with Sebastian and Lucy. They all then get in with Jessica sitting in the passenger seat, Christina and Diana are in the back seat with Nallely in the middle, Will and Mark are in the middle seat with Will in the middle and Mark behind Jose. They leave the park and Will leans forward between Jose and Jessica. "Hey, you going for Rosie, right?" he asked.

"Yeah, right now, chill," answered Jose, driving out the park parking lot.

"Alright, but when we get to her house don't honk, okay?" asked Will distinctively, sitting back at his seat.

"Um, okay?" answered Jose, raising an eyebrow.

They get to Rosie's house and Will texts her that they're outside. All of a sudden, everyone sees Rosie throw a backpack out of her second story window, then gets out that window climbing down a trellis, runs across the front lawn, gets into the van, and sits down. They all stare at her while she kisses Will.

"What the fuck?" Mark said with a shocked look on his face.

Rosie looks at Mark with an oblivious expression. "What?" she asked as if she doesn't know what she has done.

"What do you mean what? You came outta the fucking window!" said Mark clenching his eyebrows.

"Well, yeah, it's called sneaking out, for your information," said Rosie, looking at him as if he was stupid.

Mark clenches his eyebrows even more. "I know that! But what? Your parents didn't let you come with us?" he asked curiously.

"Nope, still grounded," she answered, smiling.

"I see," said Mark, looking at Rosie with guilt.

Rosie gives him a strange look. "Yeah, well…let's go. I don't wanna get caught," she said, hitting Jose's seat.

# CHAPTER EIGHTEEN

# ROAD TRIP

The friends have all packed their things on to the van and are on their way to Dunsvill. They have been driving for about six hours; they are now out of the city and deep in the desert. Jessica is fast asleep as Jose bobs his head to his music. Christina is looking out the window, while glancing at Nallely and Diana with the corner of her eye, as they hold hands in secret. Mark and Will are talking about the town as Rosie is texting her father. Lucy and Sebastian are bickering to themselves under the blanket.

Will gives out a devilish smile, then says, "I bet the kids that killed their parents are still kids. Just waiting for us in the trees to jump down and kill us all."

Mark looks at Jose in suspense, then taps his shoulder and whispers, "So, what are we going to do if we find the town and there's someone there?" he asked him.

Will chuckles. "What dude, you scared?" he asked, punching his shoulder.

"Nah, I'm just saying. What if we aren't alone?" he asked again.

Jose takes a glance at Mark through the rearview mirror. "Then I guess it's a sleepover," he answered with a smile.

"You can't be serious?" said Jessica wide awake with her arms crossed.

Jose quickly turns his head toward her, then back at the road. "I thought you were sleeping?"

She raises an eyebrow and gives a small smirk. "Stupidity woke me up," she said, making a slight movement with her head, then continues to say, "We're not staying if there's people there," she finished, clenching her eyebrows.

Jose smiles. "It's a town, and I bet we aren't the only ones going over to check things out," he said, placing his right hand on her thigh.

Jessica lifts up his middle finger moving his hand off her, placing it on the steering wheel. "So, what? Are you expecting some kind of town fair or something, where there's a bunch of drunken idiots?" she asked, hitting him softly on the shoulder, "We aren't staying if there's people there, okay? There's no way," she finished, giving him a stern look.

"Aw, come on; it'll be fun," he replied, shoving her softly.

Her jaw drops. "Are you stupid?"

"Well, you did say his stupidity woke you," interrupted Mark.

"Shut up," replied Jessica, then looks at Jose with anger and says, "We're turning back now; this was a stupid idea."

Jose clenches his eyebrows, looking at her in shock. "What why? We're like almost there, Babe," he said.

"Don't Babe me; I wanna go home."

"Come on, don't be like that. We don't even know if anyone will be there."

"I don't care, turn around now," she finished, crossing her arms and looks out the window.

Jose rolls his eyes. "How about this? We're almost there and the nearest gas station is in the forest. We'll just check it out really quick after we fill up, and if there's people there we'll leave no problem. How's that sounds, guys?" he asked, quickly turning toward his friends and back to the road.

They all reply. "Yeah." ... "Sounds good to me." ... "I'm down" at the same time.

Jessica turns to them in shock. "Are you guys serious?"

Rosie gives her a lazy look. "Well, it's not like we haven't thought about that; Jose's probably right and we aren't the only ones going to check it out."

"What, no we—" Jessica started to say, but Rosie interrupts her. "Just don't worry about it, my man will protect you,"

The friends continue driving for a couple more hours. The van's clock reads 3:43 P.M. and the asphalt has turned to a dirt road. Jose then sees a dark spot stretching out and getting bigger in the horizon. "There it is, you guys!" he said, with excitement.

"Where? All I see is dirt," said Christina, looking out the window.

They all look straight ahead with suspense, trying to look for the forest, and then the entire horizon becomes thickened, and begins to form a tree line, slowly becoming brown and green. "Damn it's big. It looks like it covers the world!" said Mark looking from left to right, trying to see the end of the forest.

Once they arrive at the start of the forest, Jose comes to a slow stop and looks around. The forest is extremely large, with trees standing at about seventy to a hundred feet tall, and seeming as if there is only one way in.

"What's wrong?" asked Jessica, looking around with him. "I don't see anything, you're freaking me out," she said, hitting him.

Jose gives a big smile. "I'm just looking at the open lane, before we go into the unforgiving forest," he said, looking at all his friends.

"I thought it was called the Unmarked Forest," replied Christina.

"Unmarked Forest, unforgiving forest, the fuckin' forest, I don't care what it's called. We're leaving if there's people," said Jessica with frustration.

"We'll be fine," he said, driving slowly into the forest. "Trust me. We might not even find the town anyways. And I also got my dad's big ass tents just in case."

Jessica hits him again. "You said we would leave!"

"If we find the town and there's people, Babe, damn," he replied, rubbing his arm.

As they continue to drive into the forest the desert disappears behind them, while Jessica looks through the van's passenger side mirror and takes a deep sigh.

The friends all laugh and talk to each other while driving deeper into the forest, trying to get Jessica to lighten up and enjoy herself. It doesn't take long till Jose reaches the gas station, parking next to a gas pump. The gas station is small containing an old minimart, with two pumps each having one nozzle. There's a ranger Jeep and two forest rangers sitting on a bench, near the front entrance having a smoke.

One of the rangers gets up and approaches the van. "Hey, there, heading to the campsite?" he asked, putting out his cigarette in the ashtray near the gas pump.

Jose gets out and shakes his hand. "Yeah, we're spending the weekend," he answered with a smile. "We just need gas."

"Well, you kids be careful, and make sure you follow the signs. The road splits a little down the path," said the ranger, giving a slight nod.

"Thanks," replied Jose, then walks toward Jessica. "Can you put fifty in…" he looks at the gas pump, "one?" she gives him a cold glare, "Please," he finished with a smile as he hands her the money.

She squints her eyes at him. "You're lucky I need to use the restroom," she said, grabbing the money and opens the van door aggressively.

"I have to go, too," said Lucy.

All the friends head into the minimart except for Jose, Mark, and Christina. Jose waves Mark to come to him. He rolls his eyes and gets out of the van.

"What bro? I'm trying to…you know," Mark said with an impatient face.

"Calm down, I need your help," said Jose, opening the hood to the van.

Mark clenches his eyebrows. "With what?"

Jose looks into the engine with a smile. "I need you to tell me if anyone comes by," he said, fiddling at the back of the engine.

Mark becomes worried and looks at Christina with a nervous smile. "Um, is everything okay?" he asked.

"Yeah, I'm just going to make the thermometer say it's over heating," he replies, finishing up with the engine. He looks at Mark and smiles as he dusts off his hands.

"Why?" Mark asked with confusion.

Jose chuckles. "This way we'll have no choice but to stay if we find the town," he said, closing the hood. "Don't tell anyone, okay?" he finished with a wink. He then sees his friends come out from the minimart and says, "Alright, get in, and if anyone asks what I was doing, just say I was checking the oil."

Mark takes a step toward the van, then turns back to Jose. "You think there's going to be people there?" he asked.

He shrugs his shoulders. "No idea, but better safe than sorry. Oh, and treat her good, alright? Be a real man," he said, putting gas into the van waggling his eyebrows.

Mark gets back inside the van sitting back down with a concerned look. She looks at him, noticing something is wrong; and the rest of the friends then get in soon after filled with energy.

"What did he want?" she asked as the friends continue laughing and having fun. Mark doesn't respond. "Hello?" she said, waving her hand in front of his face.

Mark shakes his head and looks at her. "Huh? Oh, um, nothing. He just told me to treat you right," he said, with a weak smile.

"Aww don't be scared, he won't do shit," she said, rubbing his shoulder.

Jose then gets in the van with enthusiasm and starts the engine. "Alright, there's no going back now," he said, smiling at his friends.

"Shut up," said Jessica, hitting his arm.

Once the van begins to move, Lucy lays back down and pulls on Sebastian's arm. "Come here and talk to me. I have a feeling it's going to take a while," she said, with a smile.

"As you wish, my queen," replies Sebastian with blushed cheeks.

"What? Did I just hear what I think I heard?" asked Christina in shock, turning over and looking down at Lucy.

"Why you listening to our conversation, huh?" Lucy asked.

Christina giggles. "Making sure I don't hear any monster noises," she said, covering her smile with the van seat.

Lucy rolls her eyes and says, "Oh, shut up, we don't do it all the time."

Will turns around and joins in on the conversation. "Well, it seem like you do, like come on."

Nallely then quickly puts here attention to them. "Yeah, like member that time we went to the movies, what did Sebastian start doing to you?" she asked, staring straight at Lucy.

"Oh, I know! He went down under!" said Diana, giggling and smiling.

"Oh, my—" said Lucy, covering her eyes, then down to her mouth.

Sebastian smiles. "Hee-hee, I remember that; good times…good times," he said.

"Yeah, also when we were at the park, you and Sebastian were—" Diana started to say, but Lucy shoots siting straight up interrupting her. "Okay, okay, I think we get the point, but we don't always just do that…we talk to," she said, innocently.

"Yeah, what do you guys say to each other? Harder, harder!" said Nallely, laughing.

Christina nods. "Yeah, you guys are freaks," she said.

"And so, what if we are; and we don't always do sexual things to each other, okay? We have sweet innocent love," said Lucy, holding Sebastian's hand.

"Yeah, you guys are cute together; it's like you two are meant for each other," said Rosie, smiling.

"Thanks. So, Babe, come on let's talk," said Lucy, giving Sebastian a kiss.

"Ha-ha, fuck, alright," said Sebastian, smiling.

Lucy puts her index finger on Sebastian's lips. "Ah, language, and what? Don't you like talking to me?" she asked.

Sebastian, talking through Lucy's finger says, "Yes, Babes, I do, I love talking to you," he gets the blanket ready to pull it over them. "Let's talk under the blanket though."

"Ah, fine but we are not going to do anything, okay, love?" said Lucy giving Sebastian her eyes once more.

"Yes, yes, Babes, I know, come here and give me those sopt lips," said Sebastian, about to kiss Lucy.

Lucy moves her head away rejecting his kiss. "Ha-ha what, sopt? What's that? I think you mean soft," she said, smiling at him.

"Oh, my gosh, Babe, come on," said Sebastian, looking up, then closes his eyes and puts his head down.

"Ha-ha, yes, Babe, I know you can't speak right at times, you're so cute," she said, kissing him on the cheek and pulls the blanket over them.

Continuing to drive deeper in the forest, Jose comes upon the first split in the road with an old road sign pointing at both roads. One says, "Camping Site" and the other, "Rangers' Office" being the one he takes; and within a couple of hours, they hit another split road, with a wooden pole missing a sign for one of the roads. On that road there are two metal barricades in the middle, being the only thing blocking the way.

Jose gives Jessica a big grin, then drives around the barricades. He follows the road until it slowly begins to disappear.

"Okay, there's no town. Can we go back now…please?" asked Jessica, putting her hand on his thigh.

He stays silent and drives onward.

Jessica squeezes his thigh in suspense. "What are you doing?" she asked.

He keeps his eyes ahead of him. "Finding this town," he said with determination.

# CHAPTER NINETEEN

# WELCOME

The friends have been driving for hours before arriving at the forest, all excited for their big trip except for Jessica. They have all agreed to leave the town if they come across any people. But Jose tampered with his engine's thermometer, hoping that will force them to stay for a while. As the road in the forest disappears, Jose proceeds to drive deeper into the trees.

Jessica gives Jose an angry glare. "You better turn around right now before we get lost!" she said, punching his shoulder.

"Stop hitting me," he said, then comes across another dirt road, stopping on its edge. "Aw, what? Did we go in a circle?" he asked himself.

"Good! Now just take us home," said Jessica, crossing her arms.

Sebastian takes the blanket off him and throws it at Lucy's face, and quickly sits up. "Aw, what no camping?" he asked with disappointment.

Lucy props herself up tossing the blanket to the side. "Hey, were you even paying attention to what I was saying?" she asked angrily.

He turns to her with a weak smile. "Uh, yeah, Babes, I was," he replies.

"Okay, then, what did I say?" she asks but he doesn't respond. "You know what…never mind, don't talk to me," she said, covering herself with the blanket.

He tries touching her gently. "What? No, Baby, I am listening!"

"Don't touch me," she whimpered.

"But Babe," he said, tugging at the blanket, but she holds on to it, keeping herself covered.

Jessica doesn't break her glare off Jose. "No one is having fun being in this car anymore, take us home," she said, crossing her arms.

Jose takes a deep sigh and drives on the dirt road. "Fine."

"Wait so we really aren't going camping? We drove all the way here for hours and we ain't doing shit?" asked Rosie.

Jose looks back at her. "Oh, we're going camping. Hopefully, this is the right way," he said, turning toward the road.

"Good, I don't wanna get in trouble for nothing."

While driving on the dirt road, Jose sees a large wooden sign in the distance. "I didn't see that before," he said, clenching his eyebrows, and as they get close a smile begins to grow on his face.

"DUNSVILL! A FRIENDLY LITTLE TOWN FULL OF ALL TIME FUN AND HAPPINESS" reads the sign along the side of the road.

"We're here!" said Jose relieved.

Jessica lets out a groan. "No!"

He looks at her with his big grin on his face. "Yes, and good thing, too. The engine is overheating," he said, pointing at the thermometer on the dashboard.

Jessica's jaw drops. "Why didn't you say anything? We should have just went camping if you knew it was over heating!" she said, with anger.

They see the entrance to the town and notice a man wearing a straw sun-hat, pulling weeds out from around the town's main sign. Jessica's eyes widen, and she begins hitting Jose repeatedly. "You fuckin' asshole! I hate you, I hate you I hate you! Turn around now!" she said, infuriated.

Jose steps on the breaks and grabs Jessica's hand. "Stop hitting me! It's just one guy and we need to let my van cool off...damn," he said, raising his eyebrows at her.

"I fuckin' hate you," she replied as her eyes tear up.

An awkward silence fills the vehicle as Jose drives up to the man, rolling down his window. The man stands and walks up to the driver side window, lifting his head revealing his face, then rests his arms on the van door. "Why, hello, there! And welcome to Dunsvill. We really don't get any visitors here, but when we do, they don't seem to stay long, but their spirits will stay here forever. Psh, listen to me talk and you don't even know who I am, I am Victor," he said, holding out his hand to Jose.

Jose looks at Victor's rough beaten hand. "Ah, hi, I'm Jose," he said, shaking it.

"Nice to meet you," said Victor, smiling.

Mark leans over Jose's shoulder. "I thought this place was abandon?" he asked Victor curiously.

"It kind of is," he replied with a small shrug. "Just my ma, pa, two sisters, and me who live here," he said, pointing over to their white house on the small hill.

"Cool what was your name again?" asked Jose.

He slowly turns his head toward Jose. "Victor," then gives an open smile, "well, you guys can stay in any of the other houses since they're not being used anymore," he finished, taking a step back from the van. "Enjoy your stay," he waved.

"Thanks," said Jose, closing his window, and drives into the town.

"That was weird," Christina said slowly.

"Yeah, it was, do you think he was one of the Duns?" asked Rosie, then she turns to the back. "Come on, you two, stop fucking we're here," she said, with a soft giggle.

"We're not 'fucking' damn!" yelled Lucy still under the blanket, annoyed and interrupting the question.

"Whoa, Babes, language," said Sebastian, smiling and rubbing her back.

"Oh, shut up! I'm still mad at you," she said, pushing his hand away as she comes out from under the blanket, looking seriously at him.

Christina gives Sebastian an astonished expression. "Oh, someone's in trouble," she said, with a silent laugh.

"Shut up," he replied.

Lucy hits his Achilles tendon. "Don't tell her to shut up!"

Sebastian flinches and leans against the seats. "Sorry…"

The friends are now deep inside the town, and Jose parks in front of a few abandon houses. There are many shops surrounding the area, and the neighborhood is fairly large. He looks behind him at his friends. "Alright, let's have some fu—," he starts to say but they all rush out of the van. They all grab their belongings as quickly as they could.

Diana stares at the houses and smiles. "WE CAN BE NEIGHBORS!" she said with excitement.

Jessica glares at Diana. "We aren't staying! We're leaving as soon as the car cools down, okay?" she said with sincerity.

Jose hugs her from behind and says, "Calm down, Babe, everything will be fine."

She pushes him away. "No, don't tell me to calm down, I wanna leave," she said, with anger.

Rosie puts her hand on Jessica's shoulder. "Hey, we just got here and we're all tired and frustrated. Maybe we should take a nap."

Right when Jessica is about to respond, Will comes standing next to Rosie. "Yeah, you guys rest and we'll check this place out, see what's up," he said.

Christina stands on the vans tire and says, "Can you boys help unload before you go?" she said, bouncing up and down biting her lower lip.

"NO! Why would we unpack if we're going to leave?" Jessica asked, crossing her arms.

As the young men head back to the van to unload, Christina jumps down smiling and says, "But I want my weed."

Jessica widens her eyes. "And I wanna live!" she said, with more frustration.

"If they wanted to kill us, they would have done it by now," said Rosie, trying to calm her down. "They could have easily shot us when we were in the van?"

"See, so let's just smoke and relax. I still have a lot left from when we went to the beach," said Christina, turning toward the van waiting for her bag.

Meanwhile as the friends unpack, Devin walks up to Victor who's still at the entrance of the town.

"Hey, there, brother, so did I tell you or what?" said Devin with excitement rubbing his hands together.

"Yes, Devin you were right, so are you..." Victor started to say but then he sees another car.

"Ah, what do you know," said Devin with a creepy smile.

It's James, and he drives up to Victor and Devin parking his car.

"Welcome to Dunsvill, kid," said Devin.

"Hi," said James, giving half a smile.

Victor begins to look inside James' car through the front windshield. "You come by yourself, boy?" he asked.

"Well, um kinda, the people that arrived sooner than me don't know I'm here yet," replied James, giving a crooked smile.

"I see. Well, can you get out of your car, please? I have to do a quick search before you can enter our town," said Victor, opening James' car door.

James looks at him uneasily. "Ah, yeah, sure," he said, getting out of his car.

"Son, who are you? What's your name?" asked Victor while searching the car.

"I'm James," he answered with a smile.

"Nice name," said Devin, grabbing an old rope from the floor out of James view.

"And what's your name?" asked James, being friendly.

"I'm Victor and that's my brother Devin," answered Victor, still searching James' car.

Devin wraps both ends of the rope to his hands. "We're from the Duns family," he said, with a creepy smile.

"Wait wha—?" James began to say with surprised eyes, but Devin quickly puts the old rope around James' neck and says, "Welcome to Dunsvill boy."

James gives a good struggle but it isn't enough and dies.

"What the…What's wrong with you? We still needed to ask him if…Ah, never mind, it's too late now. Take him to the house, and try not to let the others see you," said Victor, pointing to a nearby wheelbarrow. "Shit, don't want you fucking up again," he continued, keeping calm.

"Alright," said Devin, putting the dead body in a wheelbarrow, covering it with a blanket that was inside James' car.

"I'm going to get rid of the car; now go," said Victor, getting inside the vehicle.

Devin looks around him checking if anyone is around, then quickly transfers the body over to the house.

# CHAPTER TWENTY

# RECON

The friends are now in Dunsvill, and Jessica continues to show her discomfort, especially now that they were greeted by Victor. They try and ease her nerves and begin to unpack at one of the abandoned houses. As they do that, James arrives and gets dealt with by the Duns brothers. Devin is now taking the body over to their house.

Devin opens the back door to the house carrying James' body. He walks into the living room seeing his mother and father sitting on the couch, drinking tea. The coffee table has a white tarp with a tea set on top. The mother is wearing a yellow dress with a white rose in the right side of her hair. The father is wearing a black suit, white shirt, and black tie, with a fedora and a white rose pinned to its left side.

"Hey, Ma, hey Pa," said Devin.

"Hi Son...I see you got...food like always...that's my boy...you never... disappoint," said his father with a weak smile.

"Thanks, Pa," said Devin, smiling.

The mother grows a large grin on her face. "Oh, goodie, we can have our guests for dinner. Quick, Baby, plug him in so I can get started and you're going to help me."

Devin heads to a nearby room and says, "Yes, Ma," with satisfaction. He opens a door, then turns on the light, showing stairs going down to the basement, which was remodeled into a refrigerator room. The basement is large with white tiles and metal walls. There are five metal tables; one has restraints with a blood machine next to it, another has some dry blood on it with all kinds of operating tools, and the other two are labeled packaging and sorting. The fifth table is in the middle of the room; that also has restraints. Devin places James down on the table with the blood machine and hooks him up to it. He then opens a closet that has aprons and masks inside.

Back in the living room, the mother is just about to finish her tea as Victor walks into the house. "Hello, Mother, hello, Father, I'm going to see how our guests are doing, just thought my sisters would like to join me," he said.

The mother gives her son a sweet smile. "While you're there, invite them for dinner, sweetie," she said.

"Yes, Mother," he replied.

Victor walks up the stairs towards his sisters' room, and when he reaches the door, he hears, "He-he stop, stop it," giggled one of the sisters. He then opens the door, and he sees them half naked with Lesley on top of Sofia.

The sisters' bedroom has one queen sized bed with amber covers. The walls have locks of hair pinned on one side of the room. There are many whips and paddles laying everywhere, along with plenty of clothes on the floor.

"Hey, Lesley, stop messing with your sister, we got stuff to do," said Victor with a serious face.

Lesley tries fixing her hair. "Alright, so they came then?" she asked smiling, getting off from pinning her sister down. She looks up at her brother smiling showing her crooked teeth with her freckled face.

"Yes, let's go," answered Victor sincerely.

"Yes, Sir! Mister Bossy Sir! Hahaha come on Sofia, we'll wear the dresses we bought," she said, laughing and hitting Sofia's leg.

Sofia jumps out of bed with excitement. "Yay! We're going to match," she said, clapping repeatedly.

The friends have finished unpacking and are inside of the house they chose. It's a decent size house, with four bedrooms and two nonworking bathrooms. The living room is large connecting to a small kitchen and dining room. The girls are sitting in the living room, as the guys bring in the rest of their things.

"Okay, that's everything," said Will, dusting off his hands. "We'll go look around, you relax," he finished, kissing his girl on the lips.

Rosie closes her eyes as she receives the kiss. "I love you," she said, smiling.

"I love you, too," he replied.

Jose and Sebastian look at their girlfriends, and Jessica says, "Don't talk to us," crossing her arms.

"Aw, okay," said Sebastian, walking out of the house, and the rest of the guys follow.

Jessica rubs her eyebrows. "I can't believe this," she pouts.

Christina goes through her suitcase and takes out her things to smoke with. "Oh, it's not that bad," she said, starting to pack her pipe with marijuana.

"Yeah, we can have a lot of fun here, who knows," said Nallely, holding Diana's hand with a smile.

Jessica stares at them. "You can't be serious, we are in—" she started to say, but Lucy stands up and interrupts.

"Hey, I'm-a go for a walk, I need fresh air," she said, with a weak smile.

"You can't go out there by yourself," Jessica said quickly. "You can die!"

Rosie rolls her eyes and gets up from her seat. "I'll go with her; we'll die together," she said, with a small smile, looking at Lucy.

She smiles back. "Thanks, I don't wanna die alone."

"Stop!" yelled Jessica with frustration.

Lucy and Rosie start to giggle. "We're just playing," said Rosie.

"Well, don't mess around like that, okay?" said Jessica with a sad look.

As the two girls open the door to head outside, they see the boys talking with Victor and his two sisters, who are wearing matching yellow dresses with summer hats and pigtails. Rosie sees Lesley walk up slowly to Will putting her hand on his chest, up to his right shoulder as she bites her lower lip.

"What the fuck?" said Rosie, rushing outside toward Will and Lucy follows.

The rest of the girls look at each other with confusion, and head out to see what's going on.

Rosie reaches Will and pulls him away from Lesley. "Um, excuse me? Who the fuck are you?" she asked with anger.

She looks at her and smirks. "Ha-ha, I'm Lesley," she said with a wink.

"And I'm Sofia!" she said with enthusiasm.

Victor walks in between his sisters and puts his arms around them. "These are my two sisters," he said.

Rosie angrily looks up and down at Lesley. "Well, this one is really flirty," she said, holding Will's arm as she continues to stare her down.

"Hey, I didn't know you two had a thing, alright?" said Lesley, rolling her eyes and smiling at Will.

Lucy walks in to view of the conversation. "Well, we're going to look around and maybe try and find a lake," she said, trying to change the subject.

"Mm, is that so? We actually do have one, it's not too far. You can just follow the signs. But before you go, we would like to invite you for dinner," said Victor politely.

Before any of the friends can think of an answer, Diana comes from behind and says, "Okay, sure," with a smile.

"Great! I'll let you guys know when the food is ready," said Victor, smiling. "Come on, girls."

"Heh, heh, goodbye 'Cutie', see you soon," said Lesley, winking and blowing a kiss to Will.

"Bye," said Sofia, waving.

The friends all stare at Diana.

"What? I don't wanna be rude, and I'm hungry. We haven't eaten anything like all day. Just chips," said Diana, shrugging her shoulders.

"We could use some food. And you won't have to cook Jose," said Nallely, trying to get them to accept the invitation.

Jose peps up and says, "Sounds good to me!"

"Yeah! Now we have to smoke together before we eat," said Christina with excitement.

Diana holds on to Nallely's arm smiling at her. "Let's go look around and see how this town is, then find a good spot," she said, beginning to walk away.

They all start to follow Diana and Nallely except for Jessica and Jose, who are still standing next to the van. "This wasn't the plan!" she said, stomping the ground.

Jose holds her hand. "Come on, Baby, try and have fun. I'll protect you," he said, with a smile.

She looks at their hands, then at Jose, and takes a deep sigh. "Fine...I'm starting to hate all of you," she said with a weak smile rolling her eyes.

The friends walk past the nearby shops, all taking quick looks inside and exploring a little bit. Some of the stores still have some things inside, although most are completely empty. About an hour passes by and as they all turn a few corners, they see the Town Hall. The Town Hall is a large bricked three-story building, placed on an elevated six-foot foundation. It's old and looks as if it hasn't been touched for centuries.

Diana puts her hand out stopping her friends, then points straight at the Town Hall. "We so gotta hot box that!" she said, with a big grin.

They all head over passing by more stores and even a sheriff station. They climb the stairs and Diana begins to push on the two large wooden doors. "This door won't open," she said, pouting her lip.

Will inspects the doors. "Looks like it's been boarded up from the inside, I'm going to try to kick it open, stand back," he said, getting ready to bust the door open.

"Ooh, watch out," said Jose, shaking both of his hands.

Will kicks the door once and it goes flying open.

"There, come on," said Will, waving his hand for everyone to follow.

"Psh, I could've done that," said Jose, walking into the building.

Jessica gets ahold of Jose's arm. "Yeah, sure, Babe," she said, rolling her eyes smiling.

As the friends enter the building to explore, the two sisters come out from hiding and approach the Town Hall. Sofia sits on the edge of the Hall's foundation near the steps, and Lesley is pacing back and forth. "Why don't we just go inside with them?" Sofia asked, kicking her feet. "I wanna talk to them, we hardly talk to anyone."

"Because we are just supposed to check on them and see where they go, also we are not allowed in there; you know that," answered Lesley.

"Ah, yes, I know," said Sofia. Sofia then starts to hum the song her mother hums.

"You never get tired of that song," said Lesley, rolling her eyes staring at Sofia as she walks back and forth.

"Na! Mother hums it all the time when she's getting the food ready," said Sofia with a smile. "I bet she's doing it right now."

"Well, yeah, that's Mother," said Lesley.

"Well, I like it, it makes me feel happy," said Sofia with a big smile.

Lesley then stops and turns to her sister. "Ha-ha, okay. You know, the guys are cute," she said, with a small smile.

Sofia jumps up from her seat. "So are the girls, I bet they're really good at what they do," she said, biting her lip.

"Mm, I bet they are, ha-ha, too bad they got to go," said Lesley with a grin.

"Aw we can't just, um you know," said Sofia, smiling.

"Ha-ha I like the way you think, sis," said Lesley, smiling at her sister.

Inside the Town Hall the friends are in the first room. The room is a wide open hall where the town's people would go for an important meeting. All the desks tables and chairs are scattered throughout the hall, with clothing and shoes next to them. Broomsticks mops and other handheld items are also all around the room. There are two curved staircases leading up to the second floor that is a balcony setting, and a chandelier hangs from the ceiling of the second floor overlooking the first floor. A small arched perch is also overlooking the first floor that's placed in between the two staircases; that's where the mayor would speak to the people of the town. The friends are all spread out in the room searching the area, but Jessica is by the front door in shock of how the room is.

"This place is fucking old and messed up; let's go to the lake already," said Mark eagerly.

"Well, no shit, it's old, but it's pretty cool. LOOK! A PIPE!" said Nallely picking up an old pipe that was on the floor next to some clothes.

"DAMN! That's cool let me see!" said Diana looking at the pipe.

"Let's pop its cherry right now!" said Christina pulling out the bag of marijuana from her pocket.

"Fuck, yeah, the food is probably almost ready; let's smoke this shit," said Will happily.

Jessica finally breaks out of her daze, crosses her arms, and begins to rub them. "Um, you guys, none of you find it weird that there's random ass clothes all over the place?" she asked, walking up to her friends slow.

Jose starts to laugh as he looks around him. "It kinda looks like everyone just got naked and had a blast," said Jose, smiling at his friends.

They all laugh while Jessica gives him a serious look. "This isn't a joke! It's just weird, and that Victor guy and his sisters…they creep me out," she said, then looking at her friends with a weird look.

Mark looks at the clothes on the floor and says, "I don't know, I think this is all a trick. Like they put this stuff to scare people," he then looks at Jessica.

"Like, come on. There's no blood or any sign of a fight, only clothes. I think you just need to blaze and chill," he finished with a smile.

Jessica looks at her friends and sees that they all agree with Mark. "Maybe you're right…" she said with a weak smile.

Will begins to get some chairs together to form a circle. "Alright, let's blaze," he said with excitement.

Lucy begins to walk backward as she says, "I'm not going to smoke; you guys have fun. I'm-a look around some more," with a forced smile.

"What, again, Babes? It's not 'cause of me, is it?" asked Sebastian with a sad look on his face.

"No…Um, I just want to look at stuff," said Lucy, looking sad.

"I'll go with her," said Rosie with a smile.

# CHAPTER TWENTY-ONE

# TROUBLED MIND

Victor and his sisters met up with the friends and invited them for dinner. Diana accepted for everyone, and they all headed into the town to explore a little, and see if there is anything out of the ordinary. They end up at the Town Hall and decide to enjoy a smoke there, as Lucy and Rosie search around some more.

While the friends are smoking in the first room, Lucy and Rosie find themselves in the mayor's office on the third floor. The office is fairly large with a big desk and mayor's chair next to boarded up windows. There are a couple of bookcases and a couch for guests to sit on. As they look around the room, Lucy is quiet and continues to take deep breaths as she closes her eyes. Rosie walks up next to Lucy and puts her hand on her shoulder. "So, why don't you wanna smoke?" she asked.

"No reason, I just don't want weed right now," answered Lucy.

Rosie slightly tilts her head, and with a curious face, she asks, "Are you quitting or something?"

Lucy cracks a smile. "What? Psh, no," she said, shaking her head.

Rosie then takes her hand off Lucy's shoulder and throws it to her side. "Then what's up? 'Cause you're acting weird," she asked with her eyes wide open.

"The ceiling," replied Lucy with a big smile.

"Wow, really," said Rosie, rolling her eyes.

"Ha-ha, yes, really…" said Lucy laughing, but then she sees the trashcan next to the desk and throws up in it.

Rosie quickly rushes to Lucy's side and holds her hair up. "Oh, shit, you okay?" she asked, worried.

"Ah, um, yeah," replied Lucy, leaning over the trashcan and throws up again.

Rosie grabs Lucy's hair with one hand and begins to rub her back with the other. "Fuck, you're sick, huh?" she asked.

Lucy throws up once more in the trashcan, then takes a deep breath. "No, I'm okay," she said.

Rosie lets go as soon as Lucy starts to get up, then becomes confused. "Alright, then, something's wrong," she said, sliding both of her hands from the top of her head to the back of her neck.

"Nothing's wrong," she said, taking another deep breath.

"Well, you're not smoking. You just threw up, and you say you're not sick, so what's wrong?" asked Rosie, looking at Lucy with concern.

"Nothing, okay," said Lucy, starting to walk away.

Rosie quickly grabs her arm stopping her from going anywhere. "Lucy! Come on, tell me," she said, with a stern tone.

Lucy looks away at the floor and closes her eyes taking one last deep breath. "Ah…alright but don't tell Sebastian, okay?" she said, finally looking at Rosie with a sad face.

Rosie lets go of her arm and looks at her with confusion and says, "Um, okay? I won't."

Lucy heads over to the couch and takes a seat as dust flies in the air. Her eyes begin to tear up and her body starts to shake; she looks up at Rosie and says, "Um, I'm…I'm pregnant…" as one tear falls down her left cheek.

Rosie looks at Lucy with a shocked face and says, "NO WAY! Why don't you want Sebastian to know about this?"

"I'm scared that he'll leave me," said Lucy, covering her eyes to try to stop the tears.

Rosie takes a seat next to Lucy. "He's not going to leave you; he loves you. And besides he's going to find out sooner or later," she said, trying to look at Lucy's face.

Lucy quickly looks at Rosie and says, "Ah, I know…I know," then stares at the ground.

Rosie gets a hold of Lucy's hand. "Well, how long you been pregnant?" she asked.

"Like two months…and I still haven't told him," said Lucy, starting to cry.

"Hey, don't cry," said Rosie, hugging Lucy.

"But I've been keeping this from him for a long time. Shit, I'm not a good girlfriend," said Lucy, covering her face as she continues crying.

"Hey, don't say that, you are a great girlfriend," said Rosie as she embraced her.

Lucy wipes her tears and looks at Rosie. "Gosh, I don't know what to do," she said, starting to calm down.

"Well, it's okay, I get you, but I think Sebastian would like to know that he's going to be a daddy," said Rosie, looking at Lucy with a small smile.

"I will…I will tell him when the time is right, and right now I don't think it's the right time," said Lucy as she finishes wiping her tears.

"Okay, tell him when you're ready, but soon. Better you tell him instead of him finding out by himself," said Rosie, looking at Lucy's stomach.

"Yeah, you're right, I will," said Lucy with a small smile still wiping her tears.

"Alright, well, come on think happy thoughts, let's see if we can find something cool like Nallely," said Rosie, changing the subject with half a smile.

"Ha-ha, okay," said Lucy, not crying anymore.

They both look around to see if they can find anything interesting, and then Lucy comes across a box that say's "TOWN'S KEYS" inside the mayor's desk.

"Hey, look," said Lucy, waving to Rosie.

"What?" she asked.

"I think these are keys for the whole town," answered Lucy.

Lucy places the box on the desk, then opens it. The town keys are bunched together in a large metal hoop.

"Aw, cool, they look old," said Rosie, looking at the keys.

"Yeah, they do. Do you think there will be stuff out in the town to open?" asked Lucy, looking at Rosie with a smile.

"Maybe, it would be cool if we find something," said Rosie with wide open eyes.

"Well, I'll take these just in case there's something we can open," said Lucy with a smile and putting the keys in her bag.

"Alright, cool, let's go back. They should be done blazing it already," said Rosie, closing the box.

They both go back downstairs to their friends and find them laughing having a good time. Jose is spaced out, looking into the distance, as Jessica is talking about her problem with a particular girl at school, while the others are having an energetic conversation.

"Hey," said Rosie with a smile as they walk down the stairs.

Jessica is now relaxed and doesn't seem to be worried about a thing. She looks up at her two friends and asks, "Hey, hee-hee, did you two have, ah, fun ha-ha?" giggling with a big smile.

"Ha-ha, yeah, we did," answered Lucy, shaking her head and smiling.

Jose then snaps out of his daydream and turns toward Rosie and Lucy. "Oh, ha-ha hey! What's up? Oh, man, I'm so high," he said, continuing to laugh.

"Ha-ha, what did you guys do? Ha-ha, oh, ha," asked Will, smiling with a wink as he looked back and forth from Rosie and Lucy.

"Oh, Babe, ha-ha, we just went looking around," said Rosie, rolling her eyes smiling.

"Did you guys find anything?" asked Sebastian with half closed eyes.

"Yeah, Lucy found some keys," she answered.

Sebastian gets up from his seat and walks up to Lucy. "Oh, yeah! Cool, can I see, Babes? Um, please," he asked with a half-smile.

"Yeah, here, Babe," said Lucy, giving the keys to Sebastian.

"WOW! Damn there old…but ha-ha, cool. Here," said Sebastian, giving Lucy back the keys.

Will gets up and gives Rosie a hit of the wooden pipe. "Should we be going?" he asked, looking at all his friends. They all agree walking out of the Town Hall and see Victor waiting for them at the bottom of the steps.

"Hello, I just came to tell you that the food is ready," said Victor with an even tone.

"Then let's eat," said Jose, rubbing his hands together.

"Ha, follow me," said Victor with a small smile.

# CHAPTER TWENTY-TWO

# GRAND FEAST

As Lucy and Rosie were looking around the mayor's office, Lucy told Rosie her big secret, and having her promise she won't tell her boyfriend. After the emotional reveal, all the friends are following Victor making the walk up the small hill to his house for dinner.

Victor opens the front door, and they immediately see his mother, father, and two sisters, standing in the living room, waiting for them with a smile.

The mother takes a few steps toward them and claps her hands together. "Hello, nice of you to join us. I'm Silvia, and this is my husband Dannie," she said, holding out her hand towards Will.

"Um, hey, I'm Will and these are my friends," he said, shaking her hand.

The friends all say "hi" and "hello."

"There's a lot of you ha, let's go outside, and we can begin eating," said Silvia, walking into the kitchen with a smile.

They all head outside to the backyard and sit at a long picnic table, with some bread and small snacks. All the couples sit next to each other on the same side of the table.

"She seems nice," said Christina with a smile.

"Yeah, but it doesn't mean she is, I don't know but I feel like we shouldn't stay here," said Jessica, holding on to Jose.

"What do you mean?" asked Jose clenching his eyebrows.

"Just that, I don't think we should stay," said Jessica, shaking her head, "I think we should leave," then nods.

Jose was about to say something, but Victor and Lesley come out with the food and the rest of the Duns follow, except Devin. Dannie slowly walks up to his seat with a cane as he holds Silvia by the arm. Lesley places a large plate of meat on the table and sits right in front of Will. Sofia gives everyone a plate, then sits in front of Jessica and Jose. "Alright, let's eat!" said Victor, putting more food on the table, then taking his seat.

They all grab some food and start to eat. Sofia stares at Jessica, while Lesley stares at Will. Rosie notices that Lesley is checking Will out.

"So, um, Lesley, how old are you?" asked Rosie with a mad face.

The friends stare at Rosie and Lesley as if they are about to watch a movie.

"I'm twenty-eight, and my sister is twenty-two," said Lesley, smiling at Will.

"Oh, well, I didn't ask you how old your sister is, but okay," said Rosie, continuing to stare Lesley down.

Lesley rolls her eyes but continues to stare at Will. "Whatever, and how old are you?" she asked, smiling at him.

"I'm seventeen," said Rosie, doing a quick snap and wave to Lesley.

Lesley tilts her head toward Rosie. "Oh, ha-ha, sorry, I was asking him not you," she said, looking back at Will.

"Ah!" pouts Rosie.

"And what's your name again, 'Cutie'?" asked Lesley, still smiling at Will.

Will looks at Rosie, then back at Lesley, and says, "I'm eighteen, and my name is Will."

Rosie then hits Will on the shoulder; he looks at her and she has an incredibly angry look about her. Will shrugs his shoulders and looks at her with confusion. Before anyone could say anything else, Jessica sees that Sofia will not stop staring at her.

Jessica looks from side to side, then says, "Um, yes?" looking at Sofia weirded out.

"Mm," said Sofia, lost in her own world looking at Jessica.

Jessica begins to close herself off with her arms. "Something wrong?" she asked, feeling uncomfortable.

Sofia comes out of her trance and takes a couple of blinks. "What? Oh, no, everything is good, everything is just fine," she said, smiling at her.

"*Okay?*" said Jessica and turns her head away, then covers her face.

Mark realizes that dinner isn't going so well, so he takes a big bite of the meat and asks, "The food is good, Miss. How do you get it here?" smiling at Silvia.

"Why, thank you. I made sure the food had extra flavor to it, for you guys. My son goes out to gather food in the city, or sometimes we hunt here in town," answered Silvia, smiling back at Mark.

Mark swallows his food. "You hunt here?" he asked.

"Well, my son does, my girls not so much, they're learning," said Silvia.

"Oh, well, what do you hunt?" asked Mark.

"Only the best kind of meat," said Silvia, with a sort of creepy looking smile.

"We make the best out of the thickest meats, it's to die for, so to speak," said Lesley, playing with her hair continuing to look at Will as she bites her lip.

"Oh, really now?" said Rosie being rude.

Will bumps Rosie's elbow with his and says softly "Rosie," and she gives him an angry look.

"I'm getting kinda full," said Sebastian, holding on to his stomach. "Yeah, yeah, so am I," nodded Jose.

"We heading out, then, or what?" asked Mark, looking at Sebastian.

"Yeah, I guess so, well, thank you for the food, it was really good," said Sebastian, getting up and then bows his head with a small smile.

"You are very welcome, let me show you out the door," said Silvia, getting up from her seat and walks the friends out to the front door.

"Well, thank you again for having us for dinner," said Sebastian, shaking Silvia's hand.

"You're welcome; it was nice meeting all of you. Have a nice night," she said with a smile and slowly closes the door.

They all gradually walk down the hill of the Duns house to recap on dinner. Everyone is silent and Rosie is looking at Will with anger. Diana turns to her friends and says, "The food was good wasn't it?" to break the silence.

"Yeah, it was, it had an interesting flavor to it, but it was good. I don't think I ever had meat like that before, it was different," said Jose, picking at his teeth with his right pinky.

Diana puts her arm around Nallely and places her head against hers. "Well, it's always good to try new things" she said, with a smile.

"Yeah, I guess that's true, so now what? Let's split up?" asked Will, then looks at Rosie. "I saw a gun shop, I want to check it out, Babe," he said, grabbing her hand.

Rosie slowly gives him a glare. "So, I'm Babe now?" she asked, angrily letting go of his hand.

"What are you talking about?" asked Will confused.

Rosie's face becomes shocked. "You didn't even care that she was clearly hitting on you!" she yelled as the friends watch, as if they're still watching their movie.

Will puts his index finger on his lips. "Shh, hey, chill. We're still by their house," He said, softly trying to get Rosie to calm down.

"I don't give a fuck…ah, come on, let's go to your stupid gun shop," said Rosie, storming off and he goes off trying to catch up with her.

The friends continue walking and Jose giggles bumping Mark's shoulder, then stares at Sebastian. "Looks like we're not the fuck ups anymore, huh, guys?" he asked, with a smile.

"What's that supposed to mean?" asked Sebastian with clenched eyebrows.

"Yeah?" asked Lucy, letting go of Sebastian's hand.

They stop walking and are near the Town Hall.

"Well, Sebastian said he'll break up with you if you don't tell him things, and I finally got my girl to calm down and have some fun," said Jose, still smiling. "And Mark, well, we know about him."

"Jerk," said Jessica, hitting him.

Lucy's lip begins to quiver, and Sebastian tries to hug her. "Don't listen to him, Babes," he said.

"Don't…" she said, putting her hand up, "touch me. I think it might be a good idea to split up. Come on, girls," and then walks away, as the girls follow.

"Well, let's meet up back here at the Town Hall," said Sebastian with a pout.

No one answers except for Christina. "Okay!" she called out. "Sorry, Mark," she finished, following the girls.

Sebastian and Mark both look at Jose with disbelief and hatred.

"The fuck man?" asked Mark, tilting his head a little.

Jose stays quiet and Sebastian rolls his eyes and takes a deep sigh. "Guess

I have to do it today, and you guys are fuckin' helping me," he said, making a gesture to Jose and Mark for them to follow.

"Why do I have to help?" asked Mark. "I didn't do shit."

Jose pushes him a little. "Shut up."

The guys rush back to the house they picked to get Sebastian's suitcases.

# CHAPTER TWENTY-THREE

# DISCUSSIONS

An interesting dinner took place at the Duns house. The friends have been introduced to the mother and father, all having an uneasy meal. Rosie is upset with how things went when they were eating, and she's now furious with her boyfriend. Not long after, Jose causes the girls to go off on their own. Sebastian is now forced to set up his surprise for his friends, and girlfriend.

Silvia stares at the front door with a smile, as the whole family stands behind her in the living room.

"Good, good. This is good," she said, turning around looking at her sons. "They'll do perfect."

Devin steps forward. "I siphoned their gas while you were at dinner; they won't get very far if they decide to leave," he said.

She smiles. "That's my boy; now go make sure the traps are set you two. We need them alive," she said, about to walk off.

"Aw, but that's no fun, Mama," whined Sofia. "And why can't I do something?"

Silvia looks at her daughter. "No, Sofi, you need to stay away. I know how you get."

"But Mama."

"No, 'but's, okay," she said, stroking her cheek. "Now go. Lesley, come with me," she finished, walking to the basement.

"Yes, Ma'am," said Lesley, following her mother.

Sofia throws herself on the couch and pouts. "Not fair…" she mumbled.

At the gun shop, Rosie is standing at the corner of the store with her arms crossed, still angry about dinner. Will is going through the empty shelves and cabinets, trying to see if he could find something cool to take back home. The shop is small with empty ammo boxes on the shelves. Everything looks clean and neat as if people still shop there.

"I can't believe you," said Rosie as she pouts.

Will turns to her while walking behind the counter where the cash register is. "You're still mad at me? I didn't even do anything wrong," he said, as his foot hits something sticking up from the ground under a rug.

"Yes, I'm still mad at you! You didn't even care that she was being such a bitch to me! Let alone having her check you out, I bet you liked it, didn't you!" she said, as she walks angrily towards him.

"I wasn't even paying any attention to her, Babe; come on, and we were guests there, yeah, they're weird, but they fed us, what was I supposed to do?" he asked, bending over to move the rug to find a floor safe under it. Will's eyes brighten up in hopes of opening it.

Rosie looks over the counter to glare at Will. "Be a man and stand up for your girlfriend! That's what!" she said, turning away from him. Her eyes beginning to tear up, thinking that he still doesn't care since he's not into the argument, and more interested in the store.

Will then hears her make a very soft and quiet sniffle followed by a sad sigh; he gets up and walks toward her slowly, then puts his left hand on her right shoulder, and gently lifts up her chin with his right hand to look in her eyes. "You will always be my girl, I will always protect you, and I will never leave your side. And you know this, Babe. Didn't I prove that to you at the beach?" he asked, putting his arms around her waist bringing her close to him, looking deep into her eyes.

Rosie looks away and makes a quick small smile. "You don't have to prove anything to me, I just want you to stand up for our relationship," looking back at him.

"She already knew we were together, I can't make her do anything," said Will.

Rosie then gets angry and pushes him away. "That doesn't mean you are not interested! FUCK, MAN, all I wanted was for you to tell her to stop.

That's all…" she said, as she walks away looking out the store window, trying to hold back her tears. Will walks up behind her and tries to hug her. Rosie pushes him away. "Don't touch me!" she says as her tears come running down her cheeks.

"Come on, Babe, don't be like this, you know I love you. Trust me, she doesn't make me look at her the way I look at you," he said, with a calming voice, slowly getting closer to Rosie. Will reaches out his hand and wipes her tears away.

She relaxes. "I know, Babe. I'm sorry it's just a lot is going on all at once on this trip," she said, leaning against the wall as she covers her face.

Will grabs Rosie's right hand. "Then talk to me, Babe," he said.

Rosie glances at Will, takes a deep breath, and says, "Just girl stuff with Lucy," not telling him about the pregnancy.

"Oh, I see now, you're on your thing," said Will, being serious about his guess.

"What the—? No!" said Rosie surprised with what is coming out of her boyfriend's mouth; she then puts a small smile on her face and says, "Never mind, Babe, I'm sorry for bugging you. I love you," kisses him, "go back to your store, you loser," and starts to look around the store herself.

Will gives her a blank expression, then walks back to the safe he found under the rug and says, "Hey, Babe, come look at what I found," as he waves his hand for her to come.

Rosie walks around behind the counter and see's the safe embedded into the floor. "Cool, can you open it?" she asked as she examined the safe.

Will stares at Rosie with half-closed eyes. "I don't have the keys," he said.

Rosie's eyes widen. "Lucy found some keys when you guys were smoking, remember? I'll text her," she said, taking out her phone. "Aw, no service. Well, come on, let's go look for her," she finished getting up.

As Will and Rosie look around for Lucy, the three guys are in the Town Hall setting things up from Sebastian's suitcases. Inside them are a bunch of candles, batteries, colored lights, and streamers, along with a radio and small disco ball.

Jose is up on the second floor with Mark, placing streamers across the balcony so they can be over the first floor. Sebastian is down on the first floor, placing candles in colored paper shades. "So, you think this will take you out of the doghouse?" asked Jose.

Sebastian lights a candle. "I was planning to do this anyways; calm down," he said, putting the candle in the paper shading. "We're almost done. Let me just bring the disco ball to you." He picks up some long rope and the disco ball and takes it to Jose. "You really fucked everything up man," he said, staring at him, "I'm trying to have a good time with my girlfriend," he continued, putting the rope through the hoop of the disco ball. "Ever since I fucked up with her parents, I can barely see her dude."

Jose rolls his eyes. "Chill, dude, she won't be mad forever," he said, grabbing the end of the rope. "Why you doing all this anyways?" he asked.

"I just wanna do something special for Lucy," he said, turning on the disco ball and hangs it over the balcony, then walks to the opposite side so it would be in the middle of the room. "Tie it on the railing!" he yelled out.

Jose and Sebastian tie down the disco ball, having it drip down a bit over the first floor.

Mark runs downstairs and looks up at the ball. "This is pretty cool," he said, smiling. "Still not gonna dance, though."

Jose laughs as he walks down the stairs. "Christina's gonna make you man, trust me," he said, picking up the radio. "You brought some music, right?" he asked, putting some batteries inside it.

Sebastian comes down the stairs. "Yeah, I'll just plug my phone in," he said, looking around.

The hall is partly decorated with blue and purple lights, and streamers on the walls and balcony. The desks are placed together making a big table, having the drinks, chips, and candles with red paper shades.

"You didn't bring soda or anything?" asked Mark, looking at all the drinks on the desks.

Jose walks up next to him. "Aw, damn, I forgot to bring some," he said, patting Mark's back. "Sorry, bro," he finished with a smile.

"I think you can use a drink. It's been like two months, right?" asked Sebastian.

Mark sighs. "Yeah, but I'm not going to drink yet, man. I still can't stop thinking about what happened at Will's party."

Sebastian smiles. "Yeah, a lot did happen at that party," he said, thinking back in time, then walks toward his suitcase and says, "That reminds me," as he goes through it and takes out a purple rose. *Nice, it didn't get crushed*, he thought to himself still with a smile. He then grabs more of the colored lights. "Alright, let's put the last of these," he said, handing them to Mark and Jose, then grabs a banner.

As the guys are decorating the Town Hall, the girls arrive at the sheriff's station. The station is a three-room office type building. The front entrance room is the secretary's desk, beyond that is the sheriffs and deputies office and a holding cell. Jessica, Christina, Diana and Nallely are talking in the sheriff's office, while Lucy is by the secretary's desk looking at them through the broken wall window, thinking about her boyfriend leaving her for being pregnant. Jessica feels Lucy's eye on them, and when she turns toward her, she quickly glances at the secretary's desk. She starts to look around trying to make it seem as if she wasn't staring. They continue their conversation with Jessica having an expression of disbelief. Lucy opens the top desk drawer and sees a note that falls from the bottom of the drawer. She picks up the note and begins to read it:

"Ricky,

I don't know how you can ignore the amount of missing people in the past week. First, Mrs. Willium's husband disappeared when he went out hunting with Robert Duns and his son in the woods, then little Ronnie tells me that his little sister goes off with these two girls. Now to make things worse my son hasn't shown up for work and he's never late to open the shop. You need to do something about this, talk to the boys. They were the first ones with Mr. W when he went missing. I want my boy, sheriff."

Lucy's eyes widen up and then Jessica does a short, soft screech. "No fuckin' way! Lucy, Lucy! Diana and Nallely are together!" she said, waving at her with excitement.

"What? No way," said Lucy, walking to them putting the note in her pocket.

Diana smiles. "Yeah, we been together for over two months," she said, kissing Nallely's hand.

"You kept this secret for two months?" she asked with a small frown.

Nallely blushes from the kiss. "Yeah, it kinda started at Will's party. But please don't tell him or the other guys. I'm not ready for them to know," she said, with a small smile.

Christina does a small shrug. "Well, Mark kinda knows. We saw them when we were out late last night," she said.

"Yeah, apparently Mark and Christina had a good time. You like him," said Jessica with a smug look at her.

"Oh, shut up, he's a dork," she said, with a blush.

Will and Rosie then enter the building. "Hey, Lucy! We've been looking for you! We really need to talk to you," Rosie said with urgency.

Lucy freezes in place. "Why?" she asked with concern. *Please don't tell me Will knows*, she thought to herself.

"We just really need you; and just you," replied Will.

"Oh, um, okay," she said, taking a deep sigh, *He knows*, she thought. "We'll see you guys later," she finished, walking toward Will and Rosie.

"Wait. Where you guys going? What's going on?" asked Christina tilting her head.

"We'll be at the gun shop, but we need to be alone with Lucy," said Rosie, holding on to Lucy's arm.

"I guess we'll see you guys at the hall thingy?" asked Jessica.

"Sounds good. Bye!" said Rosie, pulling Lucy out with her.

# CHAPTER TWENTY-FOUR

# PROM

Will and Rosie went to the gun shop and had an argument, then Will found a safe that they think can be opened by the keys Lucy has. Sebastian decorated the Town Hall with Mark and Jose to throw a surprise party for Lucy, who was at the sheriff's station with the rest of the girls. Rosie and Will end up finding her and are now taking her to the safe, as the others head back to the Town Hall.

The sun has completely set, and the full moon is shining bright. A warm breeze fills the air as music can be heard outside, coming from the Town Hall as the girls walk up to it.

"Do you hear that?" asked Christina. "I think it's a party," she smiles looking at her friends.

They enter the Town Hall seeing the decorations and drinks. There is even a banner hanging from the small arched perch, between the two staircases that reads "PROM NIGHT." The boys are on the balcony and yell out, "Surprise!" as they come in.

The girls all have shocked expression. "What's all this?" asked Nallely, holding on to Diana.

"A party," said Mark as they walked down the stairs.

"Well, duh, but why do you have the banner from our prom?" she asked.

"I took it," answered Sebastian.

Christina clenches her eyebrows. "Why?"

Sebastian stares at the front door holding his purple rose. "It's for Lucy. Where is she?" he asked looking at her.

Christina gives an open smile and looks at her girl-friends. "AW! That's so cute. She went with Rosie and Will to the gun shop, I don't know what they're doing," she said, then she looks at the rose. "Is that for her, too?" she asked with a smirk.

Sebastian starts to blush. "Yeah. I'll be back, okay? You guys have fun," he said, walking out the door.

Jessica looks at the drinks. "You guys been drinking?" she asked.

Jose picks up two beers and hands one to her. "Not yet; we were waiting for you," he said, giving her a wink.

She rolls her eyes. "You mean Sebastian was waiting for Lucy," she said with a smile taking a drink.

Christina opens a bottle of vodka and pours some in two plastic cups. "Hey, Mark, come have a shot with me," she said, holding out the cup.

"I don't think that's a good idea," he said, looking at the cup, then at her.

"Oh, be a man and take the damn drink," she said, moving it toward him.

He grabs it and looks at his friends. "Um," he stands still not making a move.

"You heard her, bro," said Jose, placing four cups on the table, "Here we'll join you," he continued grabbing the vodka from Christina and pours some into the cups.

Nallely and Diana pick up their drinks. "Yeah, come on. Sebastian said have fun," they said, at the same time.

"And this time you have someone to 'dance' with," said Diana, giving him a wink.

Jose raises his cup. "To an amazing night and let it not end in death!" he said with a giggle.

Jessica clenches her eyebrows at him as they all take their shot.

Rosie and Will are taking Lucy to the gun shop, and Lucy has ahold of both her elbows with an uneasy expression.

"Um, so what's up you guys? Why are we going to the gun shop?" she asked looking straight at Rosie with wide-open eyes.

Rosie smirks. "Will found a safe," she said.

Lucy lets out a sigh of relief. "Oh, and you need my keys, huh? I thought something crazy happened," she said, letting out a soft chuckle.

"Yeah, maybe one of the keys will open it and we'll find something crazy," said Will with a smile.

They arrive at the gun shop and show Lucy the safe. "Why is it built into the floor?" she asked.

"You're asking the wrong person," he said.

Lucy takes out the old keys that she found at the Town Hall, and with her friends looking over her shoulder, she opens the safe with the first key she try's. Her face brightens up from what she finds inside; there is a loaded six shooter revolver, a hunting knifing, and $8,000 in hundreds.

"NO. FUCKING. WAY!" said Will, pushing Lucy aside to get a better look, and then grabs the money and gun.

"Wow, Babe! Looks like you got lucky, huh?" asked Rosie with her eyes all open, looking at the cash.

"Yeah, I did! Um…here, Babe, we both found it," said Will, handing Rosie $4,000 and the hunting knife.

"Yeah, but it was Lucy's keys that opened it, and what am I going to do with a knife?" asked Rosie.

Will hands Lucy $2,000. "True, here, and just keep it for your collection, Babe," he said, referring to the knife.

Lucy puts her hand up in rejection to the money. "Oh, no, I can't take it, you found it," she said.

"No, I wouldn't have opened it without your key so keep it," said Will, smiling.

Lucy then gives Will a smile and takes the money. "Okay, cool, thanks," she said.

Rosie looks at her stack of money. "Here, so, it will be fair," she said, handing her another $2,000.

"Ha-ha what no, how is this fair?" asked Lucy, looking at all the money.

"I have a knife and he has a gun, and you might need it more than me," said Rosie, raising her eyebrows at her, "so just take it please," she extends her arm more towards Lucy to give her the money.

Lucy's eyes water up a bit and she looks at Rosie's eyes. "Thank you," she said, as her voice slightly cracks.

"Okay. But keep this to us; don't let the others know," said Will.

"Alright," the girls said.

They all put their money away and Will puts his gun in his pants near his right front pocket.

"Babe, you should take the bullets out before you blow your dick off, ha-ha," Rosie said raising her eyebrows.

"Ha-ha, good idea," said Will, taking the bullets out, putting the gun back in his pants, and ammunition in his pocket.

Sebastian then opens the door to the shop startling them. "Hey, Babes, I was looking for you," he said with a weak smile holding the purple rose behind his back.

Lucy rolls her eyes. "What do you want?" she asked.

Sebastian takes a small step forward. "I wanna ask you something," he said, taking a hard gulp.

Rosie and Will watch them as if they're watching a movie now.

Lucy tilts her head a little. "Well, ask me," she said with attitude.

Sebastian reveals the rose. "Would you go to prom with me?" he asked, giving her the flower.

"Aw," said Rosie, holding on to Will's arm.

Lucy takes the rose and rolls her eyes. "My parents already said I'm not going remember," she said, crossing her arms.

He smiles and says, "I know. That's why I brought it here."

"AAAAAWWWWWW!" yelled Rosie shaking Will.

"Are you serious?" asked Lucy with disbelief.

Sebastian nods and gets ahold of her hand and takes her out to the Town Hall.

They get to the steps of the building and hear the music. "Are you serious?" Lucy asked softly trying to hold back her smile.

Once inside they see their friends dancing with drinks in their hands, including Mark. Lucy begins to cry softly to herself as she sees the prom banner; she looks at Sebastian then at the purple rose. "You didn't have to," she said with a nervous smile.

"I wanted to," he said, holding her by the waist and looking deep into her eyes. "I know it's been hard to hang out, and I know things aren't easy for you. So, I just wanted to do something to show that I love you."

Rosie shakes Will again as they continue watching them. "Aw," she said, quietly.

Lucy's lips starts to quiver as she smiles, and tears fall down her face. "I love you, too," she said, giving him a big kiss. "I'm sorry for being a pain, Babes," she hugs him tightly and takes a deep breath.

Sebastian rubs her back as he holds her. "Does this mean you'll go to prom with me?" he asked, kissing her forehead.

"Say yes!" yelled Rosie.

She smiles and says, "Yes, Baby," then gets ahold of his hand, "dance with me," and she leads him to their friends that are dancing.

Rosie looks at Will blushing. "This is so cute," she said, squeezing his hand. "I guess we're at prom again."

Will kisses her hand and says, "I guess we are," and takes her to dance.

About a half hour passes of dancing and drinking; everyone is having a great time as the music plays. Nallely and Diana are up close to each other as they dance, they look deep into one another's eyes and bite their lips.

Diana glances at the second floor, then at her friends. She notices everyone is love struck with their significant other. "Hey there, Beautiful, wanna go upstairs?" she asked with a wink.

Nallely smiles. "Okay, Gorgeous," she said, blushing.

The two of them rush up the stairs giggling with Diana taking the lead. They go to the nearest room and close the door behind them.

Christina bumps and grinds on Mark as he holds two drinks in the air. She turns around and grabs him by the shirt. "You know what's better than prom?" she whispered in his ear.

He continues to bounce to the music. "Uh, no, what?" he asked beginning to breath heavily.

She bites her lips. "The after party," she said, with an evil smile, "Come on, let's go to the lake," then leads him out the front door.

Jose takes Jessica to the desks with the drinks and opens two bottles of beer. "So, you're finally having fun?" he asked handing her one.

Jessica rolls her eyes. "A little I guess," she takes the drink. "I still wanna leave," she said, with a weak smile.

Jose takes a deep sigh. "How about we go for a walk?" he asked, holding her hand.

"Are you crazy? It's dark outside," she said.

"No, it's not; have you seen the moon? I've near seen it so bright, and don't get me started about the stars," he said, raising his eyebrows.

"It is beautiful, huh?" she asked, taking a sip.

Jose kisses her hand. "Not as beautiful as you," he said, making her blush. "Let's go for a walk, so you can make all the stars jealous."

Jessica's face turns red and tries to hold back her smile. "You're so dumb," she said, with a soft giggle.

Jose chugs his beer, then leads Jessica outside.

Four friends remain dancing, and a slow song begins to play. Lucy has her eyes closed as she embraces Sebastian closely, swaying slowly from side to side. She takes deep, slow, breaths as she smiles, feeling safe and secure.

She takes a peek at her friends and sees some have gone. "It looks like no one likes your party," she said, smirking at him.

Sebastian looks around, then kisses her nose. "Do you like it?" he asked.

"No, I love it," she said, blushing and giving him a big kiss.

# CHAPTER TWENTY-FIVE

# WANDER

Sebastian has set up all his decorations at the Town Hall and created a prom, for his girlfriend Lucy. He went out to find her at the gun shop with Will and Rosie. They all head back to the Town Hall to see the party Sebastian made, and start dancing to the music having a few drinks. But then some of the friends end up leaving to enjoy the moon light.

Mark and Christina are quietly walking along a dirt road, as Mark is nervously checking her out from the corner of his eye. Christina is holding on to his arm while she looks up at the sky. The stars are bright but quickly get covered by the leaves from the trees, darkening the path toward the lake.

Mark takes a gulp. "Um, should we be leaving everyone behind?" he asked.

"What are you scared?" she asked with a chuckle.

He looks around trying to see past the darkness. "Uh, I just think it would be cool if they came with us," he said, with a nervous tone.

She smiles. "Aw, don't tell me you're scared," she said, spanking him.

Mark flinches. "Ah, no," he said, giving a weak smile. "I just think they would like to join."

"I'm going isn't that enough? You complain too much, just enjoy the moment," said Christina, giving Mark a little shove. "Besides, I wanna be alone with you. Don't you wanna be alone with me?" she asked, touching his chest and looking into his eyes.

Mark begins to sweat. "Um, ye...yeah," he stuttered, "of course I do," he said, standing up straight and flexes his chest a little.

Once they arrive at the lake, Christina gazes into Mark's eyes causing him to quiver. He reaches in for a kiss, but she pushes him away and begins to take off her clothes.

"What are you doing?" asked Mark in shock with his mouth open.

"Getting in the water what does it look like?" replied Christina, being sarcastic as she takes off her shirt.

"But why are you taking off your clothes?" he asked, baffled.

"Well, duh; I don't want them getting all wet, and then having to walk around dripping with water. Besides, it's not like you haven't seen me naked; we go skinny dipping all the time," she replied as she sits on a rock taking off her underwear.

"But that's with friends," he said, with wide eyes.

She rolls her eyes and smiles saying nothing. Mark stands there staring at her with his mouth still open, as she gets in the water and stops to where it is at the middle of her stomach. She faces Mark and takes off her bra and tosses it on the top of the rock she was sitting on. She lowers herself so her breasts are covered in the water. "So, are you coming in or what?" she asked as she goes completely underwater.

Mark is still standing in awe, trying to figure out if what just happened, happened. He soon snaps out of his trance and starts to take off his clothes.

"What's taking you so long?" she yelled out while playing in the water.

He finishes getting undressed; but leaves on his boxers and joins Christina. She swims up to him and gets really close almost touching lips, then splashes water in his face and swims away.

As they enjoy themselves in the lake, someone is spying on them from behind the bushes waiting silently.

Jessica and Jose are holding hands while walking through the woods. Jose is looking around the trees and bushes, as Jessica is talking to him about how she feels about the town.

"Those people are weird, this town is weird, these woods are creepy, this whole place is just not right, Babe," she said, but he doesn't answer. "Why don't you ever listen to me," she finished, hitting his arm.

He rubs his arm. "Huh? Sorry, Babe, I was looking at the wilderness," he said, with a smile.

She squints her eyes at him and says, "I don't like this place."

"Why not?" asked Jose.

"I just have a bad feeling about this place, like something bad is going to happen, I really think we should go," said Jessica with a worried face.

"The van is too far, and nothing is going to happen," said Jose as he stopped walking; he looks into Jessica's eyes, "come here," he continues pulling her to him and holds her close, "Nothing is going to happen, okay? And if something does happen, I'll protect you," he finishes, kissing her on the lips.

Jessica blushes. "Alright, well, now what do you want to do?" she asked.

"Let's go deeper in the woods and 'explore' and stuff," said Jose giving her a wink.

She rolls her eyes with a smile and asks, "Okay, um, what time is it, Babe?"

He takes out his phone, then answers, "Eight o'clock," looking back at her.

"Okay, thanks; but be quick," said Jessica with a giggle.

Jose just smiles and kisses her hand, and they head off deeper into the woods. They are both walking through leaves and bushes but as they go further, Jessica trips on something.

"Ow," she said, getting up from the floor.

"You okay?" asked, Jose helping her.

"Um, yeah…what I trip on?" Jessica asked, annoyed. She looks and picks up a human skull, then drops it immediately and begins to scream. "AA-AHHH! WHAT THE FUCK!" she said, crying, rushing to Jose's arms.

"Oh, shit," he said, staring at the skull and the skull staring back at him, with the jaw broken off from the left side.

"See…h-h-h-ah…n-n-now, c-c-can, w-we-e, go…p-p-please!" cried Jessica, holding and burying her face into Jose's chest.

Jose continues to stare at the human skull while hugging Jessica, he then looks up and sees something through the trees that looks like a large machine.

"Hey, it's okay, don't cry." said Jose holding Jessica tightly trying to comfort her.

Jessica pushes away from his wet shirt and cries, "What do you mean okay? That's a dead person's head, a fuckin' human skull Jose 'okay'," as she gave a devastating look at Jose while he was focused on the large object. "Babe! I'm talking to you," she said, shaking him, trying to get his attention.

"I know…" he quickly looks at Jessica and then starts to move towards the object. "Follow me I found something," grabbing her hand to lead her deeper into the woods.

"NO!" said Jessica moving her hand way from Jose with anger. "I wanna leave now!" she relaxes. "Please," she finished as her eyes are tearing up.

"We will; I just wanna see what's over there. You coming or you walking back by yourself?" asked Jose, leaving Jessica behind.

"You're such an asshole!" she yelled, following him.

Once Jose and Jessica get to the machine, they find the missing construction workers remains and their construction equipment. Jessica starts to cry in fear and Jose with his eyes wide open says, "Oh…my…shit, okay, let's go now, we have to leave," then grabs Jessica and walks back to get his friends to tell them what he found.

Jessica and Jose are running back to town, but Mark and Christina are still at the lake, being watched. They have finished swimming and are now lying on the ground near the water and some bushes. "You know, you're kinda cute," said Christina, getting closer to Mark.

"Ha-ha just kinda?" asked Mark, smiling biting his lower lip. Mark kisses Christina and they start to make out. Christina starts to go into Mark's boxers, and Mark begins to caress her breast. They are about to have sex not knowing that they are being watched by Sofia.

"Ah-yeah, mm fuck yeah, harder. Ah!" moaned Christina.

Sofia takes out her knife, kisses it, and creeps up behind Mark.

"Ah-mm, yes," moaned Christina.

Sofia grabs Mark's hair and stabs him in the stomach.

"AH!" yelled Mark in agonizing pain.

"Ah! What the fuck! AHH!" screamed Christina in fear and having Mark's blood splash all over her, as the knife comes in and out of his body. Mark, not dead yet, tries to fight back. Christina scared out of her mind runs away naked, leaving Mark behind.

"Hahaha die! Die! Hee, hee, hee," laughed Sofia as she repeatedly stabs Mark and rips him apart. Mark is now dead, and Sofia starts to chase after Christina. "And where do you think you're going cutie!" she yells as she swings her knife in the air.

Back at the Town Hall, Nallely and Diana are still in the room on the second floor, as Will and Rosie are sitting down at the desks having a drink, and Sebastian and Lucy are still slow dancing together.

Lucy stops and looks into Sebastian's eyes. "Babe, can I ask you something?" she asked with a small smile.

Sebastian holds her by the waist. "Of course, Babes," he said, returning a smile.

She takes a few, deep breaths. "Do you see us together forever?" she asked.

"Past forever, Baby," he said, kissing her on the forehead.

Her smile grows and she begins to blush. "Would you…start a…family with me?" she asked hesitantly.

He clenches his eyebrows. "Well, yeah, when we're older," he answered. "Where is this coming from?" he asked.

She closes her eyes and leans on his chest. "I just wanna know you'll stay with me no matter what," she said, smiling.

Sebastian holds her and rests his head on hers, then says, "I'm not going anywhere."

"You promise?"

"I promise, Babes."

Lucy takes another deep breath. "Babes, I really need to tell you something," she said, touching his face. "Um, Babes, I'm…we…you're gonna—" she continued, but Christina burst through the door screaming her lungs out.

She slams the door quickly putting a chair to try and lock the door behind her. The friends all look at her in shock.

Will immediately stands up dropping his drink. "What the fuck? Where's your clothes, and why do you have blood all over you?" he asked, freaked out.

Christina begins to pace back and forth. "Uh, she…she got Mark…I think she killed him," she said, crying as she tries catching her breath.

"What do you mean 'think'?" asked Rosie, walking up to Christina.

"Um, uh, I ran away…I didn't mean to leave him I was scared and she's coming!" said Christina, wiping her tears.

"Wait? You just left Mark? What the hell is wrong with you? What you couldn't help him?" yelled Will.

"I'm sorry I…" Christina began to say but Sofia starts to hit the door. "Ah! It's her!" she screamed.

"Shit," said Will, taking out his gun and six bullets.

173

Sofia yells as the chair begins to break. "Hey, come on, open the door. I just wanna play...ha, ha, ha!"

Will stumbles to put in five bullets and drops one. "Shit, fuck!" he said, panicking.

"Come on, hurry up, Babe!" said Rosie freaking out.

"Fine, be that way!" she yelled, kicking the door open and then, BANG, BANG, BANG, BANG, BANG, CLICK, CLICK. Sofia covers her upper stomach with her hand, then looks at it, seeing blood. She looks at Will, who is still pointing the gun at her, smiles at him and falls backward on to the floor.

"Is...is she dead?" asked, Rosie still afraid.

Sebastian goes up to Sofia and puts his two fingers on her neck. "Yeah, she's gone," he said, getting up.

"Shit, you killed her!" said Lucy freaking out.

"Well, it was us or her, and she already killed Mark 'cause of this one right here," said Will angrily, pointing at Christina. "Here. Put this on, bitch," he continued as he takes off his shirt and throws it at her face, causing her to cry.

"Hey, stop it! You made her cry, who knows what could have happened if she stayed there. She could have died, too, she was scared and didn't know what to do and if she would of died, we wouldn't know that these people are going to try to kill us!" Rosie said, yelling at Will.

Will calms down, looking at the body, then at Rosie. "Fine, whatever. I guess you're right," he said.

Rosie hits Will in the chest. "No, I am right. So, don't you yell at her and go off calling her a bitch!" she said, hitting him once more.

"Okay, okay; come on we got to go, they must of heard the shots so they'll be here soon...and I don't wanna be here when they come, put the shirt on Christina," said Will, picking up his last bullet.

Nallely and Diana come rushing out the room on the second floor. "What the fuck was tha—" Nallely started to say as she fixes herself but sees Sofia's body. "AAAAAHHHHHHHH!" she yelled, falling back into Diana's arms.

"What the...fuck happened?" asked Diana with wide eyes looking down at her friends.

"Mark is dead," said Will, staring at Christina.

"What, how? What the fuck is going on?" she asked as she walks down the stairs holding Nallely, covering her face with her hand.

"This can't be happening, this can't be happening, this can't be happening," Nallely mumbled into Diana's chest.

"Ask this one over here," said Will, glaring at Christina.

Rosie throws a random old shoe at him yelling, "Stop! It's not her fault!"

Sebastian holds Lucy tight as she cries in his arms. "Look, we can't fight right now. We need to find Jessica and Jose and get the fuck out of here," he said.

They all quickly walk out of the door to look for their other friends, hoping they were not killed.

# CHAPTER TWENTY-SIX

# ALL NIGHTER

**PART ONE**

The friends have enjoyed a makeshift prom Sebastian made with the help of Jose and Mark. Everything was going well until some started to leave the party to be alone. Jessica and Jose found the remains of the construction workers, and Mark was killed while spending time with Christina at the lake. Christina ran back to the party as Sofia chased her. Will shot Sofia dead, and the friends are now frantically running to find Jose and Jessica.

At the Duns house, Silvia is still with Lesley in the basement butchering the remains of James. They look at each other with concern as five faint bangs can be heard.

"Go check on your sister." said Silvia as she puts some meat in a plastic bag.

"Yes, Ma'am," she said, walking up the stairs and goes into the living room, seeing that Sofia has gone. She comes back down to the basement and quickly says, "She's not here."

Silvia closes her eyes taking a deep breath, then looks at her daughter with a blank stare. "Go find your brothers," she said, turning on a machine with a small satellite dish. "And don't do anything stupid. We need them alive," she finished with her face slowly turning angry.

Lesley nods and rushes out the front door, as Silvia picks up the butcher knife continuing to cut more meat while humming her song.

Victor is speed walking past old buildings, heading toward the sound of the gun shots with Devin right behind him. "You think Sofia took a gun?" asked Devin, trying to keep up.

"I don't know; but if she did, oh, I'm-a kill her," said Victor with his eyebrows slightly clenched as he sees a blood trail to the Town Hall.

Getting closer they hear music playing from the Town Hall. "You think they're still here?" asked Devin.

Victor puts his index finger to his lips. "Shh," he said, silently walking up the steps.

"But we can't go in there," Devin said quietly, waiting at the bottom of the steps.

Victor stops at the entrance of the Town Hall not saying a word.

"What is it?" asked Devin, slowly walking up to his brother, then stands next to him, immediately seeing their sister lying on the floor. "Sons of bitches! They killed our sister," he said, quickly. "How did they get a gun? You think they brought it from their home?" he asked.

Victor looks around the room at all the decorations examining the area. He sees bullet shells on the floor, and the bloody knife in Sofia's hand.

"Well?" Devin asked again.

"I don't know, but this made things a lot more complicated," he answered.

Lesley comes by seeing her brothers at the entrance of the Town Hall. "Hey, what happened? I heard…" she begins to say but stops when she sees her beloved sister on the floor covered in blood. "What! Sofia!" she yelled running inside and falls on her knees, hugging her dead sister's body.

Devin reaching his hand out toward her. "Sis, get out of there! Everything will be okay; we'll get them, okay?" he said, trying to cheer her up. "Sis, sis," he went on trying to get her attention.

"Ha-ha-ha-ha-ha, you're damn right…they're going to die," she said, grabbing Sofia's bloody knife that she used to kill Mark, then looks at her brothers with an evil smile and tears falling down her cheeks.

The friends are on the road of the house they picked, rushing to the van. Noise is then heard coming from the woods. "You hear that?" asked Sebastian, stopping in his tracks.

Will gets his gun ready as the rest of the friends stand watching with suspense. Jose and Jessica then come rushing out from the bushes holding hands.

"Aw, thank goodness," said Sebastian with relief. "Hey, we got to go!" he said.

"Yeah, I know; where's Mark?" asked Jose.

It gets quiet for five long seconds.

"He's dead…" said Lucy, holding on to Sebastian.

"What? How?" asked Jessica with puffing eyes from crying.

"There's no time we have to get out of this place!" said Rosie.

"Yeah, she's right. I gotta go to the house for the keys first. Wait, where did Christina go?" Jose asked, looking around.

Will turns behind him and sees Christina running out of the house straight to the van. "Christina! Christina! Christina!" yelled the friends as they run to the van trying to catch up to her.

She gets in Jose's van and drives off; she sticks her head out the window and yells, "I'm sorry, I'm sorry!" then sits back and begins to cry as she looks down at her lap, still driving fast. She wipes her tears and whispers, "I'm sorry" and looks up and sees a tree. She screams in fear and hits the tree, crashing out the front window, hitting headfirst on the tree trunk. She cracks her head open, causing blood to come out.

The friends get to the van and all have their jaws open. "Oh, shit, Christina!" said Rosie, covering her mouth with her hand.

"Fuck, the van! How are we going to get outta here?" Jose asked upset. He gets in and starts it. With a smile on his face, he backs up, but the van comes to a stop and dies. Christina's body falls off the hood of the van.

"Hey, man! What the fuck? You dropped Christina. Couldn't you wait till I took her down?" asked Sebastian madly glaring at Jose.

"Hey, sorry, but we don't have time. We have to get the fuck out of here, but the van's fucked up," said Jose, hitting the steering wheel, then lays his head on it.

Sebastian picks up Christina and puts her down gently and says, "Rest in peace, Christina," and goes to Lucy to cheer her up.

"Are-are-are are we going to die?" she asked, holding Sebastian tighter and tighter.

"No, Babe, I'll make sure nothing happens to you," he answered, kissing Lucy's head.

Rosie takes out her phone. "Fuck! Still no service!" she said, throwing her arms down.

Will grabs her phone and begins to dial 9-1-1. "Yeah, but sometimes you can still call the cops. This might work," he said, putting the phone to his ear. The phone begins to ring. "Yes, yes, it's working!" he said, with excitement.

Operator: "Hel.o wh.t .s yo... ..."

Will begins to tell the operator the situation, but it is not going through clearly.

Operator: "He..o i. a.yone ...re. Ple.s. spe.. cle..ly. Hel..? He..o? Um, we ca.t tr...t.. ... (static)."

Will hangs up and begins to pace back and forth. "Fuck! Okay, we can't go anywhere now, it's getting dark, and they probably know the woods better than us." He then stops and looks at his friends. "So, it would be best if we wait till morning. It's a big town; we just have to stick together," he said, getting ahold of Rosie's waist bringing her close.

"And what if they kill us?" asked Jessica terrified with her eyes on Christina.

"That's not going to happen. We have to fight back and hide," said Will, thinking to himself.

"And where the fuck are we going to hide?" asked Jose.

"I have no idea, but we shouldn't stay here come on. We'll get what we need at the house, and we have to be quick," said Will, running off and holding Rosie's hand.

Meanwhile, as the friends head off to grab some of their things, Victor and Devin are following the blood trail left behind.

"So, who's going to tell Ma and Pa about Sofia?" asked Devin.

"I don't know yet; for now, we don't say anything," replied Victor, focused on the blood.

They arrive at the lake and quickly find Mark's body laid out near some bushes. His innards are out of his body and lower half is in the bushes.

"What do you know...you weren't that hard to find, huh?" Devin asked, picking up Mark's body reviling his missing parts. "Ha-ha, wow, fuckin' Sofia," he went on with laughter.

Victor looks at his watch. "Yeah. Now come, let's take the body to the house. I'll tell Ma and Pa about what happened," he said.

When they get to the hill of their house, they see Lesley dragging a body behind her.

"What do you have there, sis?" Victor asked curiously.

"A friend," answered Lesley with an evil smile. "It seems like they tried to leave but crashed into a tree, and this one went flying out the window. Hee-hee, poor thing was left behind half-naked," she went on with laughter. "She came, too, when I was dragging her ass over here, but she lost her shirt on the way here." She lets go of Christina's foot. "She won't stop saying 'sorry'."

Devin places Mark's body down and runs over to Christina with excitement. "HA! Looks like she busted her head open," he said with a big smile.

Victor looks at the two bodies. "Okay, both of you take these two dumb bitches to the basement," he said with a serious face.

"But what about the others? I don't want them leaving. I want them dying!" said Lesley with a fiery rage.

"I doubt they'll go in the forest now that it's dark; they'll just get lost, and we know these woods better than anyone. I'm guessing they're waiting somewhere till daybreak if they're smart," said Victor, smiling.

"And if they're not?" asked Devin.

"Then we go hunting," he said, looking at him. "Now come on, we're wasting time; take them inside," turns to Lesley. "I need to tell Mother and Father the news."

They enter the living room and see their mother and father sitting on the couch, drinking tea.

"So...two...kills already...we said...we want...them alive," said Dannie, looking at the bodies.

Victor places his hands on his sibling's shoulders. "To the basement, and stay there till I come for you," he said, pushing them forward a little causing them to walk. "Um, Mother, Father. I got bad news," he said with a sad face.

"What do you mean...bad news?" asked Dannie, sitting up straight and clenching his eyebrows.

Devin and Lesley head down in the basement and Victor stands at attention.

"It's about Sofia; she's dead," Victor said looking down at the floor away from his parents.

Silvia yells in shock, "What?"

"She was shot. Her body is in the hall," Victor said, finally looking at his mother.

She immediately gets up from the couch. "That place is off limits," she said with anger.

Victor lowers his head. "Lesley went inside to mourn our loss," he said.

Silvia's eyes widen, and the room is silent for a couple of seconds, and then Dannie slowly gets up from his chair and goes upstairs to his room.

"Pa?" Victor said with concern.

Silvia pours herself some more tea. "Leave him. With me to the library, now," she said, walking off to another room.

Victor follows her and Dannie comes out of the room with a double-barrel shotgun.

"You...all of you stay!" said Dannie, quickly heading to the front door using the shotgun as a cane, not realizing he is now alone. Once out the door he loads his gun with one shell.

"You killed my...daughter!" he yelled as he shoots a shot in the air.

The friends are getting their things together at the house as they argue about what to do next. Everyone is in the living room except for Jessica whose pacing back and forth in the kitchen. "Fuck, fuck, fuck, fuck...what are we going to do you guys? This isn't a game anymore," she said, then goes into the living room with her friends. "We can die you guys. Like Mark and Christina!"

Rosie stares at the floor with tears falling from her eyes. "I still can't believe they're dead," she said, wiping her cheek.

Diana holds Nallely in her arms to comfort her. "Maybe Christina is still alive. Do you think we should go back?" she asked.

"Her head was busted open, and she wasn't moving," said Jessica with her eyes tearing up.

"But we didn't really check. Maybe she was knocked out, maybe..." Diana said then was interrupted by the gun shot.

"Oh, shit they got a shotgun!" said Will in fear getting his gun. "Stay here and stay low. I'm gonna try and take them out," he says as he heads to confront Dannie.

"What the fuck are you crazy? They have guns!" said Sebastian, silently yelling.

Will turns to him and puts his index finger to his lips, then walks out the door.

Sebastian takes a deep breath and follows Will, but Lucy grabs him by the arm before he leaves. "Where do you think you're going?" she asked.

"I have to help him, Babes; he can't be out there alone," he said, looking into her eyes.

She gives him an angry glare. "And leave me alone? No, Baby, stay here with me please," she begged.

He kisses her on the lips. "I'll be back, okay?" he said as another gun shot is heard. His eyes widen and looks at Jose, saying, "Stay with the girls," then rushes outside.

Lucy holds her hand out to him and falls to her knees, letting her tears fall down her face. Rosie is still staring at the ground, paralyzed to what is happening. Diana continues to hold Nallely, and Jose tries to comfort Jessica.

Sebastian catches up to Will behind one of the houses near the Town Hall. Dannie shoots another shot in the air, then reloads.

"It's a double barrel shotgun," said Will, quickly looking at Sebastian. "He just finished reloading. I'm going to run across the road and get behind that building," pointing at the town's clinic, "He should shoot once, and then I want you to go around the other side of the house and throw this at him and take cover," handing Sebastian a fist sized rock.

"What? You're craz—" Sebastian began to say but Will begins to run to the other side of the street. "Fuck," he said, then heads to his position.

Dannie easily spots him and struggles to yell, "DIE!" then he shoots at him.

Will quickly dives for cover behind the clinic, but his right calf takes a hit from the buckshot. "Aah!" he screamed in pain.

"Now...show yours—ugh!" Dannie was about to say, but Sebastian hits him with the rock on the side of his shoulder. Dannie turns around and shoots his gun again, then gets ready to reload, but Will peeks out from around the corner and shoots him in the back of his neck. He falls forward and has a difficult time breathing, slowly bleeding out. Will limps up over to him, grabs his shotgun, and hits him in the head with the butt of the gun.

Sebastian runs out from behind the house to approach Will. He quickly notices Will's leg wound. "Dude! You got shot man! Are you okay?" he asked, covering his mouth.

"Yeah, I'm good. Just have some buckshot in my leg," he replied, showing him his right calf. He then goes through Dannie's pockets and finds three shells. "Mhm, come on, let's go," he said, getting up and starts to head to the house.

When they arrive back to their friends, Lucy rushes to Sebastian's arms. They all see that Will got hurt and Rosie quickly gets up and runs over to him. "Shit, Babe! Are you okay? I'm so sorry. I should have said something," she said, hugging him as she weeps.

"I'm okay, Babe," said Will, grabbing her by the shoulders and then kisses her on the lips. "May I use your knife, please?" he asked as he held out his hand.

Rosie gives him the hunting knife they found in the safe. Will begins to take the buckshot's out from his leg and Jessica vomits.

Sebastian rubs Lucy's back as she cries. "How did you know what to do, Man?" he asked.

Will takes another pellet out and grunts as he says, "My dad."

"Damn," said Jose.

"Focus, we have to keep moving," said Will as he takes out the last buckshot.

"What the fuck, man? You're shot and it's getting darker. What the fuck are we going to do? Where the fuck are we gonna go?" panicked Jose.

Rosie hands Will her summer sweater knowing that he will need it. "Calm down. I'm fine; trust me. It's not that bad, I can still run," he said, as he rips a strand of cloth from the sweater then wraps his leg.

Nallely instantly jumps up and says, "The hidden bunker! Let's find that thing. Maybe we can hide there for a while."

"Oh, yeah, good idea. Go somewhere we have no clue where it's at," said Jose sarcastically.

"Shut up, Jose, that's a good idea. We'll look for it. Maybe these monsters stashed some supplies there, maybe even some ammo and more weapons. We just have to hope it's on this side of town," said Will, getting up from the floor. He begins leading them deeper in the neighborhood.

## ALL NIGHTER

## PART TWO

The friends are stuck at the town now that the van is totaled, and with Mark and Christina gone they are all trying to stay calm. Will and Sebastian both take out the father Dannie, and they are all now looking for a place to hide and find supplies.

Back at the Duns house, Devin and Lesley are still in the basement with Christina. She has been restrained facing up on the middle table, her wound is clean, and she has an IV attached to her arm. Her eye lids flicker and her lips quiver, while Devin glides Sofia's knife over her torso.

Lesley is sitting on a chair with Mark's body on her lap. "Would you like us to have some fun with her, boy?" she asked, looking at his lifeless eyes then moves his mouth and says in a deep voice, "Yes, please! have your way. Do what makes you happy." She giggles and looks at Devin. "You heard him brother, make me happy," she said, with an evil smile.

Devin inserts a seven-inch knife between Christina's legs. Blood runs down the table as she is quietly moaning in pain, barely clinging to life. "Mm, you have a sexy ass body," he said, moving his free hand up her stomach to her breast. "Too bad you're practically dead," he grins as he quickly moves the knife up to the middle of her chest. Christina's organs bulge out of her as her eyes and head twitch.

Lesley bounces in place with excitement and moves Mark's mouth again. "Yes, more, more, show me more!" she said, with her deep voice.

The basement door opens, and Victor comes down the stairs. He looks at Devin, then at Christina who tries to turn her head to look at him.

Lesley stands dropping Mark's body. "What's going to happen, brother? Is it okay to kill them now?" she asked, clenching her eyebrows.

Victor walks up to his sister and places his hand on her cheek. "For you… yes, it's that time. Go, have fun while you can," he said, rubbing the wrinkles next to her left eye.

She smiles big then rushes out the basement. Devin puts the knife down on the table with Christina.

"Ma wants me, doesn't she?" asked Devin.

Victor nods.

The friends are walking alongside the neighborhood and the forest. As they continue Nallely trips over something covered by leaves. "Oh, fuck," she whispered, and Diana catches her.

"You okay?" asked Diana.

"Yeah," she answered, looking at the area she tripped on and sees a metal handle. "You guys, I found something!" she said, turning to her friends.

Jessica mumbles to herself. "Please don't let it be another skull…"

"What is it, Babe?" asked Diana as she looks at the ground.

Nallely dusts the dirt and leaves off a large metal door. "I think it's the bunker; help me open it, yeah?" she asked, leaning over.

"Tell the guys to do it. Hey, Sebastian, Jose, open this," said Diana, pointing at the door.

"Okay, move," said Jose, moving them aside.

Sebastian and Jose open the floor door to a dark tunnel. "It is the bunker…" Sebastian said quietly to himself then turns to the others. "Come on, you guys. Hopefully we'll find something useful," he said, taking a step inside.

They all enter the bunker using their phones for light. Its pitch black and no one can see a thing. The bunker smells oddly pleasant. "It smells like candles," said Jessica, taking a few sniffs of the air.

"Yeah, it does," Lucy said, finding a light switch and turns it on.

With the way visible, they see a wooden door. Jose approaches it and a slight noise can be heard from the other side.

Rosie quickly and quietly asks, "What was that?"

Jose puts his ear against the door. "Sounds like humming," he said, with concern.

"Let's get outta here then; they might be here," said Jessica, terrified.

"No, I wanna see who it is," said Jose, reaching out for the door handle.

She grabs his arm before he could touch the handle. "No, you always wanna see everything. Let's go," she said, softly getting annoyed. Jose uses his other hand to crack open the door, and she freezes in shock.

Jose peeks inside while everyone waits for him to say something, but he stands there not saying a word.

Jessica tugs on his arm and says with a loud whisper, "Stop playing games and let's go!"

"Guys…you have to see this," said Jose, walking into the room, and the humming gets louder, sounding more frantic.

"Baby no, please don't do this," she whined.

Will let's go of Rosie's hand and walks in. "Oh, shit…" he said.

They all go in and see people nailed against the walls, dressed up in formal clothing with nice hair. All their eyes and mouths have been sewn shut and nails ripped clean off. Their limbs are broken and bent in different directions, all humming the same song. The room is lit with scented candles smelling like roses and a table is placed in the middle with a hammer, large nails, and some rope.

The friends stand in horror and Jessica covers her face then beings to cry. "What the actual fuck? This is going to happen to us, I know it. We're all fucked," she mumbles through her hands.

Jose stands paralyzed with his mouth open, looking at each person's face. Before he could examine all of them, Diana hits him on the arm. "Go comfort her," she said, giving him an angry glare.

He shakes his head and glances at Jessica. "Oh, right," he answered, then walks up to his girlfriend. "I'm here, Baby," he said, embracing her.

Nallely turns pale and begins to walk slowly toward one of the hanging people. She then begins to cry. "I'm sorry, I'm so sorry," she turns and looks straight at Diana. "I shouldn't have gotten mad when she called," she said, with a cracking voice.

Diana gives her a confused face. "What are you talkin—" she started to say but then sees Adriana's mother behind Nallely. "Oh, no!" she said, running to Adriana's mother. "Mrs. Aguilar, can you hear me?" she asked.

She hums as loud as she can through her stiches.

"It's me Diana," she said, then turns to her friends and says, "We have to help her!"

Jose tilts his head. "How the fuck are we going to do that? She can't even walk!" he said, jerking his head forward.

"We can't just leave her here! She's my friend's mom!" she yelled as she gently touches her face. "Don't worry, we'll get you outta here," she told her.

Will closes his eyes for a second and takes a deep breathe. "He's right, there's no way we can take her with us," he said, turning his head away from her.

Diana stomps the ground. "Why the fuck not?" she asked with anger and tears falling down her cheeks.

"We don't have the van anymore, and we don't know if it's okay to take her down," he said.

"What do you mean?" she asked in horror.

Will takes a deep breathe in frustration. "Look, I'm sorry, but we just can't help her. Maybe if we get out of here, we can—," he started to say, but Diana cuts him off as she struggles to comprehend the situation. "NO! We can't lose anyone else!" she yelled out.

"LOOK AT US!" he yelled back, pointing at the others.

Sebastian is holding Lucy in his arm as she cries into his chest. Jessica has her eyes closed, trying to hold back her tears as Jose rubs her back. Nallely is quietly mumbling to herself in sadness. Will continues to point at the others while embracing Rosie covering her face.

Diana moves her mouth but does not say a word. She turns and looks at Adriana's mother. "I'm so sorry," she said, softly.

Will walks up to the table and picks up the hammer.

"Dude, you just said we can't take her with us," said Jose.

Will rolls his eyes. "We came here for supplies, and this is what we have," he said, picking up the rope and large nails. He goes up to Sebastian and gives him the hammer. "Here bro, hopefully you won't have to use it," he said, giving him a weak smile.

Lucy looks at her boyfriend with watery eyes. "Babes, I'm scared," she said, holding him tighter as she looks at the hammer.

Will then gives Jose the rope. "Why does he get the hammer?" asked Jose with offense.

"Here," said Will, handing him two large nails. "Stop complaining." He gives the rest of his friends a nail each, then takes another deep breath. "We have to leave, find a good place to camp. I already have some ideas for the stuff we have."

The friends begin to walk for the exit, when they get to the metal door Will stops and looks at everyone. "Alright, I'll check if everything is okay out there," he said, holding Rosie's hand and kisses it.

Rosie slightly blushes and looks deep into his eyes. "Be careful," she said, with a worried face.

"I will, Babe," he said, smiling at her then opens the door outside.

Lesley is near the bunker following the footprints the friends left behind. She is carrying a short sword with her and is wearing all black. She hears the squeaking metal of the bunker's door, then quickly climbs up a tree.

Will does not see anyone as he scopes out the area. "Okay, it's all good," he said, waving his hand to his friends.

They get out of the bunker and start to walk back in the heart of the town.

Will is at the back of the group with the shotgun, not knowing that Lesley is following them on the roof tops. The friends go into a nearby two-story

house except for Will. He stands pointing the gun around the corners of buildings. He turns on his light from his phone and starts looking around, he then
walks forward away from his friends.

"Will, are you coming or what?" asked Jose.

"Yeah, hold up, don't come outside," said Will, putting his hand up.

"What? Why?" asked Rosie looking through the door edge of the house,
concerned for her boyfriend.

Will looks around, making sure the area is clear. He sees nothing but still
feels uneasy. Lesley then drops down and lands silently behind Will, then kicks
his wounded leg. Will screams in pain, shoots one shot in the air, and takes a
knee on his wounded leg. Lesley hits him in the back of his head with the handle
of her sword, then takes the shotgun from the barrel, and points the tip of her
sword at Will's neck. She then shoots one shot at the house's windows and slams
the gun against the wall of a house, breaking it. "Get up, sweetie," she said,
raising Will's chin with her sword, slowly forcing him up from the ground.

"Babe!" Rosie yelled in terror.

Lesley grabs hold of Will's right arm and puts the swords blade across his
neck. "If anyone of you fuckers come out here, I'll slice his throat right open
you hear!" she yelled with an evil smile.

"Babe, no!" yelled Rosie in fear trying to run out to him but her friends
hold her back.

"Come on, sexy, I'm taking you somewhere safe," said Lesley, kissing Will
on the cheek leading him somewhere.

Rosie attempts to run after him, but Diana grabs her by the arm. "I'm
going after him," said Rosie in tears.

"You heard her! If you go, she'll kill him!" said Diana with fear.

"And if I don't try to save him, he'll die!" she said, crying.

Sebastian grabs Rosie's other arm. "We'll think of something, okay? We
have to stick together," he said.

Rosie jerks her arms away. "We aren't together without Will!" she said,
then leaves the house to save her man.

Lesley quickly takes Will to the Town Hall and ties him to a wooden chair.
She grabs a seat herself and sits down, looking into Will's eyes. "You're so cute,
you know that?" she asked, touching his face. Will moves his head away from
Lesley's hand. "Aw, why do you have to be like that, Sweetie? I'm trying to be

nice, and besides, I'm better looking than that bitch you're with right now. I can do things I bet she can't do," she went on putting her left leg over Will's right shoulder. "I'll teach you things you haven't even heard of," she finished, whispering in his ear.

"Fuck you, hoe!" said Will with anger.

Lesley moves her leg away. "Hey, that wasn't nice. How about this…if you're so worried about cheating, I'll bring her here and kill her slowly in front of you. Once she's dead, you'll be all mine. My own little slave," she said as she touches his chest.

Will begins to struggle in the chair. "If you even touch her, I'll kill you!" he said, spitting at her.

Lesley puts her index finger on his lips and says, "Shh, you're mine now." She reaches in to kiss Will on the lips but then Rosie grabs her hair.

"You fuckin' whore!" Rosie yelled, taking out her hunting knife.

Lesley punches Rosie in the face and gets on top of her grabbing her knife. She is about to stab Rosie, but Will frees his left leg, and kicks Lesley in the shoulder falling back breaking the chair. He quickly stands up worried for he did not see what happened after he kicked Lesley. He takes a big sigh of relief when he sees Rosie standing over Lesley's dead body, having the knife in her stomach.

Rosie rushes over to Will. "Babe, you okay?" she asked, hugging him.

They embrace each other and Rosie puts both hands on his face gazing deep into his eyes. Will smiles. "Yeah, I am now, thank you, Baby," he said, kissing her on the lips.

"Let's get out of here," said Rosie, pulling Will's hand.

Will and Rosie walk out the door, and Silvia is there outside against the wall. She grabs Rosie from behind and puts a knife to her neck, walking backward into the Town Hall.

"Hey, no, please leave her alone!" Will cried out slowly, going back inside.

Silvia's mouth drops then puts on a big smile. "You and your friends killed both my daughters and my husband. You were supposed to be a part of something wonderful," she said, pushing the knife against Rosie's neck even more.

Will puts his hand out. "Please stop, just let her go," he said, with a tear falling down his cheek.

"Like you let my daughters go?" she asked.

Rosie's lips quiver looking at Will. "It's okay, Baby," she said, as tears fall down her face.

"Shut up!" Silvia yelled with anger, sliding the knife across Rosie's throat and lets her go. She then points the knife at Will so he would not go to her.

Will reaches out to Rosie, and cries, "No!" as he watches her hold her throat trying to stop the bleeding.

Rosie falls to her knees looking at Will weakly. She holds out her hand in pain trying to reach out to him. She moves her mouth trying to speak.

Will drops to his hands and crawls to her. "No, don't talk, Babe," he cried, reaching for her hand.

Their fingers touch then her eyes start to close.

"No! Babe! Babe!" cried Will, getting closer to her. "Stay with me, don't close those eyes," he holds her in his arms and covers her neck trying to stop the blood. "Look at me, Babe! Look at me!"

Rosie dies and Will rests his head on hers then cries to himself.

Silvia laughs. "You're pathetic," she says and walks closer to Will.

Will, without looking up, says, "You killed her," crying softly, too weak to get up.

"Yes, I did," said Silvia with a serious face watching Will cry.

Silvia takes her knife and stabs Will in between the shoulder joint. He screams in pain, and she then stomps on his knees breaking them.

"Just kill me, you crazy bitch!" he yelled out.

She cuts both sides of his cheeks. "Don't worry, my boys are preparing for our smolder," she said.

"What are you talking about?" he asked, trying to move.

Silvia continues to give Will small cuts on his body. "It saddens me we weren't able to consume you and your friends, so you're going to help me find them for my sons, mmm," she said, with a smile licking the blood off the knife.

Will looks at her in disgust and confusion.

She cuts a design on his forehead. "Oh, don't give me that face. If I remember correctly, you loved the taste," she said, then cuts off Will's pinky. "Here have some more," she forces it in his mouth while he screams.

## ALL NIGHTER

## PART THREE

The friends searched the house they are held up in. The front and back doors are barricaded with couches and chairs. They are in one of the second-floor bedrooms panicking to themselves. The girls are all sitting on the bed and Jose is pacing back and forth. Sebastian is looking out the window able to see the Town Hall. He sees Will and Rosie come out the building. "I see them!" he said, with excitement.

The girls jump up and rush to the window. "Oh, thank goodness," said Lucy, hugging Sebastian.

They then see Silvia come out from the shadows beside the entrance grabbing Rosie. "NO!" he yelled, hitting the window.

"What's wrong?" asked Jose, worried.

Sebastian turns to him. "I think Rosie and Will are dead," he said, softly.

"You don't know that!" said Nallely holding on to Diana. "Will, Will, save her!"

Jose comes up to the window, and they then see Victor and Devin walk up in front of the Town Hall with shovels and a wooden pole.

"Who are they?" asked Jessica with wide eyes.

"I think that's Victor," said Jose, squinting his eyes.

"But who's the other guy? How many of them are there?" she asked, hitting him.

"I don't know," he said, softly.

They continue to watch and see Victor dig a hole standing the wooden pole in it. Devin then starts drawing a circle design around the pole.

"What are they doing?" Jessica asked, hitting Jose again.

"I don't know!" he yelled. "Fuck," he said, rubbing his arm.

Diana points at the Town Hall. "Look!" she said, as Rosie's body is thrown down the steps.

"NO!" cried out Nallely, burying her face in Diana's chest.

Silvia then comes out, dragging Will by the collar of his shirt.

Lucy places her hand on the window. "Will! We have to do something!" she said, shaking Sebastian's arm.

Silvia ties Will's arms to the top of the pole, then gives him three large cuts down his torso. She takes her hand and rubs his bloods all over his chest.

She finishes by smearing the blood over her face; and takes a seat in front of him inside the circle.

"Babe!" cried Lucy, shaking Sebastian's arms even more.

Sebastian stares out the window in shock. "I don't know what we can do, Babes," he said, then looks at her. "Will's really fucked up and we don't even have a gun anymore."

The brothers stand to the left and right of Will and their mother, outside the circle. They put their hands out and look up at the night sky. The circle ignites in flames and spreads inward burning Will and Silvia alive.

"WHAT THE FUCK?" said the friends as their jaws drop.

Jessica walks away from the window and franticly paces about. "You gotta be fuckin' kidding me. Did they just kill...they burned...where the fuck, how the fuck did they start that fire?" she asked, holding on to her head.

Before the friends could give a response, they all begin to sweat, and smoke starts to come inside the room.

"What the fuck (cough) is this?" asked Jessica as she coughs. "I knew we shouldn't have come here!" she said, starting to cry.

Nallely opens the room door.

"NO, WAIT!" yelled Sebastian but a small burst of fire rushes in, slightly catching Nallely on fire.

Diana runs to her and quickly puts out the fire and pulls her away from the flames.

The fire slowly starts to spread in the room.

"Fuck," said Sebastian, holding Lucy tight.

"I don't wanna die," she whimpered.

Jose then gets his rope and ties it to the bed, tossing the other end out the window. "Come on, you guys, over here!" he yelled, waving to the others. "Sebastian you first," he said, putting his hand on his shoulder.

"I'm not leaving Lucy," he said, clenching his eyebrows.

"She'll go next bro, now go!" he yelled, pushing him to the window.

"NO, she goes first," he said, with anger. "I'll be right behind you, Babes," he said, stroking her cheek and hands her the rope.

"You better," she said, grabbing it.

Lucy climbs down and Sebastian follows, Nallely went next then Diana. Jessica is staring at the fire in shock, not able to move as the fire is now spreading throughout the room.

Jose holds her gently by the cheeks. "You need to go down right now, okay?" he said, looking into her eyes.

"I can't," she said, in horror while watching the flames behind him.

"Fine," he said, climbing down.

Jessica runs to the window and looks down to him. "Don't leave me please!" she yelled.

He gets to the ground and yells, "Just come down!"

Sebastian pushes him. "You left her up there?" he yelled.

"She'll come down."

Jessica looks behind her and sees Victor come through the flaming doorway. "JOSE!" she yelled.

She climbs out the window and gets ready to go down, but Victor grabs her by the hair.

Jose grabs the rope and gets ready to climb up. "BABE!" he yelled.

Victor then takes a knife out from his pocket and stabs Jessica in the back of the neck.

"NO!" Jose screamed in terror, as Jessica's glasses fall, hitting him on the face.

Sebastian pulls him down. "We gotta go man!" he yelled.

Jose pushes him and says, "But Jess—" but was interrupted as Jessica's headless body falls next to them.

Nallely and Lucy scream their lungs out and Diana says, "We need to get the fuck out of this place…fuck morning!"

Sebastian grabs Lucy's hand and puts his other hand on Jose's shoulder. "We really gotta go," he said, looking up and sees Victor climbing out the window.

They run off trying to escape from Victor and Devin. They get near the end of the neighborhood and take a rest beside one of the houses. "Where are we gonna go?" asked Nallely in fear as she holds on to Diana's hand.

"We have to find the Ranger Station or something," said Sebastian, leaning against the wall.

Jose sits on the floor and begins to rock in place. "They killed Jessica, they killed her man," he said, softly in shock.

Sebastian places his hand on Jose's shoulder. "I know," he said, sadly.

Jose stops rocking and hits his knee with his fist. "They're killing everyone man, we have to get outta here," he said, madly.

"We're going to get outta here, okay?" said Sebastian calmly.

Jose's eyes begin to tear up. "This is all my fault. If I would have listened to Jessica, we wouldn't be in this," he said, sadly.

"Hey, bro, chill, it's not your fault. You didn't know this was going to happen. You just wanted to find something for us to do and you did, and now we just have to get the fuck outta here," said Sebastian.

Jose takes a deep breath and then Jessica's head falls from above, landing in front of him like the skull Jessica tripped over in the woods. He jumps up with fear as he looks in Jessica's lifeless eyes.

The girls scream in terror and Sebastian stands in shock, he looks up from where the head fell and sees Victor on the roof top with a machete. Before he could warn the others, Victor drops down and hacks Jose from behind his skull. Nallely and Diana run off, and Sebastian grabs Lucy's hand and follows them. Jose takes one more second staring into Jessica's eyes, then Victor kicks his back to free his machete. Jose falls to the ground cross eyed and mouth, barely moving; Victor then begins to stomp on his head, smashing his brains in.

Sebastian and the girls get to the end of the neighborhood and head into the woods. Nallely and Diana are a few steps ahead with their phones barely lighting up the way. As they run a metallic sound is heard, along with loud cracking and breaking, and Nallely suddenly falls to the ground screaming for her life.

"Ah! Please help me!" she cried.

Lucy shines her cell phone down at her and sees that she stepped in a bear-trap.

Nallely's left leg is severely injured, with her bone completely broken coming out the skin. She holds on to her knee as she looks at Diana while she cries in pain.

Diana begins to try, and pry open the trap with all her might. "It won't fuckin' open!" she looks at Sebastian with tears falling down her face, "Help me!" she yelled as her hands start to bleed.

Sebastian stares at Nallely's leg and makes a face of disgust, he takes off his shirt then bends down and examines the bear trap, he wraps his hands up and tries to get it open. As he pulls at the jaws of the trap Nallely screams in pain while blood gushes out of her. The trap does not budge and when he lets go the jaws clench tighter. "I don't think I can't take this off," he said, in a panic.

They look at each other as Nallely whimpers in pain. Diana beings to get angry and tries to open the trap again.

Lucy shakes Sebastian's arm. "You have to help her, Babes!" she said, eyes tearing up.

He glances at Nallely's leg. "Babes...I don't even know if we can take her with us," he whispered.

Nallely's eyes widen. "NO! Don't leave me!" she yelled, then grabs Diana's shoulder. "Please don't leave me," she whimpered, looking deep into her eyes.

Diana continues to pull at the jaws of the trap. "I'm not leaving you, okay? I'm staying right he—" she was saying as a machete comes flying and stabs her in the back, penetrating her heart.

Nallely's eyes widen up and her face turns pale. "Diana?" she asked with confusion.

Diana drops forward on top of Nallely. "Ah! Get up! Wake up! Please Love!" yelled Nallely.

Sebastian picks Lucy up over his shoulder and starts running.

"Don't leave me!" cried Nallely, screaming.

Lucy begins to hit and kick Sebastian while screaming. "NO! DIANA! NALLELY!" she yelled with tears.

"Babe that guy is coming for us now come on!" said Sebastian as he carries her over his shoulder.

Nallely's screaming abruptly stops.

Sebastian puts Lucy down as she continues to hit him. "You left them! You left them!" she yelled.

He grabs her gently by the head. "Yes, and now you gotta leave me," he said with watery eyes.

"What?" she asked, quietly crying.

Sebastian gives a weak smile while he looks deep into her eyes. "Babes, listen to me, okay?" he said, moving his hands to her cheeks to wipe her tears away, "I want you to run," gives her a kiss on the lips, "run as fast as you can, okay?" he gives her another kiss, "Go!" he finished, giving her a slight push, taking out his hammer.

"No, Babes!" said Lucy grabbing his hand.

"Babes, there's no time! Go, I'll be fine, now go!" he said, tugging his hand away.

Lucy looks at him with tears in her eyes and asks, "One last kiss?"

They kiss each other goodbye, and Lucy runs off into the woods.

She uses her cell phone to light the way and comes across James' car; as she gets close, she trips and her phone falls right on top of another beartrap, triggering it. She stares at her broken cell for a quick second then gets in James' car. She looks around for the keys and luckily finds them in the cup holder then starts the car.

Victor then jumps in front of the car. "Ah," yelled Lucy, stepping on the gas. Victor tries to hang on to the hood of the car, but Lucy makes a hard turn and Victor goes flying off and hits against a tree. Lucy drives and runs into the Ranger Station just before running out of gas. She gets out of the car and rushes to the door banging on it.

"Help! Help!" yelled Lucy as she banged on the door as hard as she could.

A ranger wearing a camo uniform and holding a rifle answers the door. "What? What's wrong?" he asked with urgency.

Lucy hugs him for being an authority figure. "My friends! They're all dead!" she said, crying into his chest.

The ranger quickly raised his arms when she hugged him. "Wait what? What are you talking about?" he asked with confusion.

Lucy backs away and tries to collect her words. "Um, we...we went to... Dunsvill...and now they're all dead, but my boyfriend is still there! You have to help me!" she cried.

The ranger looks at Lucy with regret. "Oh, ugh...um we're not authorized over there," he said, feeling sorry for her.

"You gotta be fucking with me! Please! He's going to die!" she pleaded in tears.

The ranger looks at her and sees that she has been through hell. "Alright, hold on," said the ranger, walking back inside. When the ranger returns, three others come out as well, holding rifles. "Okay, let's go," he said.

They all get into the ranger's Jeep and drive off.

# CHAPTER TWENTY-SEVEN

# RESOLUTION

A long night has transpired, and the friends have been hunted b
family. Everyone has seemed to be killed except for Lucy who fou
Ranger Station. She gets them to take her back to town and try an
her boyfriend.

They arrive at the town and Lucy immediately leads the rangers
bastian. "Come on! This way!" she said, with urgency.

As they rush through the main road of the town, they come across
tina, who has been crawling on the ground with her guts trailing beh
"Hel...p...meee," she moaned, holding her hand out to them.

Lucy covers her mouth. "Oh, no, Christina, I'm so sorry, I need to fin
tian," she said, slowly walking away. "I'm sorry, I'm sorry," she repeated t

The main ranger looks at the others. "You guys do what you ca
and call for help, I'll follow her," he said.

Lucy takes the ranger to the area her and Sebastian split up.

"Where was the last time you saw him?" he asked as he followed her fro

She passes by some trees with a worried look in her eyes and s
over here, we went into the woods and..." but was interrupted by
cough. "Babes!" she said, running to the sound of the cough and
follows. Lucy sees Sebastian sitting against a tree and rushes ne
"Babes! You're bleeding," she said, holding on to Sebastian's blood

Sebastian gives a weak smile. "Ha-ha, yeah, I know," he said, moving his right hand away from his stomach where he was stabbed.

"Oh, no, Babes, it looks bad!" she said, with her eyes wide open.

The ranger sees Devin's body on the floor, with his head face first in a bear trap and the claw part of the hammer in his leg.

"Who's this?" asked the ranger.

"The guy who killed our friends," answered Sebastian.

The ranger walks up to Sebastian to examine the wound. "Um, I don't know if we can do much for him," he said, looking at Lucy.

"No! Do something!" she yelled.

"He has to go to the hospital and there isn't any near here," the ranger said, and Lucy began to weep. "Ah, I'll see what I can do; wait here I'll get the first aid," he said, running off.

Lucy gets ahold of Sebastian's hands and they look deep into each other's eyes. "Babes, everything's going to be okay," she said, as tears fall down her cheek.

He reaches out his left hand to wipe her tears. "I don't think I'm going to make it," he said, trying to keep his eyes open.

"Babes no! You have to...you're going to be a dad!" said Lucy, still crying.

Sebastian looks at Lucy in shock. "What?" he asked, confused.

"Yeah, we're having a baby," she said, crying, giving a little smile.

"I'm going to be a dad?" he asked with a weak smile as a tear falls down his cheek.

Lucy returns a smile. "Yeah," she said, while tears fall down her face. "So, you can't go, okay? You need to stay here with me." She embraces him.

Sebastian closes his eyes as he wraps his arms around her. "I'm going to be a dad," he said, then takes a deep breath. "I want you to know that I will always be with you (cough)..." he struggled to say, then coughs out some blood.

Lucy starts to panic. "Babes, no, stay with me!" she cried, gently holding on to his face.

He caresses her cheek and says, "I...I...I lo...love...love you," then dies.

Lucy shakes his body. "Babes! Babes! Wake up...please wake up," she cried, then hugs him and weeps softly. "Babes...Babes...one last kiss..."

The ranger comes back. "Alright, I got the first aid and help is on the way. The cops should be here soon with a copter, move aside and I'll see what I

can..." The ranger sees Lucy crying over Sebastian, who is dead. "Oh, damn, I'm sorry," he said in a sad tone.

Time passes, and the cops arrive. There are cop cars and a helicopter in the middle of Dunsvill, and an officer is talking to Lucy.

"I want you to I.D. the rest of the bodies for me," said the officer, writing stuff down in a notebook.

Lucy is continually wiping her tears. "I don't know if I can," she said softly.

"Please, you would be helping us out a lot," said the officer.

"Um, alright," said Lucy sadly.

The officer takes Lucy to the bodies they found. Lucy cries out loud when she sees all her friends' dead bodies, knowing she will never see them again. After she calms down, she I.D.s her friends and the Duns; but sees one of the Duns is missing.

"Wait? One's missing!" said Lucy freaking out.

"Well, we looked all over this place, and there's no one else," said the officer.

"Well, there's people trapped in a bunker, and I'm telling you there's one asshole missing!" yelled Lucy.

"We will do what we can to find them. Do you know their name, and where's this bunker?" asked the officer.

"I think Victor and it's over there," said Lucy, taking the officer to the bunker.

They procced to rescue the tortured victims and search the woods for Victor. They find the construction site and some abandoned cars, but no sign of Victor.

"We are going to put you in a witness protection program, okay?" said an officer to Lucy.

Lucy begins to lose her mind. "What? You can't find him?" she yelled.

"Calm down, we are doing what we can. We are going to take you home now," said the officer.

• • •

Months later, Lucy is in the hospital giving birth.

"Push, push!" said the nurse.

The baby comes out.

The doctor holds up her baby, so she could see. "It's a boy," he said, with a smile and handing over Lucy's baby.

Lucy grabs her baby and looks into his eyes. "A boy," she said, smiling down at her baby.

"Do you have a name now or do you want time to think?" asked the nurse.

"No, I have a name, Sebastian," Lucy said with a smile. "I'm-a name you, Sebastian."

Rain and darkness fill the city, and a man wearing a trench coat walks up to a two-story house and knocks on the front door.

"Yes? Who is it?" asked a man answering the door, trying to make out who it is.

"Hello, cousin," said the man, smiling.

"Victor? Ha, is that you?" asked the man, smiling.

"Yeah, may I come in?" asked Victor.

The man opens up his door and throws out his arm. "Yes, of course; it's freezing out there," he said, inviting Victor inside. "I was expecting you some-time next month."

"Ha-ha, sorry for coming so late, Raymond, this couldn't wait," laughed Victor as he walked in. "It's time," he ended with a serious face.

To be continued…